THE
WHISPERING
GIRLS

BOOKS BY JENNIFER CHASE

JENNIFER CHASE

THE
WHISPERING
GIRLS

bookouture

Published by Bookouture in 2025

An imprint of Storyfire Ltd.
Carmelite House
50 Victoria Embankment
London EC4Y 0DZ

www.bookouture.com

The authorised representative in the EEA is Hachette Ireland
8 Castlecourt Centre
Dublin 15 D15 XTP3
Ireland
(email: info@hbgi.ie)

ISBN: 978-1-80550-101-5
eBook ISBN: 978-1-80550-100-8

For Donna, who has taught me what true friendship is

PROLOGUE

In the dead of night along a windy country road in the middle of nowhere, a white utility van slowly turned down a side trail barely wide enough for any car. The vehicle bobbed and weaved, inching along, pushing through. The bright lights were the only illumination through the thick trees, leaving an eerie spattering of red light as it went.

The van abruptly stopped when the trail narrowed and it was unable to drive any farther, the engine revving as gears ground to a halt. Steam rose in the cooler outdoor temperature, surrounding the vehicle. Cutting the engine but leaving the headlights on, a man got out: lean body, average height, wearing blue jeans, long-sleeved flannel shirt, baseball cap, and well-worn work boots. There was a lighthearted air to his step as he walked to the back of the van, as if he were on a fun day out.

His looks were unremarkable and he could disappear into a crowd, but despite his jaunty walk there was a rage lurking just beneath the surface. Taking a moment, he stared out into the darkness. The forest seemed to whisper to him its secrets and demands. The evening was still, frosty, the trees remaining quiet as the cool air brushed against his face, though he perspired. Several times he unconsciously curled his fingers into tight fists and then released them—part of his ritual as the forest welcomed him.

He opened the doors to reveal an old rolled-up rug. The man pushed up his sleeves and pulled it out, dropping it on the ground. He began to slowly unroll it with his boot, revealing a mass of heavy plastic tarp... and inside it, the shape of a body.

Picking up one end, the man easily slid the tarp toward the front of the van. The headlights shone on the lifeless distorted face trapped beneath the plastic. She had long dark hair, pale waxy skin, and a frozen terrified expression with fixed and wide eyes that stared back, making it almost impossible to escape her gaze. It almost appeared as if she had been surprised by her fate.

The man moved to the back of the van again and returned to the light with a large white bucket, a rope, and a backpack. Pulling on a pair of gloves, he began to unload various items from the bucket and put them into the backpack for transport. He took his time, seeming undaunted about being out in the open at night.

Finally satisfied, he shut off the van's headlights, and the area went dark. He waited, unmoving, savoring the blackness, as if it gave him strength. After a few more minutes, he slung the backpack over his shoulders, secured a strap around his waist, and then switched on a headlamp, affixing it over his cap to light his path. He easily dragged the body into the forest. The sound of something heavy sliding along the rural path had an eerie echo, making it difficult to know where the noise was coming from. It sounded here, there, and everywhere. The flashlight beam flickered in between the trees, like a bulb that was beginning to burn out, until it became completely dark again.

ONE

Tuesday 0700 hours

Katie Scott sat in a comfortable chair on the back deck sipping her morning coffee while watching the sunrise. The warm colors of the morning didn't counteract the cold and the incoming clouds. The weather forecast said some snow flurries were possible today and tomorrow. With a blanket wrapped around her, she took a deep breath. No matter her mood or what was going on in her life, there was one simple thing she never took for granted—watching the sun come up. There were always new brilliant hues of orange and yellow highlighting the forest all around the cabin, celebrating that it was a new day when anything was possible.

Katie's long brown hair was down around her shoulders, gently tousled from a restless night, when she'd napped less than three hours. She was still dressed in pajamas and thick socks and didn't have anything on her agenda today. It was difficult for her to not have anywhere to be or be working on a new case, but she was learning, with some difficulty, to take the much needed time off to relax—something she hadn't done in a while. Even this time, it wasn't by choice, but an order from her superior that she take two weeks immediately.

Katie was a detective for the Pine Valley Sheriff's Department and she headed up the cold-case unit. She and her partner, Detective Sean McGaven, had worked many cases with a perfect solve record—at least for now.

Katie closed her eyes. Like most days, she still saw the victims and killers, their faces, the crime scenes, and the collateral damage flashing through her memory. She made peace with herself a long time ago that the memories and images would never completely disappear from her mind. They were a part of who she was and that was what made her a strong detective.

There was a low whine. Katie reached down to pet her black German shepherd, Cisco. He had been by her side ever since she did two tours in the Army as a K9 explosive detections team. She had been extremely lucky to be able to bring Cisco back with her, with a little help from her uncle (and now boss), Sheriff Scott.

Not only did she bring back Cisco, but also post-traumatic stress. A mental state that was more like a grief cocktail with highs and lows at some of the worst possible times, but she didn't let it stop her from performing her job. She was determined it was to be a reality that would take a back seat to her life.

Cisco sat up in front of Katie. The jet-black dog with amber wolf eyes watched her with curiosity, slightly tilting his head. It was clear he felt Katie's moods.

"Good boy, Cisco," she said. She got up from her chair and stood at the railing looking out into the forest. The brisk air touched her face, but in an odd way it was comforting. Maybe she would go for a walk and clear her head. Or maybe she would make pancakes and stay inside contemplating her life.

Probably not.

Katie knew she wasn't going to be able to do nothing for

two weeks. The area she was staying in was beautiful, but the Echo Forest was really quiet and isolated. A friend of her uncle had offered the nice two-bedroom cabin and it had seemed a perfect place for her to take the time she needed. However, as she stood in the silence, she wasn't so sure. She had spent only one night there so far, and as she looked out at the immense forest, her serene surroundings, she was already calculating the days and hours until she would be heading home.

Several loud thumps against the cabin jolted Katie back into the present.

Cisco instantly turned his focus toward the interior of the house. His body stiffened and a low grumble vibrated from his chest. He stood still, taking in sight, sound, and smell to catalog the incident.

Katie instantly moved quietly back into the house with her cop instincts alert and grabbed her Glock from her suitcase. Straining to listen, she didn't hear any more sounds despite expecting to hear another thump, a voice, or even footsteps. But it remained hushed.

Cisco padded lightly behind her, watching her back.

Katie slipped out of her pajamas into a pair of jeans and a hoodie, quickly pulling on her boots. Her mind seemed to always jump to criminal activities instead of thinking it might just be the trees swaying against the cabin or a forest creature making its way across the roof.

She inched from her bedroom to the living room and then stopped at the front door. Pausing there, she listened. No other sound. Her nearest neighbor was a couple of acres away and she wasn't sure if the occupants lived there year-round—it was most likely vacant. There wasn't a convenient peephole in the door to see if someone was out there. Instead, her hand grasped the deadbolt lock and she quietly eased it clockwise before gripping the doorknob.

Furious knocking broke the tense silence. The rapping was fast and frantic, rattling through the cabin.

It startled Katie, causing her anxiety to rise. Her breath became shallow, and her hands tensed.

Cisco rapid-barked.

She turned to the dog. "*Nein, bleib,*" she said in German to command the dog to stop barking and to stay in place.

Cisco immediately stopped and stood in position. His eyes fixed at the door.

With her gun down at her side, but ready if she needed it, Katie said, "Who is it?"

There were soft cries. "*Please...*" said a female voice. "I... I... need your help."

Katie's first thought was that someone was trying to bait her as a ruse to get her to open the door, but that was her cop way of thinking. Everything wasn't always the worst-case scenario.

She turned the doorknob and opened the door. A teenage girl, who looked to be about seventeen to eighteen years old, stood there staring at Katie, her eyes wide. The girl wore jeans, a long-sleeved T-shirt, and a jean jacket. Her fur-lined leather boots were laced up to her knees. Her long blonde hair was braided and gently laid over her right shoulder. She had several piercings on her ears and wore a leather choker with unusual beads.

"What's wrong?" said Katie glancing around to make sure there wasn't anyone else.

"Please help me..." The girl eyed Katie's gun. "Please, I saw your car... There's a..." The teen was clearly distraught and had obviously seen something.

"I'm Katie. Can you tell me what's wrong?"

"I found a woman in the woods. She needs help."

Katie's interest heightened, but she still wasn't sure if the girl was making complete sense. "Where?"

"She's just a ways. Please... you need to come and help."

Katie glanced back to where Cisco waited. "What's your name?"

"TJ."

"Okay, TJ, show me where this woman is." Katie grabbed her phone and keys from the small wooden table by the door. She wondered why the girl hadn't called the police for help. Katie slipped the Glock in her waistband. "Do you have a phone?"

She shook her head.

Katie thought that was strange, that a teenager didn't have a cell phone—or at least didn't want Katie to know she had one.

"Please hurry," said TJ as she began to walk down the gravel driveway.

Katie closed her cabin door and locked it, leaving Cisco behind. She wasn't sure what was going on, so she decided not to bring the dog. It was one less thing to worry about.

"This way..." the girl said.

Katie had to jog to keep up as they weaved their way around trees and across overgrown areas. The brisk morning brought out a strong aroma of oak and pine trees, pushed around by the slight icy breeze. Katie made a mental note of the route they took, as the trees and winding areas began to all look the same.

They moved through the wooded area for less than ten minutes before TJ abruptly stopped, her arms at her side. It was as if her feet were glued to the forest floor.

Katie could see that she was shaking and her eyes were filled with tears.

TJ then raised her arm slowly and pointed. "There," she barely whispered.

Katie looked to where she indicated and instantly sucked in a breath. She blinked twice to make sure she was really seeing what she thought she was.

About twenty feet away was the body of what appeared to be a woman hanging in a pine tree, her feet barely a foot above the ground, the body swaying slightly. Katie could see bright pink nail polish on her toes and fingers. It was clear by the condition of the body and its disturbingly pale-bluish color that the woman seemed to have been dead for a while, more than a couple of hours. She was dressed only in pale-pink panties and a thin white T-shirt, and there was a brown burlap sack over the woman's head.

The rope around her neck made an eerie creaking sound against the branch as the body rocked back and forth.

TWO

Katie's instincts and law enforcement experience kicked in. She quickly assessed the surrounding area since it was officially a crime scene. She scanned the areas where the killer could have brought the body and the ways they could have exited. A barrage of questions rapid-fired through her mind.

How far did the killer bring the body?

Did the killer bring her here and then kill her?

Who was she? Did she live in town?

She turned to the girl, who couldn't take her eyes away from the body. "TJ," said Katie, "did you disturb anything? Did you touch anything?"

The girl shook her head.

"Are you sure?"

"Yes."

"Who is the sheriff or chief here?"

"I'm not sure."

"Police? Do you know any names?"

"I... I... think Officer Cooper is the chief."

"This is now a crime scene. I need you to stay right here and don't move, okay?" said Katie.

The clearly traumatized girl slowly nodded, keeping her eyes fixed on the body.

"You have to be strong, TJ. I'm a police detective for the Pine Valley Sheriff's Department. I'm going to take a brief look so that I can report the overall scene to the police, so they'll know what and who they will need. Okay?"

"Yes."

First and foremost, Katie didn't want to disturb any evidence, but she knew this small town most likely didn't have the manpower or resources to conduct this type of investigation. The more information and facts she could glean the better.

"It's okay. Just take a deep breath and wait right there. Do you know who it is?"

"No," she said quietly, not making eye contact.

Katie turned her focus back to the body. There was something about the scene that unsettled her—it was as if she had seen it before but she was unable to remember where or how. She would wrack her memory until she recalled.

She checked her cell phone and found it had only one bar of reception. It meant she might have to go back to the cabin to make the call.

Katie slowly and deliberately walked in a straight line to the body. She planned to exit the area by the same route. Using her cell phone, she took a few photographs in a sweeping motion. She wanted to get the overall view, which included how she guessed the killer entered and exited the area.

It was difficult to not look at the pink nail polish on the woman's toes. It gave identity to the body, which made it more challenging to be objective. Despite that jarring image, Katie moved closer.

There were no signs of lethal marks on the victim—no obvious stab or bullet wounds—that Katie could see. The body had blue and purplish markings, indicating she had been killed less than a day before, but a medical examiner would make a more accurate account.

Katie looked back at TJ, who still stood in the exact same spot. The girl's face remained set in horror at the scene. Her dark-blonde hair was wet and matted.

Katie didn't have gloves, so she pulled out an unused tissue from her pocket. After taking a couple of breaths, she gently took the edge of the burlap sack and lifted it a couple of inches. She could see that the neck was heavily bruised, implying the woman had been strangled.

TJ said something Katie didn't understand. The girl's voice was barely a whisper. "*The Woodsman*, no, no, no," the teen kept saying.

Katie turned to her. "Woodsman? Is that what you said?"

She nodded.

"What do you mean?"

"The Woodsman..." TJ pointed to an area next to the tree where the body hung.

Katie turned and saw what the girl was referring to. On the side of the large tree trunk, along the ground, there were some gathered forest items. At first, Katie assumed them to be random, but studying them closer they seemed to be purposely arranged. Was it for the killer? Or for the victim? Carefully taking a couple of steps, not wanting to get too close and contaminate the area, Katie bent forward. Three pine cones, several sticks, berries, a rock, and some leather strings surrounded by a padding of pine needles were arranged in a way that wasn't random. There were many possible explanations. Anyone could have left the display—hikers, neighbors, or kids.

But the more Katie looked at it—the more her gut instinct told her the killer had left it.

It was a totem of some sort, which meant that the killer was trying to tell them something that only made sense to him—or maybe it was a warning. Katie didn't want to think the worst, but she was afraid that there would be more victims.

She quickly took another photo and then turned to talk to TJ, but she was gone.

"TJ?" She jogged around the area where she'd last seen her. "TJ?"

Making her way back to the cabin there was no sign of the girl.

The Woodsman...

Even as Katie thought of the name there seemed to be a faint whisper in the trees. The temperature dropped, which caused snow flurries to float around her.

THREE

Katie had returned to the cabin and was able to get through to the Echo Forest Police Department. She spoke with a young woman who was obviously the receptionist. The woman had identified herself as Libby and assured Katie that Chief Cooper was on his way.

Katie decided to wait at the cabin for the police. She didn't want to leave the body and crime scene unattended, but she didn't have any way of sending a GPS marker of the exact location in the forest due to the spotty reception. She would have to lead the chief to the area. She paced back and forth as the minutes ticked down. There were no sirens or cars approaching. She looked at the photos of the victim, area, and the totem several times, trying to put together some type of preliminary profile, but there wasn't enough evidence yet to do so.

Snow began to fall. Light fluffy pieces.

"Oh no," she whispered. She needed to get something to cover the scene otherwise the snow would either bury any significant evidence or soak it. She ran into the cabin followed closely by Cisco, who sniffed her with interest. "You have to stay here," she said.

She searched for anything she could use. Finally, in the kitchen storage cupboard she found several tarps still in their bags. She grabbed them, some bungee cords, a hammer and nails, and a tent complete with poles, then left the cabin, running as fast as she could back to the crime scene. If the police came in the meantime, they would have to wait for her at the cabin.

She worked quickly, assembling a makeshift covering to protect as much as she could. She was able to drape the tree trunk and use the tent poles with the tarps and nails to keep the snow off the hanging body. Another tarp covered the totem area. That was the best she could do for the obvious evidence, but she cringed about other possible evidence that wasn't immediately visible.

Katie then jogged back to the cabin, expecting to see the police, but there was no one. She sighed and dialed the police department, but this time the phone went immediately to voicemail. She wondered where they were.

Almost forty-five minutes had passed since Katie had spoken to Libby and before she had secured the crime scene. The snow flurries had stopped, which was the only good thing. Katie walked back and forth, inside and outside, the cabin—pacing and processing what she had seen, trying to make sense of everything.

She finally heard cars approaching. One moment they seemed close, but then they seemed to be farther away. She had forgotten that the town was called Echo Forest because sound traveled strangely around the area. Realizing the truth of the name, she continued to wait for the police.

Finally, two police sedans arrived along with a large white truck. It was more than Katie expected, which was definitely a good thing. A tall man in his fifties wearing a police uniform got out of the lead car. His shaggy brown hair seemed out of place, with most police officers wearing their hair short or in crew cuts. He casually looked around and then fixed his attention directly on Katie.

"Detective?" said the first man. "I'm Chief Cooper." He extended his hand.

The sound of Cisco barking from inside the cabin cut the awkward silence. Another police officer exited his vehicle. The stocky man walked up the driveway.

The chief turned as the man built like a tank joined them. "This is one of my officers, Banning."

Katie nodded and shook both of their hands. She couldn't help but notice that they scrutinized her almost in a way that a cop would a suspect.

"I just arrived yesterday and I'll be staying here for two weeks. I'm Katie Scott, a detective from the Pine Valley Sheriff's Department."

"Reason for your visit?" said the chief.

Katie was taken aback. That was hardly a priority at the moment. "Vacation time," she said.

"Seems odd." His tone was officious.

"What do you mean?"

"Two weeks is a long time. Most would go somewhere that was more of a vacation area," said the chief. "Not much to do here."

"I needed some peace and quiet." Katie was becoming more suspicious about the line of questioning and didn't appreciate having to explain herself. And why hadn't the chief immediately asked about the body? That seemed very odd to her.

"So what's this about a body?" said the chief, finally, but with a hint of sarcasm.

Katie glanced to the other officer. He stared at her.

"At about 0815 there was a knock at my door. A teenage girl

stood there upset and said her name was TJ and that she had found a woman in the woods."

"Did you get any more information about the girl?"

"No. She took me to the location," she said. "Follow me." Katie wanted to get moving so she could get back to her relaxation time.

As she moved through the trees, the area around her seemed to change. It was lighter now the snow had stopped. The trees, leaves, and ground seemed to brighten. When Katie reached the crime scene everything was exactly as she had left it.

"Did you do this?" said the chief, indicating the tarps. It was clear he wasn't happy.

"Yes. It had started to snow and I didn't want any evidence ruined."

"By the looks of it that's exactly what you did."

"Excuse me?"

"You've traipsed all around setting up your tent without authorization and showing a complete lack of professionalism."

Katie was annoyed to say the least, but she decided to tread lightly. She was in someone else's jurisdiction, and she wasn't a trusted person. She could almost see his point.

"Just what kind of detective are you?" said Officer Banning. He fidgeted with his uniform on his bulky body and then ran his fingers along his beard.

"I'm a cold-case detective."

"I see. Not used to active crime scenes, I guess," said Chief Cooper.

"I commend the visiting detective's initiative," said a voice behind them. It belonged to a sandy-haired man in his forties, fit, medium-build with a crew cut and dressed in snow gear. His footsteps made noise in the light snow due to his heavy hiking boots. His eyes were dark, making a striking contrast with his hair.

Katie turned her attention to him. She wondered why he

wasn't in uniform. Then she noticed he was carrying a medium-sized plastic case. "Forensics?"

"No. I'm Dr. Jack Thomas. But everyone just calls me Jack."

"This is Detective Katie Scott from the Pine Valley Sheriff's Department, *cold-case* unit," said the chief.

"Nice to meet you," said Jack.

There was an uncomfortable silence.

Katie decided to fill in the gaps. "After I followed TJ, she showed me the location of the body. It looked to be a teen to early twenties with a burlap sack over her head. There is also a strange type of totem next to her. I walked in one way and exited that same way"—she indicated her route—"and when the snow began, I returned from the cabin with something to cover everything from the weather."

"Quick thinking," said Jack.

Katie turned to leave them to their work and crime-scene investigation.

"Where are you going?" said the chief.

"Back to my cabin."

"You wait right here until I can verify who you are." He turned to the other officer. "Go grab your kit."

Officer Banning left.

"I'll be at the cabin if you have any questions for your report," Katie said.

"No, you're going to stay here where I can keep an eye on you."

"You can call Sheriff Wayne Scott at the Pine Valley Sheriff's Department," she said. "I'm sure you can get the phone number."

Chief Cooper grimaced as he looked at his phone, probably due to a sketchy signal. "Scott? Any relation?"

Katie hesitated for a moment. "He's my uncle."

"I see." The chief kept moving until he could make a call.

Katie shook her head.

"Don't worry about him. He doesn't particularly like strangers, especially intelligent and very capable ones. Trust me, he does grow on you." Jack smiled. "I promise."

Katie watched Jack move around the crime scene like a pro. He carefully entered and peeled back the tent to the body and carefully examined the woman, not removing the burlap bag. She wondered why the medical examiner's office was conducting a crime-scene investigation. Wouldn't they wait until the body was back at the morgue?

"Excuse me, but I didn't realize the medical examiner's office came to crime scenes," said Katie.

"They don't."

"So are you verifying the time of death?"

"Something like that."

"You *are* a doctor from the medical examiner's office?"

"No."

Katie was confused. "You *are* a doctor?"

"Of course. I'm a doctor of veterinary medicine."

Katie stared at him, unsure if she had heard him correctly.

He chuckled. "I do come out on calls like this, which are extremely rare, before the body gets transported. I think the last murder was more than fifteen years ago. And, unfortunately, we can't transport immediately due to personnel and road issues today, so she'll be put up in a freezer at my practice. Oh, but don't worry, I've taken a crime-scene investigation course a few years back. Mostly out of curiosity. I sure didn't think it would come in handy."

It took a lot for Katie to become speechless. A veterinarian was running a homicide crime scene and the police didn't appear to know much about how to conduct the investigation— at least in the typical sense. She could hear the chief talking to someone, but he was nowhere in sight. She looked in every direction.

"It's the way sound travels around here. You'll get used to it, otherwise it will drive you crazy," said the vet.

Katie nodded. She hoped the chief was talking to Sheriff Scott, so she could get back to the cabin and put this behind her. As much as she wanted to take over the investigation, that wasn't why she was there.

Katie watched Jack open the plastic case, which revealed a digital camera and some minor supplies for performing a crime scene investigation: all types and sizes of bags, containers, tweezers, gloves, measuring devices, and chain-of-custody bags.

The cool air blew a breeze through the trees, causing Katie to shudder. She needed to dress more warmly and in layers if she was going to spend time outside.

"You cold?" said Jack.

Katie nodded. "So tell me, how long have you been a vet and crime scene technician?"

He didn't answer her right away. After taking photographs of the body, he carefully put bags over the victim's hands and feet. "About as long as I've lived in Echo Forest."

"I see," she said.

Chief Cooper returned. "Your boss has volunteered your services if needed. You're going to be on-call, so don't leave town unless you clear it with me first."

Katie frowned. It wasn't as if she didn't want to dive into a murder investigation, but she was beginning to think her uncle was correct in having forced her to take some time off.

"How long did you book the cabin?" asked the chief.

"Two weeks, like I said."

"Hmm."

"I can see you're in good hands. If you don't need anything from me, I'll let you conduct your investigation," she said.

Officer Banning returned to the area.

"Make sure you submit your report," said Chief Cooper.

"Report?"

"Of how you came to find the body." He handed her his business card.

"Of course. It was nice meeting you both." Katie turned to walk away. "Oh, do you know TJ? She was shaken up. You might want to make sure she's okay."

"Can't say I know her, but don't worry, I'll be asking around. I think I know how to do my job."

"Does 'the Woodsman' mean anything to you?" she said, thinking of what the girl had whispered over and over.

"Nope. Should it?"

Katie shrugged.

"And I've never heard of any teen around here named TJ," said Jack. He seemed to be watching Katie with curiosity.

Katie thought that was strange since the town had barely five hundred residents and she had assumed the girl was a local out in the woods for a walk. She thought small towns were more likely to know a lot about each other's business. She turned and left the crime scene—the image of the young woman hanging in the tree burned into her memory.

FOUR

Tuesday 1135 hours

Katie had just finished unpacking her things and cleaning up the kitchen. She kept trying to put the homicide out of her mind. It wasn't her case and it wasn't her responsibility.

Cisco followed her around the cabin, whining once in a while. He wanted to make sure she didn't forget about him.

Though Katie initially didn't want to get involved in the homicide investigation, it was, after all, the type of case that was her expertise. Maybe she could just check out some things as she wrote her report. She sat down at the kitchen table with her laptop computer and quickly powered it up, deciding to grab another cup of coffee before sitting down again. The crime scene buzzed through her mind.

Cisco whined once more and then curled up at Katie's feet.

In order not to forget what happened, Katie typed up her report from the time TJ knocked on her door to the time the police arrived. She found an email for the police department and sent her report and contact information.

She then began checking out the town of Echo Forest. She didn't know exactly what she was looking for but wanted to try to get a feel and understanding of the area. She also checked out the website for the police department. She didn't find much, but it did refer to Chief Beryl Cooper and his bio stated that he had grown up in Colorado working as a police sergeant for Colorado Springs Police Department. He then moved to Echo Forest five years ago after being appointed to the position of chief.

Katie continued to scroll through the site, but it was mostly highlights and not much substance. She let out a sigh. Maybe she'd have better luck with the so-called Woodsman.

Typing in this name, and ignoring all the results about hunters and lumbermen, she found a ton of information including movies, books, and various blog articles that were based on a type of mythical monster that stalked people, namely children, in forests. There were artistic renderings and people's accounts, which seemed to cross over into other countries.

She then narrowed the search to the specific area and across three surrounding counties. After scrolling through several pages, she found an article from almost fifteen years ago written by local newspaper *The Pine Cone* that featured "the Woodsman." There wasn't much to the article, but it did say a woman was found dead about five miles from where Katie was staying. The case had remained unsolved and the article suggested that something powerful had murdered her. The commentary inferred that something in the forest had killed her—and it had then gone on to cite "the Woodsman." The article wasn't very helpful; it was more from the writer's point of view. Katie couldn't find anything about local folklore or any evidence related to the cold case. It was all too cumbersome to try to pinpoint what she was looking for. It frustrated her.

Katie leaned back in the chair and took a sip of coffee. There was nothing glaring or conclusive, but she found it troubling that TJ had been so terrified of what was most certainly a well-spun tale. It could have been stories she had heard growing up—or, though unlikely, it could be something more.

"Well, Cisco... what do you say? Should we go on a hike and check out the location of this cold case from fifteen years ago?"

Cisco immediately jumped up, wagging his tail.

She dropped the location into her phone and hoped the spotty cell signal would be available when they got there. Even if she found nothing, it would still be nice to get out for some fresh air.

Before closing her laptop, Katie decided to check out something. She typed in *Jack Thomas, veterinarian, Echo Forest, California*.

A simple website popped up. It showed some stock photographs of cute dogs and cats. There was an image of an older warehouse with a sign out front: "Thomas Veterinary Clinic."

Katie put the address into her phone: 1216 Timber Road.

"C'mon, Cisco," she said.

The jet-black dog hurried to the front door, not missing a step. He breathed heavily at the doorknob.

Katie tucked her Glock into the holster underneath her sweater and jacket—just in case. She checked her phone and was surprised she hadn't received a text message from her uncle —or anyone else. She thought at least her partner, McGaven, would have checked in with her by leaving a funny message. But her phone was quiet. She supposed everyone was giving her rest and privacy.

Katie and Cisco climbed into the Jeep. Cisco stood in the back seat behind Katie, staring straight over her shoulder. His tail wagged and every few minutes he let out a whine.

The little bit of snow that had come down earlier was now melting. The roads were completely clear and the only evidence of the previous flurries was spotted along the tree branches.

It took about ten minutes before she came to the downtown area. She passed a couple of trucks with single drivers and one utility van. The traffic was nonexistent compared to what she was used to in Pine Valley. The main street was scattered with a few stores and was about a mile long with adjacent side streets where the grocery, hardware, and supply businesses were located. She decided to stop and get some groceries just in case the weather hit harder overnight.

When Katie was back behind the wheel, her GPS told her to turn onto a gravel road and then travel farther west. The longer she drove the more rural the area became. She had just passed the five-mile marker, which was near a hiking trail entrance. There were no other cars parked. She wasn't sure what she would find, if anything, but she wanted to get a sense of what had attracted the killer to use the densely wooded area to dump a body.

After making sure the Jeep was secured and locked, she and Cisco headed to the trail. Cisco trotted about five feet ahead, stopping once in a while to sniff something of interest. She tied the dog's leather collar around her waist in case she needed it.

Katie looked at her phone, which amazingly had a signal, and which showed that she was close to the described location. But it wouldn't give her the exact coordinates. Either way, she estimated they were near the site.

Katie slowed her pace, then stopped and surveyed the area, wondering how different the forest was from fifteen years ago. In the article there weren't any details about the crime scene, just that a woman had been murdered. No name. No details of the scene. No cause of death. No mention of any suspects and so forth. Just that it was a cold case. The article seemed to be a mishmash of information, and most of it not informative.

The air was cold and the bitterness of it stung her face, but the wind was so slight as to be almost perfectly still. The forest area around her was quiet—too quiet.

Katie noticed that Cisco had stopped and was staring straight ahead. His body was tense, unmoving, looking with intensity at what appeared to be nothing.

Katie's arms tingled. She thought she had heard something, but then dismissed it. It wasn't because of anything she saw, but rather, something she sensed. She looked around a few minutes, but was satisfied it was a combination of the cold weather conditions and that she was surveying an area that was once a crime scene.

"Cisco..." she said.

The dog hesitated, but then turned, wagging his tail as he approached Katie.

She took another few minutes to look around. It was definitely an overgrown area, but the walking path had been kept clear—most likely by the county for hikers. She didn't have anything to go on and there wasn't anything obvious she could scrutinize and she couldn't even identify the exact location. Katie sighed. The clouds blocked all the daylight. The temperature seemed to drop more, making her shiver. Maybe it was a stupid idea, trying to fill her boring days with something she could sink her teeth into, such as a cold case.

"C'mon, Cisco." She headed back up the trail as Cisco effortlessly trotted ahead.

That's when she heard it... a soft whisper in the wind, "*Katie...*"

Katie spun around with her hand on her Glock, expecting to see someone, but there was no one there. She continued to take a slow three-hundred-sixty-degree scrutiny of the forest. There was nothing.

Cisco had moved close to her. She felt his warm body at the

side of her left leg. His body language had changed, becoming vigilant. She took a few more minutes until she was satisfied there was no one there.

Katie took a breath and continued toward her Jeep. One thing was for sure, she had definitely heard her name. She was not imagining it.

FIVE

Katie sat in her Jeep across from 1216 Timber Road, where veterinarian Jack Thomas had his practice. She watched and waited as the police chief and a van left, leaving only a large specialized truck that had compartments and a covered bed. She assumed the vehicle belonged to the vet.

Cisco was sniffing the grocery bags hopefully. "Leave those alone," she said fondly.

For some reason, as she looked at the warehouse converted into a veterinary hospital, everything about the crime scene and the victim weighed heavy on her mind. She wasn't sure if it was because now she had nothing to do, no place to go—and a homicide victim left next to her vacation cabin had piqued her interest. Her curious mind kept pushing the strangeness of the entire situation: TJ coming to her door, the town so small that the local veterinarian was the crime scene technician, the body stored in the vet's refrigerator waiting to be picked up by the county medical examiner's office.

Cisco whined and poked his head toward Katie.

"I know... I know..." She scratched the big dog's ears. Katie knew Cisco was bored too, also not used to having so much downtime. She opened her door and stepped out. "I'll be right back," she told him.

Katie crossed the street and walked to the vet's office. She didn't realize how big the old warehouse building was—it even had a second story. From what she could tell, the office was all downstairs. She noticed there was attractive landscaping, neat and tidy, the blooming plants dormant due to winter approaching. There was also a fenced-in area with tables that were stacked against the building for the winter. There was a modern staircase leading up the left side. She wondered what was up there. One thing at a time, she told herself.

She couldn't shake the uniqueness of the entire situation and the uneasiness she felt moving around the town. Tingling extremities, shallow breathing, and slight dizziness were trying to make their presence known but she fought hard to keep level and calm. It often happened when she faced the unknown or something she couldn't figure out, and had learned that these anxiety symptoms sometimes would indicate something was going to happen even before she knew it.

Katie walked to the entrance, which had two large swinging doors. She pushed open one of them, triggering a low buzzing noise.

The main area was large, warm, and inviting. There was no receptionist and it wasn't clear if there usually was one. The long check-in counter was the centerpiece and there were cute gates on each side for entering and leaving. The built-in furniture matched a more rustic environment, reminiscent of a barn, which was fitting. The chairs and benches had easy-to-clean colorful cushions. There were many photographs of animals and their owners on the walls varying in size—dogs, cats, horses, pigs, and reptiles.

Katie stopped and gazed at the pictures.

"Detective."

She turned and saw Jack standing behind the counter. "Hi."

"Everything okay?"

"Yes."

"I heard a dog barking in your cabin earlier."

"That's Cisco."

"German shepherd?" he said, smiling.

"How did you know?"

"I know that bark anywhere."

"I'm sorry to come by without calling..."

"No problem," he said and walked through one of the gates. "I sense something is troubling you."

"Actually, I was curious about the crime scene. But now..."

"Now once you're here you think maybe you were a bit overzealous?" he chuckled. "Detective..."

"Please, call me Katie."

"Katie," he said. "I'll answer any questions you have. But I don't know how much I can help."

"I think you can." She could smell the aroma of some type of tea.

"I'm sorry. Would you like some tea?"

It was as if he had read her mind.

"Yes," she said, glancing out the window at her Jeep.

"Did you bring your dog?"

"Yes, he's in the car."

"It's going to get colder. Bring him in."

"Well..." She didn't want to stay long.

"I just have two boarded dogs, but they're in another area. And another dog, Abby, is in my office."

"Okay." Katie didn't like leaving Cisco and she thought the area would be fine for him.

It took Katie a couple of minutes before she returned with Cisco heeling at her side. She walked through the main door as the dog curiously sniffed around.

"Wow, he's a beauty, and has an obvious even temperament. Is he a police or military dog?" Jack approached Katie and handed her a steaming mug.

Cisco glanced in his direction, but didn't seem interested in the vet, though he kept close to Katie.

Katie took a sip of the tea. "This is delicious." She paused, not initially keen to share her personal life, but then said, "Cisco and I were an explosives K9 team in the Army."

"Well, I've seen a lot of dogs and their companions, and I can tell you two have a very special bond." He seemed to study Katie. It was clear he wanted to ask more questions about her Army tours, but he kept quiet.

Katie nodded, continuing to drink her tea. Her hands warmed and she didn't have those annoying anxious feelings anymore and began to relax, which was something for her.

Jack leaned against the counter. "I don't think you came here for tea. What's on your mind?"

Katie remained quiet, gathering her thoughts. She knew she had to tread lightly because she didn't know Jack or how the town conducted its crime scene business.

"You're concerned about the homicide investigation?" he said.

"Yes. I want to do whatever I can to assist."

Jack stood up and took a step toward her. "Why do I think there's more to it than that?"

"What can I say? I'm a cold-case detective—mostly homicides."

"And you're on a vacation and there was a body dumped right next door."

Katie nodded.

"I can see your point." Jack opened one of the gates, as Cisco seemed eager to find out what was on the other side. He watched her with curiosity. "C'mon. I'm sure you want to look at the body and ask some questions."

Katie tried to figure out the vet. She was quite sure there was more to his story. "I don't want to intrude on your work schedule."

"I don't have any appointments until 4 p.m."

Katie followed him. "Thank you."

Cisco happily shadowed them.

Katie was impressed by the layout of the building. It was clearly thought out. There were several private exam rooms, storage supply closets, a sitting area for animal parents, and two or three private offices. The floor remained a rustic wood that looked to be original.

"How long have you been here?" she said.

"The building belonged to my aunt and uncle. They had a hardware and feed store, and there were six apartments upstairs." He took their mugs and set them down in a sink. "I used to help out here on vacations when I was a kid."

"So you're not from here?"

"No. I grew up in Sacramento. But I spent a lot of time here."

"What made you want to set up practice in Echo Forest?"

"Why not?" He smiled. "I love it here. I spend most of my professional time as a mobile vet. There are a lot of farms and ranches."

"And you're also a crime scene technician," she said. "How do you know how to do that?"

"My secret is out."

Katie chuckled. "What do you mean?"

"I actually went through the police academy, but decided to go another avenue instead."

Katie nodded. "I see." She thought that was interesting, going from being a cop to a veterinarian. "Being true to yourself."

Jack stopped just before a large door and looked at Katie. "Yeah, exactly. Most people don't get that."

They stood for an awkward moment.

Katie realized the door was a large freezer. She turned to Cisco and said, "*Platz... bleib.*"

The dog immediately lay down and stayed in his position.

"German commands?"

"Yes."

Before opening the door, Jack grabbed a file from a wall holder. He handed Katie the file. There were two sealed evidence boxes stacked just to the left of the door, which had the proper chain-of-custody paperwork taped to them.

"Where is this evidence going?"

"To the state lab for processing, since this area doesn't have lab facilities."

Katie opened the file, where there were photos and information about the victim and condition of the body. "How did you get all this information so fast?" She couldn't believe what she was reading. It was complete with the name of the victim. Nineteen-year-old Theresa Ann Jamison. "I don't understand."

"According to Officer Bobby Clark, he recognized the girl. Apparently she was a friend of his sister."

"So there's been a positive ID?"

"That's my four o'clock appointment. Her cousin is driving in from Pine Valley to ID the body."

Katie's mind spun with uncertainty. Even in Pine Valley, where there were more personnel, they didn't get all this information so quickly. "Chief Cooper seemed to indicate that they didn't know anything about the victim."

"I don't know what to tell you. I was given the information and filled out the paperwork for the investigation, per the chief. Basically my part is over after the body is picked up tomorrow and transferred to Raven Falls, which is the county seat. They have a medical examiner."

Katie reread a few pieces of information. Theresa was a

longtime resident of Echo Forest. "I guess they'll be able to do an autopsy?"

"That's my understanding." Jack then pulled the large silver lever and opened the door.

Katie waited for Jack to enter first. The immediate cold whipped out, taking her by surprise and almost causing her body to stop mid-step. Her breath caught in her throat. Even though it had been cold outside with some snow flurries, it didn't compare to the large refrigerated room.

The overhead lights immediately turned on when they were inside. The illumination made everything appear almost colorless. It was like entering a decompression chamber. Next to the refrigerator system was a freezer used to accommodate animals that had passed or were euthanized.

Katie shivered and looked at the gurney supporting the outline of a body in a heavy plastic bag.

"Are you looking for anything specific?" said Jack.

His voice almost made Katie jolt—it sounded hollow and lifeless inside the closed room.

"I'm not sure," she said. That wasn't completely true, but she wasn't going to show all her cards just yet—if ever.

Katie wanted a closer look at the injuries to try to get a better understanding of the killer. Jack unzipped the body bag and folded back the plastic. The girl's hands and feet were protected by plastic bags, but the pink fingernails were still visible.

As always, Katie did not look at the victim's face immediately. She focused on the girl's neck and the impressions that indicated ligature marks. Then Katie leaned closer and her eyes trailed to the victim's face. She sucked in a breath and stood up straight. The room seemed to spin and everything became oddly fuzzy around her. She couldn't believe what she was seeing.

Still staring at the young victim's face, it as if she was looking at TJ—the young woman who came to her door for help.

SIX

Katie sat in a colorful molded chair near the front counter. She was mad, embarrassed, and still weak, which made her even angrier. She had never fainted or become close to it before. It wasn't looking at a dead body. It was the fact that the young woman resembled the girl who had pounded on her door. It wasn't just a resemblance—she was a twin or doppelganger of TJ.

Cisco sat at her side. He remained calm and comforted Katie as best as he could.

What was going on? It was like a parlor game.

Jack brought her a bottle of water.

"Thank you," she said and began to drink. It was difficult to make eye contact with the vet. Just as she didn't know much about him, he didn't know anything about her. "I'm sorry. I've never been this unprofessional in a case." She stood up, having regained strength in her body. A little wobbly, but she was going to push through it.

"Rest," said Jack. "When was the last time you ate?"

"Early. Just a bite and some coffee."

Jack frowned. "I see."

"I'm fine. I have groceries in the car. I'll eat when I get home."

He studied her for a moment. "I get the impression you're not only tough, but a bit stubborn."

Katie was going to protest, but she laughed instead. "Maybe."

"You're on a vacation. Take care of yourself."

"I appreciate your time. I guess I'll be hearing from the chief if he needs help."

Jack went to the front desk. "Give me your number and I'll send you a text."

"For?" she said.

"I'll send copies of everything I can. Save you the trouble of asking later on."

"Are you sure?" Katie knew the chief was most likely going to solicit her help. He wouldn't have a choice.

"Of course. You're a police detective. I'm sure you know how to keep things confidential."

Katie smiled and quickly wrote down her cell number. "Thank you."

"My pleasure." The vet watched as Katie and Cisco left his office.

Katie drove into the gravel driveway at the cabin. The entire drive she kept rehashing the victim's startling resemblance to TJ. She got out of the Jeep, grabbed the two grocery bags, and entered the cabin. The afternoon was definitely colder than it had been earlier in the day.

Cisco whined, but this time it was because he wanted his dinner.

"Isn't it a little bit early?" she said, smiling at the dog.

Katie organized her food and decided she would make a skillet stir-fry with the rotisserie chicken and vegetables she'd bought. In less than twenty minutes, she had fed Cisco and was sitting down to eat. Everything smelled great; she hadn't realized how hungry she was until she began eating. She opened her laptop and searched to find anything about the homicide, but she found nothing. She tried social media and the local news station. Nothing. It seemed odd. It would be difficult to keep this kind of crime news quiet—especially in a small town.

Katie finally closed her computer and sat for a moment. She had the urge to call McGaven and her uncle to discuss the case. Why? It wasn't her case, and the Echo Forest police probably weren't going to ask her for assistance.

"Oh, Cisco..." The black dog sat up and perked his ears at the sound of his name. "I'm sorry... this whole vacation and relaxation thing is going to be hard. Who knew?"

Katie wandered into the small living room, where there were DVDs and CDs on the shelves. She decided to watch a couple of movies and hoped it would take her mind off the homicide, TJ, the chief, and Jack the veterinarian. But as hard as she tried to watch a movie, the investigation kept flashing through her mind.

It was barely ten when Katie dozed off on the couch. The movie had stopped running and the cabin was quiet. She fell deep asleep and didn't wake until almost five, when Cisco jumped on the couch, startling her awake.

"Cisco!" she said.

The dog barked several times as he jumped on the couch.

"Why are you all wet?" Her hands touched the cold dog and his sopping paws.

At first, she thought he had been outside, but then Katie

quickly stood up and immediately her feet sank into a couple inches of icy water.

"Ugh..." Katie moved quickly to the kitchen area in her drenched socks and could see there was water coming from under the sink. She flung open the lower cabinet doors.

The pipes had burst.

SEVEN

Wednesday 0645 hours

Katie loaded her Jeep with her things and planned on having a nice big breakfast in town while figuring out what to do. She wasn't sure if she should just return to Pine Valley or try to find somewhere else to stay nearby.

Katie had spoken with the cabin owners and they'd extended their apologies. There would be a maintenance crew coming in to take care of the house and the pipes, but unfortunately for Katie they wouldn't be arriving anytime soon.

After locking the cabin door and leaving the key where instructed, Katie climbed into her Jeep. She paused a moment, staring at the cabin and then glancing around. The crime scene was still very much on her mind and the victim was still as disturbing to her as it had been the day before.

Cisco poked his head at her.

"All right, let's go..."

Katie drove into town where there was a diner, the Sunrise Café, which had a large neon "open" sign in the window. She pulled up next to several trucks and other vehicles. It appeared to be a popular morning place. She found a table by the window where she could keep an eye on her Jeep and Cisco, who was snoozing on a blanket on the back seat. She ordered a large coffee and the special "farmer's breakfast," which was a little bit of everything. Still feeling the chill throughout her body, she welcomed the hot coffee.

Looking around while waiting for her food, Katie noticed that several patrons stared at her. She wondered if she looked that out of place or if they just wondered who she was and why she was alone. She politely smiled back.

Katie decided to scroll through her phone to find any nearby vacation rentals but there were only small motels. It looked like she was going back to Pine Valley. She didn't mind, but she did feel in a way that she was ignoring the homicide—it was a crucial phase of the investigation. Why did the victim look so much like the person who had found her? That haunted her. The images, crime scene, and investigation kept pulling her back in—it was who she was. But there was nothing she could do and it seemed the decision to leave Echo Forest had already been made for her.

The diner's door opened, and Jack and a police officer Katie hadn't seen before entered. A rush of cold air whipped through the diner. Jack immediately saw Katie. He walked over to her as she scrolled for other accommodations.

"Good morning," he said.

Katie looked up and saw Jack with a big smile on his face. "I suppose it's a good morning," she said.

"Katie, this is Officer Bobby Clark."

"Nice to meet you, Officer Clark," she said.

"Ma'am," he said and nodded. The officer went to get a couple of coffees to go. He had short dark hair and a well-trimmed beard, which was the opposite of his fellow officer from the crime scene.

"Aren't you up bright and early for someone on vacation?" Jack asked.

"Not by choice."

Jack frowned. "Everything okay?"

"My cabin's pipes burst this morning."

"Oh, no."

"I'm contemplating whether to drive home to Pine Valley or to try to find a place to stay nearby."

"Any prospects?" he said.

"Unfortunately not." She put down her phone. "You both are welcome to join me." Glancing around the diner, she thought it might keep people from staring if she was with the town's vet and one of its police officers.

Officer Clark returned with a large coffee in hand. "Catch you later," he said to Jack. "Nice to meet you," he said to Katie. The officer left.

Jack pulled out a chair. "You sure you don't mind?"

"No, please sit down."

The waitress approached the table with Katie's breakfast. Katie began to dig in immediately. She was hungry and figured the food would help give her the strength she needed today. Plus it was delicious.

"The usual please," said Jack to the server. "Now, what do you plan to do?" he asked Katie when they were alone again.

Katie sighed. "Well... the cabin is definitely out. It will take a while to completely dry out and I'm not sure how long to repair the pipes."

"Unfortunately, bursting pipes aren't anything new around here..."

Katie didn't speak. She could tell he had more to say.

"I may have a solution, though."

"What do you mean?"

"I'll show you after breakfast," he said cryptically.

"Okay." She was curious, but cautious.

The waitress brought a large plate of pancakes and bacon for Jack. They ate in silence. Katie was lost in her thoughts of not only the homicide, but where she was going to land for the rest of her ordered vacation.

It wasn't as cold as the previous day, with a bit of sun shining. But Katie was still chilled. The weather didn't seem to bother Cisco as he happily trotted along with her and Jack.

"Where are we going?" she said.

"You'll see."

Katie and Cisco followed Jack around the veterinary warehouse and climbed the stairs Katie had noticed yesterday. The new railing and steps led to a large landing and balcony overlooking a creek in the back. It was quite picturesque, even in wintertime. A sign read: "Echo Forest Lodge."

"What is this?"

Jack punched in a five-digit code at the door and opened it. "Take a look."

Cisco didn't wait for them as he bolted inside. Katie could hear the dog's nails clicking on what sounded like hardwood floors. She quickly stepped inside as Jack turned on the lights.

"Wow..." she said looking around. "Did not see this coming."

It looked as if she had stepped into a four-star hotel. She was greeted with beautiful hardwood floors, built-in shelving, two sitting areas with leather couches, two large rustic chandeliers, and high-end artwork of bronze statues of cowboys and horses. There were rugs in designs of brown, black, and white on the floor, and a large front desk with intricate carvings was placed almost center of the large room. There was a long hallway where she assumed guest rooms were located.

"What is this? It looks like a resort," she said as she walked around inspecting the décor.

"That's what I was going for."

"What happened? I mean, why isn't this place booming?"

"Nothing. It's usually booked during the spring and summer. Winter not so much—at least not yet. I'm trying to find some guides that would take guests on hikes, tours of historic areas, and maybe skiing."

Cisco was interested in one of pillows on the leather couch and then went to check out other areas.

Jack laughed. "As I said before, they owned this building for a long time and it was their dream to have a really nice retreat up here and offices downstairs. Unfortunately, they didn't live to see this."

"Oh wow, they would have been absolutely mesmerized."

"You like it?"

"How could you not?"

"Originally there were six basic apartments up here that I transformed into four guest suites with this front room and a roomy kitchen and storage areas."

"Like a bed-and-breakfast."

"Something like that. It's taken a while with the construction remodel, but I've had numerous guests this year, it was basically booked for four months solid, and I'm hoping it will continue to grow."

Katie turned to Jack. "But what does this have to do with me?"

"You and Cisco are welcome to stay here. There are two suites that are ready for guests. You can have your pick. The two others are being redecorated and updated with new furniture and aren't entirely ready for guests yet."

"I—"

"It'll be quiet for you and it's a great place to relax. There are hiking trails nearby." He stood smiling, watching her reaction. "And this is an area with good cell phone signal, there's Wi-Fi too. Can't beat that around here."

"I can't..." She continued to look around amazed by the place.

"It'll be like your private resort. I'll charge you whatever you were paying on the cabin."

"No, I can't do that."

Jack laughed. "You keep saying you can't... That doesn't sound like a cold-case detective to me."

"And Cisco?"

The dog barked on hearing his name.

"He's welcome, of course."

"I don't know..."

"Follow me and take a look at the suites, each with a private bath, and you can make your decision." He walked down the hallway, expecting Katie to follow. "Since we're not booked with anyone right now, the cleaning staff comes in once a week to check everything and keep everything sparkling. My manager and cook are both retired and come in when needed."

Katie tried not to get overly excited because it seemed too good to be true. The murder was highlighted in her mind and she really wanted to stay in case she could help with the investigation. There wasn't anything else keeping her in Echo Forest—she could rest anywhere—but if the local police ended up recruiting her, this would certainly be a relaxing place to stay while she assisted them.

Jack opened one of the suites—it too had a digital keypad. It beeped five times.

"Take a look," he said.

Katie walked in with Cisco at her side. It was even more stunning than the front room. Similar in style, it too had a rustic beauty about it. All the furniture—bed, dresser, nightstands, sitting area with table, and two overstuffed comfortable chairs—appeared to be made by the same craftsman. The curtains, bed comforter, pillows, and upholstery were in earth tones with a few pops of blue and yellow. There were two big windows that looked out over the forest that backed up to the warehouse.

"This is beautiful," she said, taking a quick peek of the bathroom. It was as wonderfully decorated, with a large shower and claw-foot tub along with fresh linens and towels.

"You can look at the other one if you would like."

"No, that won't be necessary." She turned to Jack. "I can't possibly pay you what I was paying for the cabin—"

"Why not? No one is here—there's no waiting list. These rooms are just sitting empty." He moved to the window and pulled back the sheer curtain. "It's the least I could do for one of our finest."

Katie didn't want to feel as if she was getting a special deal because she was a police detective. She remained quiet and looked around. It was like going to a resort—something she had never done because it wasn't within her budget.

"C'mon, Detective," he said, petting Cisco. "This shouldn't be a difficult decision. It would be peace of mind for me, knowing a police officer is staying here as security."

Katie ran several things through her mind. "Okay," she said.

"Yeah?"

"It would be a privilege to stay here, but I will pay you."

"Great. Let me give you the codes and the Wi-Fi name." He turned to leave when his cell phone rang. "Dr. Thomas. When? Where is he now?" Jack turned to Katie with a distressed look upon his face. "I'll be right there." He hung up.

"What's wrong?"

"It's the chief. C'mon."

EIGHT

Katie drove her Jeep and followed Jack in his truck to the hospital, which was more than ten miles away. The chief had suffered a heart attack and had been taken to the closest medical facility: General Hospital just on the outskirts of Echo Forest.

Pulling into the parking lot, Katie was surprised that it was a small hospital, resembling more of an urgent care facility. She hoped the chief's condition was stable and not as severe as it had sounded.

She got out and joined Jack as they hurried to the building. There were two police cars and an ambulance parked near the entrance. The large glass door slid open and they rushed inside.

The woman at the front desk looked up. "Can I help you?"

"Chief Beryl Cooper was brought in," said Jack.

"Yes," she said and nodded.

At that moment, Officer Clark appeared.

Jack turned. "How is he?"

"Stable. It was a cardiac event, they said. But he's going to be here for a while," said the officer. His face was strained and he seemed extremely upset.

"What happened?" said Katie.

"We were going over everything for a morning briefing and then organizing duties for the homicide... and he held his chest and dropped."

"When can he see visitors?" said Jack.

"Not until later."

"Does he have family?" said Katie.

"No, he's a widower," said Jack.

"We're his family," said the officer.

"We're all family," chimed Jack.

That hit a chord with Katie. She hadn't realized how close they all were. She'd only seen that the chief wasn't happy with an outsider, a detective no less, coming into their territory. She was too busy concentrating on the crime scene, finding and protecting any potential evidence to see they all were close and worked well together.

Officer Clark turned to Katie. "He's turned over the investigation to you, Detective."

"What?" she said. "I'm just on vacation."

"That's all I know. He doesn't want FBI or other agencies coming into our town. Will you do it?"

Clark and Jack stared at Katie, waiting for her to answer.

Katie blinked in surprise. She knew she couldn't get her mind off the homicide crime scene, but now as they looked to her she wasn't so sure about the situation. "It's not that easy. Sheriff Scott needs to be informed..."

"The chief has already talked to him."

"When? I know he verified me at the crime scene, but..."

"That's what we were talking about this morning. Of course, you need to talk to your sheriff and go through your protocols."

"And... I will need some things," she said. Her mind was reeling. "And... I need my crew."

"Anything you need, we'll work it out. Officer Terrance Banning and I have been briefed to the chief's decision. Detective, you don't need to worry, we're all on board." The officer seemed honest in his statement and his eyes looked distressed.

"You have a perfect and private place to set up your headquarters at the lodge," said Jack.

"Our office is definitely too small for such an investigation," said Officer Clark.

Katie already felt the weight of the investigation. How could she deny working the case? Vacation or not, there had been a horrific murder of a young woman. And if her instincts were correct, there would be another. The totem aspect was a strong signature and would most likely prove to be a key part to the case. She felt the pull and responsibility to conduct the investigation to the best of her abilities. But there were some things that bothered her about how things got to this point.

Jack took a step closer to Katie. "Well?"

Katie nodded. "I will do everything I can."

"Great," said Clark. "Give me a list of what you need. Officer Banning and I will make sure you have everything."

"Okay," she said.

"Let's get you settled in at the lodge," said Jack.

NINE

Katie and Cisco had settled into the suite after emptying her Jeep. She had been given the passcodes for the lodge, kitchen, and her suite. The vet had left to go downstairs to attend to patients and make a trip to one of the local ranches. Jack had stressed that she was to make herself at home around the lodge and that she could set up their command center in any of the other rooms.

Katie sat down in one of the chairs and called her uncle.

"Katie," Sheriff Scott said when he answered. His voice was cheerful, which was a little unusual, because when in command his voice was matter-of-fact, so he must've been in a private area. "How are you?"

"That's a loaded question."

There was a pause. "I think it's fairly straightforward. We both know you were going to struggle with what to do with yourself on a two-week vacation."

"You know me so well." She smiled.

"What's that I hear in your voice?"

"There's already been some strange things in this case," she said.

"Strange? Like what?"

"The girl who knocked on my door to alert me to the body hanging in the tree has disappeared. No one seems to know who she is... and... the victim has a striking resemblance to her."

"I see." He paused. Katie knew her uncle was mulling over what she had told him. "Your reputation and closed cases speak volumes, Katie. My advice? Start from the beginning like you always do and follow every lead, and if you have to, turn over every rock you find."

"I need Gav."

"I've already let him know about the situation. He's just finishing up a burglary case with Detective Hamilton."

"Okay." That explained why she hadn't heard from him, not to mention he had a longtime girlfriend, Denise, who worked as a supervisor in the records' division at Pine Valley Sheriff's Department.

"Keep me posted," said the sheriff. "And Katie..."

She knew what he was going to say.

"Be careful, be mindful, and don't take everything on by yourself. Understand?"

"Thank you, Uncle Wayne."

"By the way, this doesn't count as your time off."

"But—"

"No discussion."

"I love you."

"I love you too."

The call ended.

Katie sat and thought about her great losses. Uncle Wayne was her only family. Her parents had been killed in an auto accident when she wasn't even a teen. With no brothers or sisters, she was on her own. Her family were her close friends and colleagues.

Her thoughts were interrupted by Cisco snoring from the other chair. He was curled up tight with his big paws tucked in. She watched him peacefully sleep, his breath making his chest rise easily up and down.

Katie's phone rang.

"Scott."

"I miss my partner," said McGaven from the other end.

Katie was relieved and happy to hear his voice. They had been partners working cold cases for a while and she couldn't imagine working with anyone else. They knew each other's moves, and their different personalities complemented one another.

"So I take it you're up to speed with the situation," she said.

"Yes, so far. And I'm not the least bit surprised you'd take on a homicide on your vacation. But what's the deal with you staying at a veterinary hospital?"

Katie laughed. "I'm not staying at a vet's hospital. There's a beautiful lodge located on the second floor of the converted warehouse."

"Sounds interesting."

"When can you get here?"

"I'm finishing up some paperwork and I'll be able to leave by the end of the day."

Katie was pleased he would be arriving this evening. "Great."

"Anything I need to bring?"

"Anything that would help with sorting out the investigation, and your laptop, of course."

"So what's the wildlife like there?"

Katie knew he meant the other cops and not the native animals. "There're two police officers. The chief had a mild heart attack this morning, so he'll be on the sidelines."

"That still didn't answer my question."

"No complaints. They seem eager to help."

"Hmmm. I guess I'll have to wait until I meet them."

"I'll send you the location and entry codes. It takes about two hours to get here."

"Ten-four."

She was surprised he hadn't directly asked about the crime scene. "Gav?" She took a deep breath.

"Yeah."

"It's a bad one," she said.

"I know." He remained quiet for a moment. "We've got this."

Katie closed her eyes, trying not to picture the young woman hanging in the tree. "I know."

"And we've got each other's backs."

"Always."

"See you soon," he said.

Katie took a few moments before getting up. She was so fortunate to have Gav as her partner and it had made her transition seamless to the Pine Valley Sheriff's Department and heading up the cold-case unit.

Cisco ended his afternoon nap and came over to Katie, nudging her.

"Yep," she said.

She changed into appropriate running attire with extra layers to keep her warm. She was eager to check out the trails behind the Echo Forest Lodge. The chain of events and murder board listings kept churning through her mind, and she wanted to clear her head so she could get a jump start on the investigation.

TEN

Wednesday 1410 hours

Katie decided to have a look around outside her new accommodation. It was an unusual place for a lodge and she wondered if it was profitable, although it was a great place to get away and relax while enjoying the outdoors. She noticed that Jack's mobile vet truck was gone, so she could casually look around without raising any questions. She didn't notice any obvious outdoor cameras.

Cisco paused every so often to smell the patio furniture and along the garden fencing. The furniture was stacked and organized against the building, but Katie could imagine how the area would be pretty when the pots had flowers growing, and the table and chairs were placed about. The patio was wooden decking and seemed new. She wondered how Jack was able to get carpenters and construction workers in a place so small. He must've brought in workers from surrounding towns.

Cisco whined and wagged his tail as if to tell Katie he was ready to go for their run.

"Okay..." she said to the big dog. She took a few deep

breaths and did some slow stretching before starting down the trail.

There were two trail entries that were obvious and had been well-used. Katie decided to take the left one. Cisco stayed within six to eight feet of her at his own pace, but he was never too far away. The path was wide enough for two people to walk, but the wooded areas on either side were dense and tall. Katie kept her usual moderate pace, weaving along the trail. She felt as if she were in a maze because she couldn't see anything but forest. It wasn't something she was used to, and it felt borderline claustrophobic. She supposed for some people it was part of the appeal: to feel absolutely immersed in the trees.

Katie began to relax, trying to put behind her the bursting pipes incident and thoughts of the homicide case. She knew that garnering and preserving her mental strength was imperative. It seemed ironic to her that she was practicing relaxation, not for her vacation, but for a homicide investigation.

As she kept to the path around the twists and turns of the trail, she came to a larger clearing with two benches. She stopped, but kept gently jogging in place. It was a nice spot for people to rest or to sit and enjoy the area. The trail was well thought-out.

One bench had a memorial plaque with the name *Carol Ann Benedict*. There were no dates, words, or family included. It was as if she were an angel in the forest. Katie wondered who she was and all her instincts pushed that she was someone important.

The clouds partially cleared, revealing some sunshine; even though it wasn't particularly warm, it made the walking trail seem more inviting. Katie continued jogging but realized Cisco wasn't beside her. She turned around and saw the black dog had stopped and submerged himself into the wooded area.

"Cisco," she said. He was most likely sniffing some great smells of forest creatures. "Cisco." Katie jogged up to the dog and saw that he was definitely interested in something that wasn't a part of the landscape.

"*Hier.*" She told him to come so that she could see what it was. "*Platz.*"

Cisco immediately sat still, with his unwavering attention on her.

Katie bent down and could see something tan, like a piece of fabric. She reached into her pocket and retrieved a clean tissue. Leaning farther, she gently moved the material and saw it was a type of heavier and almost industrial textile. Turning it over, there were three small areas that appeared to be blood. Her first thought was that someone had had a bloody nose or a minor injury then tossed the item, but closer inspection of the fabric suggested it was a type of burlap.

Katie stood up, contemplating if she was overanalyzing it or if it could possibly be evidence from the crime scene. She took a quick photo of it and the area where it was found before retrieving the piece of burlap. She decided to roll it up and put it into the tissue. She then tucked the rolled-up wad into one of her zippered pockets.

She paused and studied the area. Her run had been in a zigzag direction with a couple of switchbacks, so she wasn't sure the course she was taking. Retrieving her cell phone, she had a weak signal but it told her she was now facing east. She pulled up a map application that showed where she was and was surprised she was heading to the same area as the cabin.

"*Fuss*, Cisco," she said, calling him to heel as she continued her run along the path, partly to see where it would come out. Even though there was no reason to feel uncomfortable, something didn't sit right with her about everything she had just seen. Most of the time she chalked up this feeling to being a cop and almost everything seeming suspicious. Or maybe it was because of the sounds and noises in this vastly dense forest.

Katie pushed herself harder, pumping her arms, and using

longer strides. Her runs were mostly for keeping her anxiety in check and wearing down the symptoms, which usually gave her clarity, but sometimes when she went for a run during an investigation it was as if she pushed herself forward to find the clues and the killer by brute strength and endurance.

When Katie reached her limit on her high-energy push, she slowed and then stopped, still walking in place.

Cisco breathed heavily with his tongue hanging out as he too walked around, allowing his pulse to level.

Katie didn't want to go too far from the lodge, since she didn't bring water for her or Cisco. But something caught her attention ahead.

The trail ended at a narrow road that looked more like a utility road, which were common in these types of small towns. She and Cisco stepped out onto the narrow road. It hadn't been kept up. Low-lying branches and overgrown brush pushed its way onto the track.

But there were deep tire marks that appeared relatively recent. Looking at the marks, Katie assumed it to be a utility truck from the city or county. A little farther, she saw deep divots about two feet apart that didn't look as if they were from a vehicle.

There was another trail ahead but Katie glanced at her watch and saw it was getting late. Soon it would be dusk and the light would disappear. She didn't want to return in the dark because she didn't have a flashlight and didn't want to use her cell phone for the only illumination.

Katie used her good judgment and decided to return to the lodge to prepare for the investigation and made a mental note that she would return to this area with McGaven. But first she needed to inspect the crime scene zone and to map out the hiking and accessible areas.

ELEVEN

Wednesday 1545 hours

Katie and Cisco took a slower pace back to the lodge. This time she studied the path and the surroundings, musing that the killer had perfect places to stay hidden and to stage his crime scene. It became clear the killer knew the area well—so they were either a regular resident or someone who had lived in the area previously.

Katie stepped back into the patio area of the lodge, where everything was still stored in the same manner as when she left. She didn't know why she thought it would be changed, but the area, especially the walking paths, seemed to make her feel uneasy. Perhaps it was just her exhaustion.

Before going inside, she peeked out front and noticed that Jack's truck was still gone.

"C'mon, Cisco..."

Katie climbed the stairs and paused on the large landing for a moment, staring out into the forest. The creek moved along in between trees over smooth river rocks. She could imagine in warmer weather relaxing out here and listening to the tranquil sound of the water. In the distance, nestled in between trees, she could see two rooftops that appeared to be barns. There was some fireplace smoke farther away that swirled up among the treetops in a ghostlike manifestation.

Katie quickly punched in the five-digit code: 55959. The lock disengaged and she pushed open the door. Upon entering the lodge a second time, it still had a welcoming feeling. Cisco ran inside and took a few laps around the main area.

"Okay, Cisco, calm down, we're guests here..." Katie laughed, watching the dog running and then checking stuff out before opting to run again.

Katie went to her suite to gather a few things then returned to the living area—it seemed to be a good place to set up their headquarters. She found a notebook in one of the front desk's drawers and began to make a list of things they would need: crime scene report, photographs, victim information, autopsy report, and any witness reports from nearby neighbors, etc.

Katie called Officer Bobby Clark. "Officer Clark, this is Detective Scott," she said.

"Yes, Detective, I've been waiting for your call."

"First, how is the chief doing?"

"He's stable, but they're going to keep him under observation for the next few days in the hospital. He's tough."

"Hmmm. He doesn't strike me as the kind of person to take it easy," she said.

The officer laughed. "No. You're spot on about that. He wanted me to tell you that he appreciates you taking lead on this investigation."

Katie looked around the room and thought she couldn't be anywhere that was more beautiful or comfortable. "Please tell him thank you from me. He doesn't know me, so I appreciate his trust."

"Your sheriff spoke highly of you and your record speaks volumes. We're lucky you decided to come to Echo Forest."

Katie didn't say anything. She had been wondering if she had made a mistake by getting involved.

"At your convenience, he would like for you to update him in person," said Officer Clark.

"Of course," she said. "I'll need your help, though. Could you spare one or two folding tables, power strips, and some minor office supplies like pens, notepads, and file folders for me?"

"Detective, I will have these things for you in a couple of hours."

"Sounds great. My partner will be arriving this evening, so we plan on hitting the ground running."

"Got it."

"Thank you."

The phone connection ended.

Katie scrutinized the large common area, where a folding table would best fit, but then realized she was getting hungry. She set the legal notepad and pen on the dining table and headed to the kitchen, where she had put her groceries in the large restaurant-size refrigerator. The kitchen seemed extremely big for four suites and Katie wondered if Jack was planning to hold gatherings or special parties.

She noticed a door at the end of the kitchen area that didn't have any handles. It seemed odd. Always curious, Katie had to investigate. She ran her fingers around the edges and could tell that it was indeed a door. But how to open it? There were no security locks like on the front door and suite entrances. She pushed it, but it didn't pop open. Running her fingers along the edges, she detected air at the top. That was strange.

Cisco whined, indicating he was hungry.

"Wait, Cisco."

Katie got a folding two-step ladder from the corner of the room and climbed up. She took her fingers to the top of the door and pried at the wood until she heard a snap. The door had opened an inch. Quickly stepping down, she managed to open the tall closet door, which was latched from the inside.

It wasn't a storage closet, but instead a dark space. Katie leaned in and could see stairs leading down. It was quiet but there was cold air coming in from the outdoors.

Katie rummaged in the kitchen drawers until she found a flashlight. She took it and directed the beam down the stairs. The only thing she could see was light escaping from somewhere else.

What was the reason for this hidden passageway?

Was it in the original design?

Was it added later?

Telling Cisco to stay, Katie stepped inside on the small landing and followed the stairs down, which ended at two doors. One was to the outdoors and from where she felt the cool air. The other one seemed to go into the veterinary hospital, where it was warmer.

It seemed strange, but there was most likely a logical explanation. Perhaps Jack hadn't wanted guests to be able access the surgery. He still had renovations to do; maybe he hadn't got around to bricking up this old stairwell. Katie hurried back to the kitchen and secured the secret passage's door.

She made herself a chicken and rice veggie bowl as well as fed Cisco. As she ate, she thought through all the strange occurrences since she had arrived in Echo Forest. Her mind stopped on the crime scene and the peculiar totem next to the body.

Katie spent the rest of the time while waiting for Officer Clark and McGaven searching for possible meaning in killers hanging their victims and the representation of some type of ritual with the outdoor elements in the totem. She read the reports about Theresa Jamison that Jack had sent her. The young woman had been a server at the Sunrise Café and was saving up to go to nursing school.

As the day gradually moved into the evening, the lodge felt

colder. Katie sat on one of the large sofas with a blanket and perused through search results about the items at the crime scene on her laptop. First, she wanted to read through ritual killings. They usually entailed removing the victim's body parts, or the act of drinking their blood for some purpose or offering. Usually to please gods or some other type of totem. She hadn't had much experience with these kinds of killers; they were rare in this country. But that makeshift display at the base of the tree appeared to have been constructed on purpose.

Basic murder statistics reveal that men are more likely to be victims of murder than women: approximately sixty to eighty percent. Women are more likely to be murdered by someone they know compared to men. To have a local girl murdered in a small town could possibly mean the killer was someone the girl knew well—an intimate partner.

From everything Katie had studied and experienced with homicide investigations, nothing was typical, but a homicide with a totem at a crime scene was definitely rare. It was telling about the killer, she was certain.

Katie made some notes.

Totem.

Spiritual significance.

Symbolic.

She looked at the photos she took at the crime scene of the body, general area, and especially the totem. There were three pine cones, several sticks, wild berries, a rock, and some leather strings surrounded by a padding of pine needles arranged in a way that was *not* random in the forest. She wanted to read the forensic report about all the items and see if they were all from the area—or if the killer brought in something of his own.

Katie didn't want to assume what each item represented, but she found some basic meanings. She created a list on the notepad until she could get either a whiteboard or chalkboard for the investigation.

Pine cones made Katie think of many things: art, decoration, medicinal uses, and even Christmas ornaments. The pine cones looked to be the main interest by the way the piece was constructed. She read more about pine cones and found they had been known to represent many things, including fertility, resurrection, and even enlightenment.

Sticks symbolized the main origin of the vast and dense forest. Wild berries were often seen as sustenance or life. She wasn't sure if it was the right time of year, but she knew that areas like this did have wild berries. A rock could mean so many things. It was heavy, final, and could be used as a weapon, structure, or to stop the flow of water. But to use one rock seemed significant to the killer somehow.

The padding of pine needles was a means to keep everything together and it seemed to be the foundation of the construction. As for the leather strings, Katie felt they were more ambiguous.

She stared at the photo and zoomed the image in and out. There was something off about the scene, but it seemed to lend itself to something she had seen before. She knew about a couple of cases in Northern California that had had totems at the crime scene, but they were more about spiritual meanings and hexes being placed on the victim. She mulled over these possibilities.

And then there was the term that TJ had used several times. *The Woodsman...*

As soon as Katie wrote down the name, the lights blacked out, followed by a huge crash outside.

TWELVE

Wednesday 1950 hours

Katie grabbed her Glock and readied herself in seconds. A strange scraping noise emitted from one side of the lodge.

"*Fuss,*" she whispered to Cisco.

The dog immediately took his place at her left side and moved in unison with Katie. It brought back memories of their time in the Army when they had to move around and through dangerous areas.

Katie quietly went to the kitchen and found the flashlight, but didn't turn it on yet. She and Cisco moved stealthily through the common area toward the entrance. Pushing a curtain aside, she surveyed the outdoors. It was almost pitch-black and it was difficult to see the outline of the stairs and balcony, unless you knew where to look, as the outdoor lights were out as well. She hoped it was just a blown breaker and not something more complicated that would take days to repair.

The scraping sound again...

Katie released the indoor locking mechanism and quietly turned the knob. Making a hand gesture to Cisco to stay and down, she slowly pulled the door open—an inch and then wider. Her gun was directed forward.

Many things ran through Katie's mind. It was possibly burglars, since the lodge was empty most of the time. Or worse...

She stepped her left foot out and then her right. Looking down the stairs everything appeared to be black and odd shapes. If you stared too long, your eyes played tricks on you and everything seemed ominous and dangerous.

Once she had her feet planted firmly on the landing, she turned on the flashlight, aiming both her gun and the light down the stairs.

"Hi," said Officer Clark. "I didn't mean to scare you." He had a sheepish expression on his face, and had been trying to carry up two folding tables.

Katie let out a sigh and let her pulse slow to normal. "You could have sent a text." She returned inside, put her gun in a drawer, and hurried back out. "Let me help you." She left the flashlight on and targeted it on the balcony and down the stairs. It wasn't much, but it helped them guide the tables inside.

"What happened to the lights?" said Clark as he leaned the tables against the wall.

"I don't know. They just went out before you came."

"Hmm." He looked around and saw Cisco in the corner. "Is your dog friendly?"

"Depends. Do you pose a threat?" she said and smiled.

"Not right now."

"He's fine."

"Did I hear right from the chief that you were in the military?"

"Yes. Cisco and I were an explosives K9 team for two tours."

"Army?"

She nodded.

"Wow. Thank you for your service."

Katie smiled and never knew what to say when people expressed this. It brought up so many memories—good and bad. She nodded again to the officer.

"Everything okay?" said Jack, standing at the open door.

Katie startled and became mad at herself because she hadn't heard him come up the stairs. She was either hearing sound carry strangely in the forest, or *not hearing* someone walk up the stairs.

"Yes and no."

"Lights go out?" said Jack.

"Yes, just a few minutes ago."

"Strange. The clinic lights blinked but then stayed on. I'll go take a look at the breaker box. It's downstairs."

"Okay," said Katie. She remembered the secret staircase heading downstairs and wondered if she should say anything—but she opted not to.

"I'll get you some wood for the fireplace too. It's freezing in here," Jack added.

"There's more investigation stuff for you in my patrol car," said Clark.

"I'll help you," she said.

"No need, Detective. Stay here and I'll be right back." The officer left too.

Katie remembered she'd seen some candles in the kitchen and went to get them. One flashlight on the balcony certainly wasn't enough light. She lit three candles and set them on the check-in counter. The room instantly intensified in light, but it still wasn't quite enough for working.

Katie looked around the room and past the beautiful furnishings of the lodge. It seemed such an unusual place to put together their investigation. The entire town was unusual, and she still carried an uneasy feeling after her experiences in Echo Forest.

She could hear voices coming up the stairs and assumed it was Officer Clark and Jack coming back. Then she recognized the other voice.

Katie rushed out to the balcony. There was no mistaking who the other person was even in the dim lighting. Six foot, six inches tall with a light-reddish crew cut, and always there to help anyone, was her partner Sean McGaven.

"Gav!" said Katie. She couldn't help but express her excitement that he was here. It made her feel more relieved that she had her partner to work the case.

"Did you have to pick the darkest and spookiest place in town?" he said with good humor.

Clark was helping the detective bring up a large whiteboard. The officer and detective seemed like old friends.

Before they continued to bring more supplies and boxes up, McGaven stopped and hugged his partner. "Great to see you." He hugged her again.

"You too," she said.

Cisco ran up to McGaven and took a few circles around him.

"Cisco, my buddy! So glad you're here." He petted the excited dog.

"Yep. Cisco's on point."

"Let's get everything inside." Gav headed to the door. "What's with the lights?"

"Don't know. Dr. Thomas, the vet and owner, is working on the breaker box."

"Okay then..."

It took another fifteen minutes as Katie, Clark, and McGaven brought up the supplies and placed everything near the long dining table.

"This should do it," said McGaven.

"Looks good," said Clark. "I've never seen an actual homicide headquarters before."

"There's never been a homicide here?" said McGaven.

"About fifteen years ago—before my time." Officer Clark's phone rang. "Excuse me," he said and walked outside.

"This place is really nice," said McGaven. "I mean *really* nice."

"Wait until you see it in the daytime."

"And we have it all to ourselves?"

"Yes. Dr. Thomas first opened in the spring and summer, but it's quiet now."

"From what I see this place is going to do really well. It's a beautiful area." McGaven walked around and studied everything—with Cisco following.

"There are four very large suites and one is for you."

"I take it you think this is a vacation and murder investigation rolled into one... like there's no difference."

Katie laughed. She was beginning to feel better and more relaxed—and eager to get to work.

Officer Clark returned. "Detectives," he said. He was flustered and seemed to be alarmed. His voice was strained.

"What is it?" said Katie.

"There's been another murder."

THIRTEEN

Wednesday 2115 hours

Katie and McGaven along with Cisco drove in the Jeep following Officer Clark in his cruiser. As soon as Katie heard the news that a young female was found near a park hiking trail, she had visions of the victim from the day before hanging from a tree. But the report Officer Clark received didn't state anything about a hanging.

Katie quickly updated McGaven about the first crime scene. He had many questions, as did she, but they would be addressing them when they were set up at the lodge.

"You okay?" said McGaven.

Katie took a corner behind the patrol car—the red brake lights flooded her vision. "Yes and no. Is that a good enough answer?" She hydroplaned the Jeep a bit on the wet pavement, but then straightened and was now falling a little farther behind Clark.

"Whoa, Detective Katie Scott is back," Gav said smiling. "Echo Forest won't know what hit it." He kept the mood light, knowing that they were headed to something disturbing.

"Did I say I'm glad you're here?"

"Indeed you did."

Katie smiled and accelerated once again. She wondered about the crime scene, knowing they didn't have the proper tools needed to conduct the investigation properly. Her mind then wandered to the first victim, Theresa Jamison, in the refrigerator at the vet's office. There were many aspects of the case that seemed to be against them.

She slowed, taking her foot off the accelerator. "Is that it?" The area looked extremely overgrown and parking was limited. Gravel, torn-up asphalt pieces, and two large boulders that had once been used as barriers was what was left.

McGaven lowered his window and leaned out slightly. "There's the sign: Mountain Trail Pass," he said.

Officer Clark's patrol car had slowed and continued around a narrow path, passing two picnic tables. The wooden tables had become severely dilapidated due to the elements—one seating area was completely gone. There were green and black spray-painted letters and abstract symbols on what was left of the furniture.

Katie pulled into an area near the police car.

"What do you think?" said McGaven.

Katie knew that wasn't a simple question but rather an overall theory of the area and how difficult it must've been to get a body here unless the victim was murdered on scene. She worried about potential tire tracks they might have destroyed driving to the location. It was dark and she hoped Clark had some spotlights.

"I don't know if Dr. Thomas is going to get here to do the crime scene, but there are gloves, evidence markers, and some bags in the back," she said.

Cisco whined and spun around twice on the back seat.

Katie opened the car door and stepped out. The air was

cold, but not as much as it was the day before. Hoping that the weather would ease up on the frigid temperature, they had to act fast and be as thorough as possible.

Opening the hatch of the Jeep, McGaven rummaged in a plastic storage box for what they might need. Katie quickly changed into hiking boots and a heavy coat. It took most of the chill away, but the prickly goosebumps weren't from the cold but from the setting and what they were going to witness.

"Detectives," said Clark as he approached, now wearing a heavy police coat.

"Who called it in?" said McGaven.

"Don't know. They didn't give their name."

"Man, woman?"

"Libby said it sounded like a man. And he said the body was between two main trees near the entrance trail."

"Libby?" said McGaven.

"She's our administrative assistant. We don't have any other information."

Katie thought that was suspicious, but didn't want to spend any more time on it at the moment. "Do you have mobile lights?"

The officer nodded. "I have two."

"We're going to need them. Gav and I are going to do a preliminary search," she said. "We'll let you know when we need them." She hated working a crime scene at night with lights because it was easy to miss evidence.

The officer nodded. He appeared nervous, most likely due to the fact he hadn't any experience in homicides.

"Clark, we need you to be first officer on the scene. Can you do that?" she said.

"Yeah. I remember from the police academy."

"What about Dr. Thomas?"

"Jack?"

"Yes. Has he been contacted?" she said.

"It's protocol. Libby should have called or messaged him."

Katie shut the Jeep hatch and looked at Cisco, who seemed to have made himself comfortable on a blanket. "Okay," she said, readying her flashlight. "We're going to begin the crime scene investigation until he arrives."

Clark went to his patrol car to prepare the lights as Katie and McGaven headed to the area where the body had been found. Katie slowed her pace and noticed typical groupings of dense trees, but due to the clouds parting the half-moon illuminated an open area between two huge pine trees. She stopped. It was quiet. She couldn't detect any breeze. Closing her eyes, she gathered her wits, her skills, and prepared herself for what she was about to see.

McGaven had stopped six feet behind her, allowing his partner to approach the crime scene first. Then they would search and scrutinize everything as a team.

Officer Clark observed the detectives but remained at his location.

Katie opened her eyes and pulled on her gloves. She switched on her heavy-duty flashlight and pointed it in front of her, spotlighting the area between the two large trees. It was a small clearing that appeared to be natural and not prepared as a stage setting. She could see the outline of what looked like a body in the distance.

Pushing everything from her mind, Katie walked forward slowly, making sure her path was consistent and not contaminating possible evidence. It was so quiet she was aware of her breathing, which was even and calm. She noticed the area was mostly dirt with mixed small rocks in between remnants of snow. It was a little tricky to keep a straight line as she walked in. About ten feet in, the ground beneath her feet became low dead weeds mixed with soil.

Katie fanned the light back and forth, and didn't see

anything but the rural landscape. She kept moving forward. As with any crime scene, she examined everything leading up to viewing the body. It not only kept any potential evidence in mind, but it also prepared her to view the body and to look directly at the victim. It would always be difficult, but Katie had to keep her thoughts objective no matter how disturbing things could be.

There was a female body lying flat on the ground. The victim's pale skin highlighted the scene. Dressed only in panties and a T-shirt, the body was positioned with the arms straight out away from the body and legs straight and unbending, as if she had fallen backward in a trust fall. Katie's first thought was that the positioning of the body was directly opposed to the first victim hanging in the tree, and wondered if it was significant. It also seemed that there was some type of material covering the woman's face—only long blonde hair was visible. It looked wet and matted.

Katie stopped.

There were three pine cones positioned together on top of a low pile of pine needles. There was something sparkly around the gathering, and Katie saw there were also some leather strings tied securely in a knot around the pine cones. There was something familiar about this particular grouping, which wasn't more than five feet away from the body.

Katie finally stood over the victim. The ashen skin with bluish marks on the upper thighs and along the inside of the arms looked oddly out of place. There was the usual discoloring of a deceased individual, but these prominent darker bluish-black intertwining patterns were that of livor mortis, the pooling of blood after death. Katie would know more after the medical examiner did a full examination and autopsy, but she surmised it could mean that the body was transported or stored for a short period of time before being set in its final resting place.

Katie examined the body; there were no obvious indications

of punctures or means of death. She bent down and took her thumb and forefinger to the burlap fabric—then she cautiously folded it away from the victim's face.

Katie abruptly stood up. This time she *was* staring into the face of TJ, the young woman who had knocked on her cabin door.

FOURTEEN

"What is it?" said McGaven barely five feet behind her.

Katie continued to stare at TJ, remembering the pretty young woman at her door. Katie remembered she'd had several ear piercings and a leather beaded choker—all of which were now gone from her face and seemed to be incorporated into the totem.

McGaven joined her and surveyed the body. "Do you know her?"

Katie nodded. "Yes. She was the young woman who knocked on my door and brought me to the first body. She told me her name was TJ. But... that's not all; her appearance has a striking, if not twin-like, similarity to the first victim, Theresa Jamison."

"Do you know anything about her?"

"No. She disappeared before the chief showed up. When I described her, no one seemed to know who she was." Katie turned to see Officer Clark standing near his cruiser watching them and waiting. "Officer Clark, can you come here?"

The officer hesitated, but then hurried over.

"Do you recognize this woman?" said Katie.

Clark took several seconds and shook his head. "I've never seen her before."

"Could you please set up the lights?" she said. "Place them there and there." Katie indicated on each side of the crime scene area and hoped it would assist in their search.

"On it." The officer jogged back to his car.

"What do you need?" said McGaven.

"Bags for her hands and feet... and the fabric," she said. "We need to document with a cell phone until... I don't know when Jack will get here."

"Jack?"

"Dr. Thomas."

McGaven eyed his partner.

"He was the one who worked the last crime scene and stored the body until the county medical examiner's office can pick up."

"What about the evidence?"

"The chief said they have to send it to the state lab in Sacramento..."

"That seems extreme. Is there a closer crime lab that can run tests?" he said.

"I'll see what they can do." Katie looked back at TJ's face and remembered how frightened she was about the Woodsman. She would see if McGaven could work his tech-savvy skills to find out more and if there was anything to this fear.

McGaven headed back to the Jeep to get the crime scene supplies they needed. Clark readied the lights and began setting them up. Katie took a few photos of the overall scene, a close-up of TJ's face, and the totem.

When McGaven returned, headlights emerged into the parking area. Katie could see it was the white truck belonging to Jack.

Jack remained solemn as he carried his kit to the scene. He retrieved his digital camera and readied himself. "Is there anything specific in addition to the usual photos you need?"

It seemed as if something was bothering him. Katie decided not to pry because they all had a job to do. "The totem gathering and any areas that could be entries and exits for the killer."

He nodded.

"Jack," she said. "Does this girl look familiar to you?" Maybe he had never heard of a TJ, but he might remember seeing her before.

He studied her and then shook his head. "No, I don't think I've ever seen her before."

"Okay." If she'd seen TJ, someone else should have seen her as well. They just had to find them.

Katie and McGaven moved out of the way to let Jack work.

"I'm going to check out a few things around the scene," said McGaven.

Katie nodded as she watched Jack document the area. He was methodical and moved around with ease. She had been so shocked by a vet working a crime scene the first time that questions now plagued her mind. She could tell he felt comfortable and was experienced. But if the town of Echo Forest had only had one other homicide fifteen years ago, where did he get his training? There was more to veterinarian Dr. Jack Thomas than he let on.

"Detective," said Clark, "lights are in place."

"Thank you. Do you have crime scene tape?"

"Yes."

"Please rope off the area as far as the two big trees."

"You got it," he said and turned to leave.

"Oh... I know it's late, but can you update the chief or at least leave a text on what's going on?" said Katie.

"Of course."

"Where's Officer Banning?" she said.

"He's patrolling and had a couple of prowler calls."

"I see."

"Do you need him here?"

"No, I think we have it covered for now. But we are going to need some legwork of canvassing, interviewing people, and making phone calls." Reality hit Katie hard that they were in a really tiny town with little assistance, which would make everything much more tedious. Navigating this investigation would be a big learning curve for her and McGaven. Her biggest fear: more victims.

The officer nodded as he returned to his vehicle.

"I have something," said McGaven.

Katie turned and saw that her partner had been searching the surrounding area, the entrance to the hiking trail. The area was definitely unmaintained and looked long forgotten. She jogged up to her partner, who had searched an old, dented, rusted trash can. "What do you have?"

McGaven carefully pulled out a large clear plastic bag. Inside were some articles of clothing.

"Wait." She looked closer and saw faux-fur-lined boots. "Those clothes and boots look like what TJ was wearing when I met her. Jack, we need this documented when you get a chance," she called. "Is there anything else in the can?" she asked McGaven.

"It's pretty battered and I don't think anyone has used it in years..." He turned the trash can on its side and reached in farther. He shook his head. "Nothing. Not even an old soda can or bottle."

"What do you have?" said Jack.

"This bag of clothes that I believe TJ was wearing."

Jack took the appropriate photographs.

"We'll wait to take them out," she said.

"How can we do this without forensics?" McGaven asked.

"We have the best forensic person," she said.

"But John isn't here."

John Blackburn was Pine Valley Sheriff's Department's forensic supervisor and part of Katie's team. His help was integral to their solving of cases.

"That's where technology comes in," Katie said.

"Oh, I get it. We'll get him in a conference call."

Katie smiled. It was becoming more obvious that they had a bigger task than the average homicide or cold case. They would have to wear other hats in order to get the investigation moving in the right direction; otherwise, the case would be taken over by state or federal law enforcement.

"I think the doc is done with his work," said McGaven, looking over to the body.

"Then let's get to work."

FIFTEEN

Thursday 0715 hours

Katie woke to Cisco standing on the bed panting and turning in circles. He wanted his breakfast and he wanted it now.

"Oh... Cisco..." said Katie. She rolled over and saw it was already after seven. Still exhausted, her body ached, and she wanted to cover up her head to stay warm and snooze for just another ten minutes.

Cisco whined and bounced back and forth on the bed.

Katie groaned some more. "All right... all right..." she laughed. "You goofball."

Kate and McGaven had spent another couple of hours at the crime scene after Jack had finished with the photos of the body. The scene had been documented, evidence was collected with the proper chain of custody attached, and the body transported to Jack's large refrigerator, waiting for the county coroner to arrive sometime today.

They had brought the evidence back to the lodge, securing it in a safe place inside the closet before crashing out in order to get a few hours of much needed sleep. McGaven bunked in the suite next to Katie's. The lodge was still without electricity and very cold when they arrived. Jack had to buy a part this morning in order to fix the breaker box.

Katie sat up and realized it wasn't as cold as it had been last night. Jack must've been able to find the part that was needed.

There was a soft knock at Katie's door. Cisco barked and jumped off the bed to greet whoever was there.

"Come in," she said.

The door opened slowly. McGaven stepped in, dressed in sweats and a baggy hoodie, and carried two steaming cups of coffee.

"Oh, coffee..."

"Wow, I think your room is bigger than mine," he joked. He sat on the edge of the bed, handing Katie her cup. "The electricity went back on about an hour ago."

"Fantastic," she said, taking a large sip. "Jack fixed the problem."

"Jack seems cool. He brought more wood for the fireplace and built a nice fire. It's nice and toasty."

Katie looked outside. It was overcast and dreary, and she hoped it was warmer than yesterday.

"Get up. We've got a lot of work to do," he said.

"I'm working on it," she complained.

Cisco ran to the door and barked.

"I'll feed him and take him out."

"Thank you, Gav. That would be great."

"No prob."

Katie watched Cisco follow McGaven out of the suite. She needed to wake up and have a plan of attack for the day.

Katie took a quick hot shower and changed into warm clothes before she entered the grand common room of the lodge. McGaven had been busy organizing their working area.

"Thank you, Gav, for taking care of Cisco this morning."

"It's my pleasure. I love my Cisco time."

McGaven had folded a large blanket near the fire for the dog to have his own relaxing space, and Cisco was taking advantage of the comfort by snoozing quietly.

"There's some breakfast for you—it's warming in the oven," he said.

"Great. Thank you." Katie hurried to the kitchen and found a plate in the oven with eggs, bacon, and two pieces of toast. After pouring herself another cup of coffee, she returned to the work area and sat down to eat. The warmth of the room relaxed her. Not realizing how hungry she was, the breakfast was gone in minutes.

"So," said McGaven as he pushed the whiteboard over near a wall. "We need to get started."

Katie nodded. It felt strange beginning their murder board and killer profile in such a beautiful and comfortable room.

McGaven read some reports to make sense of what happened and pulled out photos and a map of the area. "Let's start with the first vic, Theresa Jamison. Nineteen, strangled, and found hanging in a tree." He put up a photo of the young woman's driver's license and one from the crime scene. "What do we know about her?"

"Not a lot until we get an autopsy report and interviews back from Officers Clark and Banning," she said. "Theresa was identified by her cousin, Shelly Jamison-Smith. She drove in from Pine Valley."

"Did she live here?"

"According to some of the interviews," she said, scanning the reports, "she had a small apartment on Spruce Street, Echo Forest, and worked evenings at the Sunrise Café."

"Okay, so it should be easy to track her last week or so," he said.

"This is a very small town. I think someone must know something important to set us in the right direction."

McGaven wrote on the board everything they had. "Okay, we need to fill in some blanks here. How did a local girl who worked a few blocks from her apartment end up in the woods dead and hanging?"

Katie studied the crime scene photos, which were good. Jack had been diligent and taken more than enough to tell a story. She frowned, looking at a close-up of Theresa's hand. "It looks like there's foreign stuff under her palm and fingers—like maybe paint? But her pink fingernails are perfect."

"Not like they would be if she had been painting something," he said.

Katie stared at the totem. The sense of urgency became more intense. They had to work fast with what they had before there was another body.

"I think there's something that belonged to Theresa included in this totem," Katie said.

"What makes you say that?"

"I noticed the second victim, who we know only as TJ, was missing her face and ear piercings—and they seemed to be included in the other display last night."

McGaven looked at photos of both victims. "You know... they do look like they're related. It's not just a slight resemblance."

Katie joined her partner. "I agree. Maybe not sisters, but cousins perhaps?"

"Though I've seen best friends without any family relation look like they could be."

"It's just a theory at this point until we get an ID on TJ," she said. The moment the girl had come to her door was still vivid in Katie's mind. "There're quite a few missing pieces until we get reports back. But there are things that tie Theresa and TJ together." Katie went to the whiteboard and began to write: *age, resemblance, physical build, hair color, strangulation marks on their necks. Crime scenes elaborate and staged.*

"The body poses are completely different, one hung from a tree and the other laid out in an open area," said McGaven.

Katie sighed. "I have so many basic questions from both scenes... but we have to wait and work with what we have." She paused. "It appears that each victim had her own specific display, how the bodies were posed, and the different totems."

"Does this tell us more about the victim or the killer?" he said.

Katie looked at her partner. "The killer."

"Why?"

"This is how the killer sees them. It's as if the killer was trying to use them to represent another crime site."

"Which also means the killer probably knew them somehow. If he was choosing them for a particular scene."

Katie nodded. "Yes. I think it means it's likely the killer lives or lived here in Echo Forest or in close proximity, hunting down his victims where he feels more comfortable. Yes, I believe the scenes mean something to the killer."

Katie and McGaven separated everything for both Theresa and TJ. Katie began to piece together the crime scenes and the evidence they had, while McGaven jumped into computer searches about the victims' backgrounds.

Katie found a rolled-up map of the town and the close surrounding areas that Officer Clark had brought them. It showed the dense parks and the neighborhoods along with businesses. It gave the detectives a better sense of the community. She taped it to the wall where they could pinpoint the crime scenes along with access.

She turned to McGaven. "One thing that TJ kept saying at the first scene was about 'the Woodsman.'"

"The Woodsman?"

"Yes. She was extremely afraid and about ready to jump out of her skin, and she kept repeating the words to herself."

McGaven seemed to ponder. "Did you try to look up anything about a woodsman?"

"I just found things from recent culture like movies, but it all seemed to revolve around urban legends and folklore beliefs where if you're caught alone or camp in the wrong place you would be visited by the Woodsman. Stuff like that. Maybe you could see what you can come up with?"

"Sure. Anything about this town I should know?"

"Not really, except the last murder was fifteen years ago, and there's not much about it. No name, cause of death, or any more details. But... I did see a memorial bench on a hiking path that said, 'Carol Ann Benedict.'"

"Interesting," he said. "But people die all the time from illness and natural causes. I wouldn't immediately think it was a murder victim."

"True. So there are a few ways we can begin because of what we have at our disposal right now: we can track down more information about Theresa; we can begin to examine the evidence results once we get them back; and..."

"Let's start with Theresa and build from there," McGaven said. "Talk to people around town and... visit the crime scene in daylight."

"With Cisco?"

"You read my mind."

Katie stared at the driver's license photo of Theresa. Her long blonde hair and dark eyes stared back at her. She wondered who she had known or when she had come into contact with the person who led to her untimely death.

SIXTEEN

Thursday 1000 hours

Katie and McGaven decided to take the Jeep instead of McGaven's truck. With Cisco in the back seat, it made it easier for the detectives to have a vehicle that could go off road and blend in.

They headed to 172 Spruce Street, apartment 112, which was Theresa's residence. According to the accounts of the police, she lived alone. Officer Clark had gone there but said there was nothing unusual to report.

"Don't forget we meet with Clark and the chief this evening," said Katie, taking a turn down Main Street.

"Yep."

Katie was relieved that the weather was moderate and not as cold as it had been since her arrival. She studied the streets, buildings, and several entrances to hiking trails they passed, and reckoned the killer must have known the area well—either by living in or near Echo Forest currently or at one time—to get about undetected.

"What's up?" said McGaven as he shifted in the passenger

seat adjusting his gun belt. The seat was almost too short for a man well over six feet.

She smiled. "You know me so well."

"You're just figuring that out now?"

"Doesn't this investigation seem a bit strange?"

"Well, let me see... our headquarters is set up at a swanky lodge in the woods, two women have been murdered and posed in the wilderness, and our backup is two officers with no experience with homicide... Oh, and the local vet handles the crime scenes and stores dead bodies in his fridge. Nah, nothing strange."

Katie couldn't help but laugh. "When you spell it out like that."

"At least our work isn't boring."

Cisco let out a bark.

"See, even Cisco thinks so," said McGaven. The detective turned in his seat to pet the dog. "You probably already know who the killer is, don't you, buddy..."

"That's a given," she said.

Katie turned onto Spruce Street and slowed her speed, looking for 172.

McGaven studied the area. "There are a lot of blind spots."

Katie knew what he meant. It was an older area where vintage houses had been turned into apartments. The trees were large and many stood like umbrellas over the sidewalk and parking areas. Native ivy and flowering plants weren't in bloom at the moment, but they would have made it difficult to see who was around if someone had been stalking Theresa in previous weeks.

Katie pulled up to the curb in between the addresses 172 and 174, which were remodeled one-story houses.

"I feel like I stepped back in time," McGaven said.

"I agree." Katie looked around at both sides of the street.

"It looks like there are four apartments: 111, 112, 113, and 114. And Theresa's looks to be around back."

"Let's go," she said and opened the door. There were a couple of whines, but then Cisco retreated and lay down in the back seat. Katie paused as she stood on the sidewalk facing the apartments. This was typical of her as they investigated, whether it was a home or a workplace. She used all her senses, focusing on the immediate task at hand. It helped to stop her from assuming anything and to check her instincts were in tune.

McGaven waited patiently at the gate. Neither detective spoke. When Katie walked to the gate, McGaven followed her through.

The fine gravel path crunched beneath their feet as they made their way to a patio that wrapped around the building. There, several pots, now empty, decorated the side in bright blues and greens. The first door said it was 111, so Katie followed the path to the right. There was a slight smell of fresh paint and the window trim and doors were glossy. That gave Katie pause.

"Looks like there have been workers here recently. Painters? Contractors? Landscapers? Maybe try to dig up who was here?" she said.

McGaven nodded.

Around the back of the building, the detectives noticed there was a slight ravine with even more trees scattered about. It would be an area where someone could get onto the property without being noticed.

"Here it is," said McGaven.

They stood in front of 112. The door had been recently painted and the apartment number had been replaced with bright gold digits. A welcome mat, a pot, and a silly gnome decorated the entrance.

Katie studied the door. "Wait."

"What?"

"Look at the doorframe."

There was a dark smudge across the frame and the siding near the lock. It was obvious someone had pried at it recently.

"That looks recent. *Really* recent," she said.

McGaven looked at it closer and frowned.

"I think we need forensics," she said.

"Call Jack?"

"This is where things get tricky." Katie looked around and then her eyes settled on the gnome. She moved it and underneath there was a single house key. "I wish people wouldn't do this." She snatched up the key.

McGaven dug out gloves from his pocket. "Call Jack. And we will be extra careful entering the apartment, making notes for any evidence that needs to be documented."

Katie immediately dialed the vet and was surprised he answered on the second ring.

"Dr. Thomas."

"It's Katie."

"Good morning. What can I do for you?"

Katie thought that he sounded exceptionally chipper today. "We're at Theresa's apartment and it looks like someone recently tried to pry the door open."

"You need documentation and possible collection?"

"Yes."

"What's the address?"

"172 Spruce Street, apartment 112."

There was a slight pause before he answered. "I can be there in about fifteen to twenty minutes."

"Great. Thank y—" The call ended. "Okay…" she said.

"What?"

"That was abrupt."

"Katie, you know we're in a very small town and people can be a little different," he said.

"I guess." She put on her gloves and then inserted the key

into the lock. The knob was stuck and it took a couple of minutes to get the door open.

"Looks like someone messed with the lock," McGaven said.

Katie pushed the door open. "Hello?" she said just to make sure no one was around. "Police. Anyone here?"

Satisfied the apartment was not occupied, both detectives stepped inside and stood at the threshold. It was a small one-bedroom apartment, which could have easily been a studio to give it a more spacious feel. There was no sofa, but a large comfortable chair with a side table in the corner, and a small two-shelf unit on the other side. There was also a bistro table with two chairs near a small kitchen with a stove, single counter, and sink along another wall. Besides the area being rather small, it still had a cozy personal feeling. There were a couple of homemade quilts, some artwork on the walls, pillows on the chair, and a pile of books on the floor. A vase of silk flowers was on the table and the kitchen was tidy, with a folded towel on the counter along with a washed plate, silverware, and a glass.

Katie moved into the room. It didn't look like there had been a struggle and the space was neat and tidy. What struck her most was that this apartment seemed to belong to someone who was happy and enjoyed her home.

Katie walked into the tiny bedroom, which had a twin daybed and small vertical dresser. The bed was made and its blankets precisely folded. Several pillows were piled in order. The dresser had a couple of figurines, some cut-glass pieces, and two picture frames. In one frame, there was a photo of Theresa and two older people, which Katie assumed to be her parents. In another frame were Theresa and a young man. They seemed close and Katie expected that it was a close friend or boyfriend.

"Hey," said McGaven from the kitchen.

Katie met up with her partner.

"I found this in the drawer," he said. "It's her address book. I haven't seen a laptop or cell phone."

"Seems strange."

McGaven thumbed through the names and phone numbers.

"Anything?"

"This looks like her parents on this page. Have they been contacted?" he said.

"I'm assuming Officer Clark has that under control."

McGaven gave her a look as if to convey that the officer may not.

Just then Katie's phone rang. "Speak of the devil." She answered it and put it on speaker. "Detective Scott. You're on speaker."

"Scott. Is McGaven with you?" said Clark.

"Yes. We're at Theresa's apartment."

"I've pulled her cell phone records."

"There isn't a cell phone or computer here," she said.

"Huh. Well, I'm looking at the call lists and it seems that there were a number of calls in the past week from a... Devin Bradley... and two days before her body was found there were at least a dozen calls from him but they lasted only five or ten seconds."

"Can you forward the lists to us?" said McGaven.

"No problem."

McGaven opened the address book and found Devin Bradley's phone number and address. Katie glanced at it.

"When we finish up here we're going to the Sunrise Café to see what they have to say about Theresa," she said. "Then we'll check out Devin Bradley."

"Okay. I'll keep you posted as things come in," said the officer. "We're in the process of contacting family."

"Thanks. We'll see you at the meeting with the chief."

"See you then," he said and ended the call.

"Is there possibly a photo of Devin?" said McGaven. "If he's her boyfriend."

"I think it's the one in Theresa's bedroom."

Katie went in there and grabbed the frame. McGaven took a photo of it with his cell phone.

The front doorknob rattled.

Katie and McGaven instantly got in place on either side of the door.

They watched the knob turn slowly and the door inch open.

Katie grabbed the door and flung it open wide.

McGaven had his gun ready.

"I guess you weren't expecting me this soon," said Jack. His expression wasn't relaxed, but he tried to make it a joke.

Katie exhaled.

McGaven said, "You are very quiet."

Jack smiled. "I can see that you two are ready for anything." He walked into the living room.

Ignoring the statement, Katie stepped aside. "Nothing suggests there was a struggle or anything, there's no sign someone had visited her. Single dishes. Everything organized."

Jack stood in the middle of the room and slowly took a three-hundred-sixty-degree turn. "You want everything documented?"

"Yes, just overall would be fine." Katie walked to the front entrance. "And this," she said and pointed to the pried area around the lock.

"Got it."

SEVENTEEN

Thursday 1300 hours

Katie and McGaven drove to the café, where there were many trucks and cars parked. It seemed to be the place to eat lunch as well as breakfast.

"I think my stomach is grumbling," said McGaven.

"Are you sure that wasn't Cisco?" she said.

"Funny." He made a face at her. "I am kinda hungry."

Katie had been lost in her thoughts about Theresa's apartment. It had occurred to her that someone could have staged it to appear as if everything was fine. The pillows, the dishes, and knickknacks were too perfect. It made a statement, but not that there wasn't anything wrong.

"I guess you aren't hungry?" he said.

Katie nodded. "But I could eat and Cisco needs a break." She decided to drive around to the back of the restaurant instead of parking in front.

McGaven remained quiet and surveyed the area. It was dirt instead of gravel or pavement. The trees led you down a slight incline where there were two available parking spaces. Katie assumed it was for deliveries and maybe the manager. She easily pulled into a space. On the farther end, there were three cars she assumed belonged to staff. Katie noticed two large garbage bags leaning against the wall near the back door. It seemed odd because the dumpster was only fifteen feet away. There was also a mop, bucket, and wet towels.

Cisco stood up and forced his big head toward Katie.

"Wait... I'll let you out in a little bit," she said. She got out of the Jeep and was immediately struck with the intense aroma of the pine trees. She took a moment.

"Front door?" said McGaven.

"Definitely."

Katie and McGaven opened the front door and walked inside. The small restaurant was busy, with every table and counter space filled with patrons. The conversation levels were high. It was obvious they were all locals and this was their regular eatery.

"Hi, can I help you?" said a middle-aged woman wearing an apron. She looked around and then back to McGaven. "It'll probably be about fifteen minutes."

"May we speak to you for a moment?" said Katie.

"Uh, sure."

They moved toward the far end of the restaurant where the extra supplies were stacked.

"What's your name?" said McGaven.

"I'm Gladys Miner, owner of this place. And you two are?" She eyed them suspiciously, noticing their badges and guns.

"I'm Detective Scott and this is my partner, Detective McGaven."

"Detectives? You have to be from out of town."

"Yes," Katie said.

"Oh... it must be about that girl in the woods," she whispered, looking around.

Katie nodded.

"We're sorry to tell you this, but she's been identified as Theresa Jamison," said McGaven.

Gladys looked shocked and deeply saddened. "Are you sure?"

"I'm afraid so."

"Oh, Lord have mercy. She was such a wonderful girl, never complained, and the customers loved her." The woman looked down, holding back the tears, rubbing her hands on her apron.

Katie saw there were two waitresses and they were busy. "I know this is not a good time, but could you answer a few questions?"

"Of course."

"When was the last time you saw Theresa?" said Katie.

"Her last shift was three nights ago."

"Did she seem different? Did she seem like something was bothering her?"

"No, she seemed like she usually did. And, if I remember correctly, it was really busy that shift. So many people coming and going with eat-in and takeouts."

"Do you know who Devin Bradley is?" said McGaven.

"Yes, of course."

"Do you know where he lives?"

"I'll do you one better." Gladys turned and went to the kitchen, clearly expecting the detectives to follow. There was a large man cooking over the grill and toward the far end was a young man prepping food. "Devin," she said.

The young man with dark hair wearing a white T-shirt and a green-and-white apron looked up and saw the detectives. He dropped his knife, turned, and ran out of the back of the restaurant.

"Devin!" said Gladys again in a surprised tone.

"I'll go this way," said Katie as she ran out of the front door.

McGaven had no other choice and followed the young man out the back.

Katie had backtracked and met McGaven almost at the same time behind the restaurant. Her partner ran after Devin, who disappeared into the woods.

Cisco barked from the Jeep.

Katie stopped. The trails seemed to parallel and most likely intercepted. She saw McGaven disappear into the trees, so she took another trail and hoped it wasn't a bad decision.

Katie hit the path running and was immediately surrounded within a narrow hiking trail. She felt the brush scratch her arms and had to duck a few tree branches. She also heard McGaven calling out for the Devin to stop. His voice echoed strangely around her and she remembered the town *was* called Echo Forest and she had heard that strange voice and soft whispers among the trees since she had been there.

McGaven was close and Katie felt confident she could pass them and then cut them off. She ran faster. Arms pumping as her legs moved swifter. Embracing the moment of a good solid run as her heavy breaths took in the splendid aromas of the forest.

Katie slowed her pace as she saw another path intercepting, so she veered to the right. Between her deep breaths and heart pounding, she couldn't make out if she still heard McGaven, Devin, or footsteps.

Approaching the main path that her partner and Devin had taken, Katie could finally hear footsteps and heavy breathing nearing her position. She stepped back and saw the white T-shirt approaching. Without another second to spare, Katie lunged out and tackled the young man.

"Let go," he said, squirming.

"Hey," said McGaven breathing hard. "You got him?"

Katie got hold of Devin and pulled him to his feet. "Stop. When we say stop... you stop! Understand?"

"Who are you?" gasped the young man not trying to pull away.

"We wanted to ask you some questions," said McGaven slowing his breathing. "We're Detectives Scott and McGaven."

Katie glanced at her partner and then back to Devin. "Who are you running from?"

"I... I... thought..."

"Thought what?" said Katie trying to get a read on him. He seemed scared, shaking a little.

His wide eyes darted back and forth from Katie to McGaven. "I thought you were..."

"Who?"

"I don't know."

"Has someone contacted you? Threatened you?" she said.

Devin took a deep breath, trying to gather his thoughts. "I've had some things go missing. Not just misplacing stuff... but strange things have been disappearing."

Katie's mind sprinted through possible scenarios. She was becoming less convinced he was a suspect. "Like what?"

"Tools, rope, and towels, stuff like that." He looked at the detectives. "Even looked like someone dug up some rocks around my cabin."

"I see," said Katie.

"And... one of Theresa's sweaters..."

"You mean Theresa Jamison?"

Devin nodded. "I thought..." He held back tears. "I thought you were here to arrest me for her... murder."

"We're here to investigate her murder. We need to talk to people who knew her and try to backtrack her last week or so," said Katie.

"C'mon," said McGaven. "Let's go back and have a chat."

As Katie and McGaven escorted Devin back to the restaurant, they all remained quiet. Katie expected a whisper to swirl around the group, but it didn't occur this time. Her thoughts immediately jumped to the conclusion that the items Devin claimed to be missing were used by the killer to stage the crime scene. It remained to be seen.

Katie and Devin sat in a back booth in the Sunrise Café while McGaven chatted with some regulars and employees about Theresa.

"Devin, tell me about your relationship with Theresa," said Katie.

"We've known each other since middle school, but when I started working here we became close. About a year and a half now."

"Had anything seemed out of the ordinary with Theresa? Did she seem moody or maybe frightened?"

"No. Don't you think I've retraced the last time I saw her and tried to figure this out?"

"When was the last time you saw her?" she said.

"Monday night. We worked the same shift together and then we went back to my place and had a couple of beers."

Katie listened intently trying to put things in order.

"This town... I found out about... about her being the... victim... this morning from my neighbor who heard it from a friend who knows one of the cops."

"I'm sorry for your loss. Had Theresa met anyone new lately? Or mentioned being in touch with someone from the past?"

"No... I don't think so... I don't know."

Katie kept her patience and noticed that question made Devin edgy and nervous. She knew there had to be something different or new that had happened in Theresa's life recently. *But what?*

"What about a neighbor at her apartment building?" she said, glancing at her partner talking with a couple at a table but not quite able to hear what they were discussing.

"I never saw them. I think one of the apartments is empty and the two others never seemed to be home when I would go over to her house."

Now we're getting somewhere... Katie saw some ways someone could have kept tabs on her at home.

"Detective, I will help in any way I can... Theresa was special. She had plans of going back to school and was saving money. She wanted to be a nurse... and now..."

Katie retrieved a small notebook and pen from her pocket, pushing it across the table. "Devin, can you write down your address and phone number?"

"Of course." He wrote them down.

"Did Theresa have any sisters or cousins?"

"No, she never said anything about her family."

"We may need to contact you again." Katie wanted to put the young man at ease until they could eliminate him as a possible suspect.

Gladys approached the table. "Excuse me. Devin, I'm going to need you to start prepping for dinner."

Katie stood up. "We're finished here." She turned to Devin. "Thank you. Sorry about the tackle."

"You have a pretty good tackle." Devin tried to smile.

Katie watched Devin walk back to the kitchen. She picked up the notebook.

"Hey," said McGaven.

"Find out anything?" she said as they walked to the door.

"Some. But I'm afraid it's mostly gossip."

"A place to start."

"What about you?" he said.

"C'mon, I'll fill you in. But first, Cisco needs a break."

"Ten-four."

EIGHTEEN

Thursday 1535 hours

Katie and McGaven drove down the long road called Pine Cone Way. Devin Bradley's cabin was farther than they had originally anticipated and that made Katie question his answers, motive, and opportunity. The detectives updated each other on what Devin and various residents had told each of them.

Cisco let out an anxious snort, pushing his wet nose toward the side of Katie's face.

"Looks like a good place out here for Cisco to get some exercise," said McGaven scrutinizing the landscape. There were wide open spaces with scattered trees, making it very quiet and private.

Katie nodded. She was still thinking about Devin and wondered if his descriptions of things that were missing from his place were a desperate attempt to keep suspicion away from him.

"Okay, you've been quiet all the way out here," McGaven added, watching his partner. "Care to share?"

"Don't you think it's a little bit convenient that Devin told me about those missing items? There's no way to verify what he had or if it went missing."

Suddenly, as if out of nowhere, a small cabin came into view. It wasn't anything that would qualify as quaint or cozy— simply put, it was old and run-down. There was also a large barn structure that dwarfed the size of the cabin.

"That's not quite what I had envisioned," she said.

McGaven had been searching for the address, along with surrounding properties, and found out it was owned by Robert and Ida Bradley. "Appears that the thirty acres and two structures are owned by family, most likely Devin's parents."

Since Devin was back at the restaurant, the detectives knew that they most likely wouldn't be interrupted. There weren't any cars or trucks, in fact, no other type of vehicles in view. It would also be, as McGaven said, a good space for Cisco to run around in.

Katie pulled up thirty feet from the cabin. She quickly got out, followed closely by Cisco.

The afternoon air was moderate. It was quite comfortable for now, but there would be more cold fronts moving through in the next few days. For now, the slight breeze blew around the acreage.

Katie stood in front of the Jeep, carefully assessing the surrounding area. If she didn't know better, it would seem as if they were out in the middle of nowhere a hundred miles away from civilization.

Cisco romped around smelling everything new. He was still never far from Katie and he usually faced her. His jet-black coat glistened in the sun, showing off his gorgeous fur as he moved.

"What's up?" said McGaven.

"Just getting a feel for the place."

"Seems familiar, doesn't it?"

"It does, but we can't search anything that's not in plain view and where there's an expectation of privacy."

"Too bad," said McGaven sarcastically. "What if the front door is open?" He raised his eyebrows.

"Seriously?" Katie turned to her partner; he rarely reacted to cases with cynicism. There was something about this town. And there was definitely a strange vibe where they were standing.

"I know, I know." He rolled his eyes.

"But I think we can get a feel..."

Cisco returned to Katie's side, tail wagging, with what looked like part of an old Frisbee covered in dirt and slobber.

"Ugh..." said Katie. "That's disgusting."

"He seems to like it," laughed McGaven.

"*Aus,*" said Katie making Cisco drop the plastic. She turned her attention again to the property. It was vast, but nothing seemed ominous or of the criminal element.

"What has you so cautious?" he said.

"Do I need to remind you of some of the places we've experienced problems?"

"No," he said. "No, you don't."

"Why would Devin want to live out here?" she asked.

"It's owned by family—so it's free probably."

"True. But there has to be another reason."

"I wonder if Theresa stayed out here with him?" said McGaven.

"Most likely. Let's go find out."

Katie walked toward the small cabin, remaining cautious and alert. McGaven remained quiet, and he too seemed watchful as they approached the house. She noticed some digging had been done close to the two structures. The trenches were long and approximately five feet deep.

"What are these for?" she said.

McGaven walked right up to them and studied the channels. "Hard to say, but they don't look recent. Looks like there's been a lot of water, you can see where the rain or snow had saturated it. It could be new drainage or some type of installed electrical or piping lines. It could be anything."

Katie stood next to him. She wasn't so sure. "Take some photos. Maybe the chief or Jack might know?"

McGaven swiped his phone from his pocket and took several photos.

Katie turned to the tiny cabin. It was only a studio or possibly had one small bedroom. Something shiny caught her eye. A small window facing them had an object hanging as a decoration.

She moved closer, mindful of not disturbing anything since they hadn't received permission to be here. Once at the window, Katie saw the object was an intricately cut crystal diffracting light and producing a rainbow of colors. It reminded her of the cut-glass pieces on Theresa's dresser.

Standing on her tiptoes, Katie peered inside. The cabin was basically one room with a closet and another door she assumed to be the bathroom. It wasn't decorated. There were a couple piles of clothes, dishes on a table, and a large, full garbage can. Not exactly a place where someone would have their girlfriend hang out.

"Anything?"

Katie startled for a second.

"Sorry. Didn't know you were so high strung today."

She turned to her partner. "This place makes me jumpy and the deep forest hiking trails here creep me out. There… I said it."

She expected McGaven to laugh or make a joke, but he didn't.

"I'm beginning to see this place is a little unnerving," he said.

"It's just a guy's place. There's nothing in there to suggest Theresa would be staying here. My feeling is he would stay with her at her apartment."

McGaven looked around. "Yeah, it seems that Devin doesn't come out here often. It's just a place to crash when he needs to..."

"Or where anyone could crash..." said Katie. "Let's check out the barn. Did you get a photo of the cabin?"

"Yep." McGaven then took several pictures of the barn structure and more of the general area and landscape. It had been overgrown, but there were signs it had been partially mowed.

Katie went into the barn followed closely by Cisco. The two huge doors were wide open and secured by two large blocks of wood. It appeared they had been there for quite some time as they had heavy dirt on them and splintered ends.

The fleeting thought of how she was supposed to be on a two-week vacation, not working, entered her mind. It wasn't that she didn't want to be somewhere relaxing and not investigating a murder. But here she was in the moment—looking for clues and a killer.

"You okay?" said McGaven.

"Yes. If I'm not, you'll be the first to know..."

"After Cisco," he said and smiled.

Cisco's ears perked up and he stared at McGaven.

Katie appreciated people caring about her, but sometimes it made her feel inadequate and unable to do her job. She pushed her vulnerable feelings aside and examined the interior of the barn. It wasn't what she'd expected.

"Wow," said McGaven mirroring Katie's thoughts.

"This is the most organized I've ever seen a barn..."

"The time it must've taken."

"But think about the time you would save when everything had its place," she said.

The detectives were mesmerized by the meticulous organization on the walls. Every single tool such as wrenches, screwdrivers, handsaws, outdoor shears, and even larger items like chainsaws, brooms, and shovels were hanging on the walls with an outline around them so you would always know where they went.

"Gives new meaning to being organized," he said.

Katie nodded. "Look here." She pointed to an area where wound-up rope once seemed to be kept.

"And here," said McGaven. "Looks like two large screwdrivers and cutting shears are missing. I guess they could be somewhere else."

Katie looked at her partner. "Someone who spends this much time organizing isn't going to leave tools lying around somewhere else."

"See your point."

"Devin told me things were missing. And this seems to match up with what he said." Katie made another once-over and took a few photos. "The way I see it, he either told me as information or he told me to throw the investigation off track."

"You think Devin is the killer?"

"It's not likely, but we have to treat everyone as a suspect. I don't see the killer being someone from out of town—it's someone who knows this area or has ties to it."

McGaven remained quiet, looking around, but everything inside the barn was visible and nothing appeared to be hidden.

"Although..." she said.

"What?"

"Devin does know the area and obviously he knows the trails well... The killer knew where to leave the bodies..."

The detectives took another couple of minutes to check if there were storage areas or even a secret room. The barn proved to be nothing more than what it was used for—there wasn't anything sinister or out of place.

Cisco barked from the yard.

Katie knew that particular bark; it meant something serious.

She hurried outside where Cisco was standing with his head down, pawing at the ground.

"Cisco," she said softly, "*Zurück.*"

The dog backed away from the area. Kneeling down, she could see there were rocks lined up, as if someone had been attempting to make a decorative outline along a flowerbed.

"What is it?"

"I'm not sure, but..." Katie looked closer. "Rocks are missing."

"Anything could have caused that and they might not have been there in the first place."

"True... but there were rocks similar to these at both crime scenes."

"Do we take one to compare?" McGaven frowned.

"Let's get some photos," she said. "You notice that the items taken are general items, making it difficult to identify if they belong here." Katie sat back and thought about everything. Then she stood up and faced her partner.

"I can see the wheels turning again."

"What does this represent?" she asked.

"What do you mean?"

"This. The property way out here. The missing tools... This whole area?"

"A place to look for clues?"

"Yes... But doesn't it seem like we're on a wild goose chase?"

"Who would do that?" he said.

"Besides the killer? I'm not sure."

"What you're saying is that someone doesn't want us poking around."

"They know we'll investigate, but once we can't come up with a definite suspect or person of interest... eventually the leads will stop and then we'll go home."

"So who wants us to go home?" McGaven said.

"At least so far, I think it's possible we're up against two people. A killer and someone who doesn't want us to find the killer. It's a working theory."

Katie took a few photos of the rock area before they headed back to the Jeep.

All of a sudden two shotgun blasts came from near the row of trees one hundred yards away.

Instinctively, Katie, McGaven, and Cisco jumped down into the ditch.

NINETEEN

Katie's heart pounded relentlessly in her chest as she sat in a crouched position in the dugout gully at the cabin. She didn't immediately hear McGaven talking to her. Her memories of her time in the Army during maneuvers into enemy territories had taken over: hearing gunfire and bomb blasts, she would never forget the sounds, the heat, and the heavily grimy environment. Her vision became dark and the colors around her were almost in black and white. The constant stress and fear infused into her soul of being captured, tortured, and killed never left her mind.

As she took a few breaths, Katie's pulse lowered and she felt the warmth and heartbeat of Cisco's body pressed against her side. The shotgun blasts had brought back their time in unfriendly circumstances, but this time McGaven was with them. It helped to ease the anxiety.

"Katie, you okay?" said McGaven. His hand was on her arm as if he'd tried to shake her back into reality.

Katie turned her head and looked at her partner. With his strong face and his eyes emanating deep concern as he continued to speak more to her, she realized that the gunfire was farther away than she had first thought.

"It came from that large cluster of trees," she managed to say, still feeling unsteady.

"I don't think anyone was aiming at us."

"Probably hunters," she agreed.

The Jeep wasn't far, so they all cautiously got out of the ditch and made their way to it.

"We're just a bit jumpy," he said.

Katie tried to sound relaxed. "I guess it's because of our previous experiences with someone shooting at us."

McGaven grabbed a pair of binoculars and looked in the direction of the loud shotgun blasts.

Three more shots sounded.

"I think there are two hunters," he said. "I can't see clearly because we're losing daylight, but I can see orange and camouflage clothing."

Katie hadn't realized how much shorter the afternoons were and how the light could change quickly. It was nearly dusk and fiery color peeked between the trees.

Katie glanced at the time. "We have that appointment with the chief soon."

As they neared the lodge, Katie saw one of the police cars leaving. Her mind finally snapped back into reality. For some reason, it was difficult to keep her head in the game with the two crime scenes. She wasn't sure if her brain was exhausted and screaming for a need for rest or if it was the strange circumstances of the town. Even at the diner, there seemed to be something amiss. The locals were nice, but there was something else just beneath the surface that troubled her.

"Back at the lodge," said McGaven. His usual calm voice and demeanor helped to continue to center Katie.

"Yep."

"Wasn't that Clark leaving?"

"Not sure." She parked the Jeep and noticed that Jack's truck was there along with another SUV. She assumed it was a late patient.

Cisco ran ahead of Katie and McGaven up the stairs wagging his tail as he patiently waited at the top. Katie punched in the code and the main door opened. The beauty of the lodge reminded her how fortunate they were to have such a great place to work.

"Hey. Check this out," said McGaven. He picked up a large pile of reports on the table.

"What is it?"

Thumbing through the files and clipped reports, McGaven said, "Looks like the forensic and autopsy reports. And a note, saying they've also been emailed. That's what I call speedy service."

"Great. Let's get these organized. I guess Officer Clark brought these as soon as they received them."

"They must've fast-tracked them."

Both detectives jumped right in to read reports and add information to the appropriate crime scene boards.

Katie looked at the autopsy report for Theresa Jamison. She quickly read through it once and then a second time more slowly, digesting everything.

"Okay," she said as she stood up and updated the board. "Do you think it's a good idea to have the murder investigation board in this front open area?"

"It's not like there are other guests. It's just the cops and Jack." He studied his partner. "Why do I get the feeling you're not telling me something?"

"It may be nothing, but I want to make sure everything is kept confidential."

McGaven moved closer to Katie. "What's going on?"

"Besides being stuck in this town with these two homicides?"

"That's not the Katie I know... You jump at solving a case."

She sighed. "Ever since I got here, things are..."

"Things are what?"

"Things seem off. Like it's all orchestrated. It's weird. I feel like I'm on the outside looking in. I don't know how else to describe it."

McGaven stared at her for a moment.

"Follow me," she said. She showed him the unusual hidden door in the kitchen and the stairs that led down to the veterinary office.

"I see what you're saying, but doesn't it seem normal that this two-story warehouse had inside stairs?"

"Okay, fine."

"Wait," he said. "Let's still seal it up temporarily or put a lock on it."

Katie looked around the kitchen. "Sure. We can do that later."

"And if you think we should have the murder board somewhere else, like one of our suites, then let's do it. We can move the files and table too."

Katie and McGaven walked back into the main area. Cisco was stretched out on the large sofa.

"Hey," Gav said. "Whatever is bothering you—let's take it out of the equation. We have a lot to deal with. Okay?"

Katie thought about it and nodded. "Okay."

"That's my partner. What do we have for Theresa Jamison?"

Katie felt a little bit better. She hated feeling vulnerable, trying to explain why things were bothering her, things that didn't seem to fit.

"I can't believe the autopsies were done so quickly," he said. "I guess they didn't have many others ahead of them."

To Katie, that seemed like another incident that was unusual.

"Most likely it had to be a priority with it being a homicide," she said. "Okay, according to the county medical examiner, Dr. Kylie Baxter, cause of death was strangulation, and manner of death homicide. There were indications of sexual assault postmortem."

McGaven took to the board and began listing things.

"Theresa Jamison, nineteen years old, good health, no scarring from any apparent operations, all four wisdom teeth had been removed, there were scars on her left upper arm and right knee," recited Katie.

"That's thorough. I'm not sure if it's important or not," said McGaven.

"It may give an indication to her lifestyle." She kept reading. "They did a toxicology report and it was clean. No medications. No illegal drugs."

"Okay," said McGaven as he continued the visual list.

"And..."

McGaven turned. "And what?"

"I'm looking for fingernail scrapings." Katie skimmed through some forensic papers. "It seems that human skin and tiny glass particles were found underneath her nails."

"DNA?"

"No, this was preliminary from the Sacramento County Forensic Laboratory... It's going to take some time for DNA testing. And the glass fragments also had blood... human... which will take some time too." Katie looked up and marveled at how neat McGaven's printing was.

"So far..." he said.

Katie stared at the list. It seemed vague, but the DNA and glass were interesting. "Theresa obviously struggled with her killer, but what were the glass particles from?"

"Don't forget if the killer isn't in the system or we don't have a suspect, we may not know who left behind blood and skin."

"It says there wasn't any semen, so the killer wore a condom," she said. "And like I said, it was postmortem."

"What does that say about a killer?"

"There're definitely familiar characteristics on the body and scene. Her face was covered, which usually indicates a psychological element to the killer—it can be good or bad."

"And the area in which Theresa was left?" he said.

"The drama and specifics of the totem left behind indicate a connection between crime scene and victim." Katie studied the board. There were things she needed to add for the killer's signature as well as behavioral evidence.

"So the killer is telling a story," said McGaven.

"Jack told me Officer Clark recognized the girl as a friend of his sister," she said. "And that's how they were able to contact family so quickly."

"I see."

"Everything is beginning to show how close-knit this area is and how unwittingly the local townspeople might be protecting the killer."

"You really think so?"

"It's a working theory, but we have to be open to anything. But that's not what bothers me the most."

McGaven stopped writing on the board and turned to his partner.

"What *really* bothers me is that we have two victims who look so much alike. No one recognizes TJ—or Jane Doe—so how did she get here or where did she stay? There's a host of other questions."

"What did the autopsy report say about TJ?" he said.

"Nothing. It's in progress and so is the forensic examination. But I do hope we get it soon."

"I suppose they only picked up the body this morning."

"I know. Maybe the chief will have some answers."

TWENTY

Chief Cooper was resting quietly when Katie and McGaven arrived. The room was dim with only two low-watt lamps illuminating it. There wasn't a nurse nearby and the hospital seemed to be deserted, but Katie told herself that was to be expected in small medical facilities with only one or two patient rooms.

"He did say around 10 p.m.?" said McGaven.

"Originally it was earlier and then he sent me a text saying to come closer to 10 p.m., for some reason."

"What do you think?" he said.

"I don't know. It's important to talk with him. I think we can trust him."

"I trust you, and if you say he's okay, then he's okay," said McGaven.

Katie looked around and still there wasn't anyone in sight, no patients, no nurses, no visitors, no security guard, and no doctors. She moved slowly into the room. McGaven stayed at the doorway and sent a text to Officer Clark.

"Chief?" she said.

He looked peaceful and had been taken off oxygen.

"Chief," she said again, glancing at the blood pressure monitor which read 120/85.

He opened his eyes and stared at Katie. At first, she thought he didn't know who she was.

"Detective," he said softly.

"If you would like for us to come back tomorrow we can. You need your rest."

He shook his head. "No, we can talk."

"I haven't seen Officer Clark yet."

He shook his head again. "Talked to him earlier."

"Are you feeling better?" said Katie.

He nodded. "They gave me something to sleep."

Katie pulled up a chair next to the bed. She glanced at McGaven, who still stood in the doorway giving them some space.

"I see," she said. Looking around the room, everything seemed the way it should be. "Do you need anything?"

Chief Cooper grabbed her hand. "Thank you."

Katie wasn't sure what he meant.

"You and your partner have been gracious to take these cases. We... we... wouldn't have been able to handle on our own..." He paused.

As Katie studied the chief, he appeared so much different than the first time they had met. Then, he was tall, commanding, and had a firm handshake. He had made it clear he was in charge and it was his town. Now, he looked thirty years older and weaker.

"We're honored to be here to help in any way we can," she said. "Is there anyone we can call for you? Or bring here?"

The chief squeezed her hand again. "No. Wife gone. No children."

"Okay."

"You need to look past people who don't know Theresa or the other victim."

She tried to figure out what he was trying to tell her. "Where should we look?"

His eyes closed for a couple of seconds and then fluttered open again. His pupils were dilated, indicating the sleeping pills or whatever medication he was given was working and most likely wouldn't wear off for several hours. "Back at the... beginning..."

"Chief, we'll come back in the morning and bring you some breakfast from the Sunrise Café." She watched him focus on her. "Okay?"

"Be careful. Only investigate and interview when you are both together..." He slurred the last part.

Katie stood up and returned the chair. "Get some rest. We'll see you in the morning." She watched the chief fall back to sleep peacefully as the monitors kept in sync.

She met up with McGaven and they walked down the hallway.

"What's going on?" he said.

"I'm not sure, but they've given him sedatives to sleep."

"I could only hear part of what he was saying."

"He... he warned us to be careful and to stay together."

"Did he say why?"

"No. But he did say to go back to the beginning. And to look past people who don't know Theresa or TJ."

McGaven didn't immediately answer.

Katie stopped walking.

"What's wrong?" he said.

"It doesn't seem right. Things are different."

"What?"

"We haven't seen anyone since we got here."

"Didn't the chief say he just received a sedative to sleep? There had to be someone here."

Katie nodded.

"But you want to make sure?"

"Yes."

McGaven looked ahead and then back behind in the hallway. "Okay. I'll go this way," he said, pointing.

"I'll go back the other way and then we'll meet up." Katie turned. "Have your cell open and put your earbuds in, okay?"

"Copy that."

Katie wasn't completely sure if her concerns were warranted, but she wanted to cross it off the list. The town and many of the situations she'd experienced seemed to be not what they were supposed to be.

She stopped at the chief's room and he appeared to be sleeping still. She could see his chest subtly rise and fall. The monitors were beeping and seemed to indicate his breathing was normal. She moved on, keeping her wits and focus alert. The only sound was her boots making a subtle squeak on the waxed floor.

For half a second, she thought they were being silly and they were wasting their time.

She passed two nurses' stations, which were also empty. Katie looked at one of the desks and it was clear—no drink, no files, no computer—and there wasn't any indication anyone had been there today. She kept moving. The next station had a personal water bottle with a cute pink cartoon character. There was a notebook and a key ring with several keys.

The lights were dark, but were on a motion system the farther she walked. There were storage rooms and some vending machines with chairs in the vicinity.

Where was everyone?

Katie could hear breathing in her ears. McGaven was moving faster searching his area and his breath seemed to be elevated.

"Gav, everything okay?" she said quietly.

"Ten-four."

"Copy that."

Katie sensed McGaven wasn't being totally honest. He must've felt uneasy about the seemingly empty hospital—she did.

There were several closed doors that belonged to doctors and another door partially open that looked like a staff lounge. Katie slowed and tried the closed doors but they were all locked. When she peered into the lounge, she saw half a dozen round tables with chairs. There was a comfortable-looking sofa toward one end. No one was in there and the tables were clean and the chairs neatly pushed up against the tables.

"Anything?" she said.

"Negative."

Katie stood in the center of the room taking a three hundred sixty turn, but nothing appeared to be out of place. She glanced into the garbage can, but it was empty and the trash bag was new. It suddenly hit her that looking at the interior of the hospital reminded her of Theresa's apartment—neat and everything perfectly in place. But there was a sanitized feeling, as if someone wanted to give the façade of what was supposed to be.

Was this what they wanted them to see?

Who?

Why?

"Gav, does everything seem to be perfectly in place?"

There was a pause from his end. "Definitely."

Katie stepped in the hallway and saw a few more closed doors. She was going to retreat to where the chief was, but then heard the sound of a door shutting.

"Gav, what's your location?"

"Near the front entrance."

"Copy that," she said.

"Why?"

"I heard a door closing up ahead of me."

"Wait there, I'm on my way. Wait there..." he said with a stern tone.

Katie looked back the way she'd come and could see the lights had extinguished, so she could only see a dark void. She knew it was common in some city or county places that after hours, the lights would reset to motion lighting to save on utility costs.

She felt cold air wafting down the hallway, coming from the back entrance. It was clear the evening temperature was dropping. Lingering for a moment, she pondered if she should check out the back ambulance entrance.

That's when she heard a sound of another closing door in front of her.

Katie stepped forward and moved toward the sound. To her relief, lights turned on above her. The fluorescent bulbs buzzed and the illumination continued to brighten. There was a linen closet. She tried the knob, but it was locked.

Turning left and entering a narrower hallway, Katie saw two restrooms. She recalled that some doors, like those on restrooms, had hydraulic mechanisms to provide a gradual closure—and that had been the sound she had heard. She was certain.

"I'm checking the women's restroom," she whispered.

"Wait for me."

Katie pressed her hand against the door. She could smell some type of cleaner that reminded her of the commercial disinfectant that was used in a medical examiner's office. It was pungent and recent. She pushed the door open and stepped across the threshold, holding the door. It was dark inside, so she waited for the light to come on. She stared into the darkness. The harder she tried to concentrate, the more the darkness seemed to push back.

"Behind you," said McGaven, giving Katie a quick startle.

Once again, Katie was always amazed at how a man six foot, six inches tall could move around like a stealthy jungle cat.

"I know I heard this door close..." she said.

"Where *is* everybody?"

"I don't know." Katie was searching around the walls and finally found the light switch outside in the corridor.

It was a moderate-size bathroom with three stalls on the right and two sinks on the left. The floors were impeccably clean with a shine that almost hurt your eyes to look at.

Katie pulled her weapon, directing it, but she was ready.

She kicked open the first stall door.

Empty.

She kicked open the second stall door.

Empty.

Against the back wall along the floor, there was something red pooling along the edge.

Katie glanced at McGaven now, directing her weapon forward.

McGaven nodded at her as he covered his partner with his gun drawn.

Katie then kicked open the third bathroom stall.

She gasped in horror.

Before the stall door slowly began to close, they saw a young woman sitting on the toilet who had been propped up leaning backward, her legs positioned like a broken marionette. Barefoot and dressed only in panties, blood trickled from her fingertips from some cuts around her shoulder and arm. Her head tilted forward and her long dark hair spilled down.

There was a message in what looked like blood written in capital lettering on the wall: *THREE DOWN... MORE TO GO...*

The stall door slowly closed almost on cue.

Katie's adrenalin pumped into high gear. "We have to secure this hospital now! Call in Officers Clark and Banning and even Jack... anyone who can help with this crime scene. EMTs, firefighters, security personnel, everyone! This facility needs to be searched and secured—completely. The chief needs to be guarded—even moved to another hospital."

Katie and McGaven began to carefully back out of the restroom, but not before a loud crash and something heavy jammed the door.

McGaven began to kick at it repeatedly and slammed into the door with his shoulder. It wouldn't budge.

Then the lights went out.

Three down... more to go...

TWENTY-ONE

Thursday 2330 hours

Katie could hear McGaven's heavy breathing in the pitch-black. The dark was disorienting and the thought of a dead body in a bathroom stall made her edgier than usual.

"Gav?" she barely whispered as if someone else would hear.

"Yeah."

"You okay?"

"Yeah," he said, still breathing hard.

Katie activated her cell phone screen to produce some light. It wasn't much, but enough. It cast a weird glow on McGaven's face and the walls.

"No signal," she said.

"Same here."

Katie turned around looking for anything that would allow them to send for help or escape. There was nothing.

"What are we going to do?" said McGaven. "We can't wait until someone finds us."

"No. We aren't going to wait." Katie took her phone and

pointed it around the ceiling. To her relief it was made up of panels about two feet square.

"What are you thinking?" he said.

"We have to get out of here." Katie pushed open the first stall door and illuminated the ceiling corner as far away from the crime scene as she could. "I think I can fit through," she said.

"I see where you're going with this..."

Katie stood on the toilet.

"Wait," said McGaven. "Come back here," he directed.

Once Katie was away from the stalls, McGaven kicked and broke the toilet seat. He then stood on the rim of the toilet and used the seat to smash two ceiling tiles. The remnants scattered but remained in that stall.

"That's what I'm talking about," she said. "Having a strong tall partner comes in handy."

McGaven dropped the seat in the corner. "And if you tell anyone..."

Despite the serious situation and another crime scene, Katie smiled for an instant and shook her head. "Your secret is safe."

It took Katie and McGaven a few minutes to maneuver. He helped her climb up and then she was safely up in the ceiling area. She made sure her gun was secure in her holster, but had to put her cell phone in a pocket facing outward. It wasn't much light, but just enough to see the outlines of the ceiling.

Katie looked down at her partner. His face reflected a variety of colors from his own cell phone. His expression seemed emotionless, but his eyes told another story.

"I'll be fine," she said. "I'm just going into another area and then I'll come down to remove whatever is at the door."

"You don't know if whoever locked us in here is actually gone."

"Of course they're gone. They used this tactic to allow them to escape," she said. Although it sounded legitimate and she said it with confidence, she wasn't so sure. She didn't want to add to the already dangerous situation.

McGaven didn't respond. They had been partners for a while and had gone through extremely dangerous and even harrowing situations. He didn't have to tell her that she needed to be careful. It was a nonverbal communication between them and it worked both ways.

Katie took one more look at her partner before she turned her focus on her risky move. Time was ticking and there were so many unknowns. She tried not to think about Cisco, but knew he was safe in the car. She carried a small remote that was a K9 door-popper if she needed the dog's assistance and it also worked if someone tried to break into the Jeep—she would know.

Taking the time to balance her weight, feeling the stability so she wouldn't fall through one of the ceiling squares, Katie inched her way forward. Her mind raced. Her heart pounded. Her hands were sweaty. Still, she moved with purpose.

Katie paused for a moment to get her bearings. Her phone only gave so much light, so there were only outlines of construction components. She felt warm air movement and realized it flowed around her. Everywhere she looked there was the grid pattern where the covering ceiling tiles fitted.

There was quite a bit of room from the grid to the roof area, but she had to remain crawling and didn't dare to stand up. She was now in the plenum compartment of the building, which was where the building joists supported the beams, and electrical wiring and boxes, ductwork, heating and air-conditioning, as well as plumbing pipes were housed. A strange buzz emanated all around her giving her the sensation her vision was affected, and her arms and legs prickled.

Katie couldn't get the sight of the body in the bathroom stall out of her mind. Thoughts whirred in her brain with theories and how the victims were connected—and who might be behind them.

And where was everyone at the hospital?

Her biggest fear was that something terrible had happened to them.

Katie got into a rhythm, pushing one knee, one hand, and so forth, daring to move a little bit faster. She saw some light through the spacing of the ceiling tiles and estimated it to be in the main hallway before the restrooms.

Once over the area, Katie paused and knew the only way to get down was to jump. Carefully balancing, she pushed two tiles until they buckled and fell to the floor below. Looking down, she could see a familiar area of the hallway. She bent forward and checked in different directions, but there wasn't a person in sight.

Katie secured her phone and gun. She then moved her body into a position where she wouldn't land precariously. Dangling her legs, she lowered herself as far as she could. Taking in a deep breath, she let go. Katie dropped quickly and hit the ground harder than she originally expected, losing her balance.

Katie sat up quickly and remained still for a moment, listening and waiting for anything that indicated she wasn't alone. To her relief, there was only quiet and a soft humming of the surrounding facilities' running equipment.

Katie got up and ran toward the restroom and found two steel bars had been jammed into the door opening by the frame. They had snugly pierced the weather-stripping just enough to jam it. It was clever and effective, which meant the killer knew what he was doing or had planned accordingly. She tried to move them and it was extremely difficult. Trying to wiggle them back and forth took a couple of minutes. Keeping watch all around her, Katie didn't want to get ambushed so kept her senses tuned.

Finally the steel bars loosened enough and dropped to the

ground causing a piercing ringing noise. Katie pushed open the door where McGaven waited in the darkened bathroom.

"You made it," he said and quickly stepped out into the light.

"Was there any question?"

"How do you want to handle this?" he said.

"We need to quickly secure this area and get everyone here out immediately and find out what's going on." She looked around the area. "We need to check the back entrance."

Katie took off at a run with McGaven following closely behind. She couldn't help but think that the killer was still there watching them, but shook it off.

They came to the emergency entrance with electric doors. Katie tried to open them, but they wouldn't budge. Seeing the emergency release button, she pressed it and the door hydraulics whooshed and slowly opened.

The cold air gusted inside, slapping the detectives' faces. They ran out and didn't see any emergency vehicles, although there were two vehicles parked.

"They have to be here," whispered Katie. She turned and saw two sets of feet near a bush. "No." She ran to them.

It was a blonde woman dressed in light blue nurse's scrubs and an older man in a security uniform. They were laid out side by side, arms down, staring up with their necks slashed.

Three down... more to go...

TWENTY-TWO

Friday 0245 hours

Katie stood near the back entrance of the hospital taking everything in that they had witnessed since they visited the chief. There were three young female victims and two hospital employees—increasing the investigation to five homicides. Her cold breath swirled around her as she watched Cisco take a break. The dog didn't want to leave her side and could easily sense her stress.

"C'mon, Cisco, let's go," she said and put him back in the Jeep with his favorite blanket.

As Katie walked back, she saw all the vehicles in the car park, which was quite different than when she and McGaven had first arrived. It felt like a real investigation and everyone working together to the same end.

There were two police cars, two fire trucks—one for the town and the other volunteer—Jack's truck, ambulance, local search and rescue vehicles, morgue van, and several hospital employee cars. More help was on standby from other towns, and if anyone needed medical attention in Echo Forest, they were being diverted to other areas. The mayor position was vacant and it had been for months, so there was no one to represent the town and oversee law enforcement. The entire hospital was considered a crime scene.

Katie had left McGaven to oversee the investigation and coordinate everyone to keep the crime scene's integrity. Everyone had a job and everyone was briefed on the confidentiality of the situation. Chief Cooper was stable, awake, and demanded that he also oversee the investigation—and he did so from a wheelchair, per hospital rules.

This was the most unusual, difficult, and disturbing investigation Katie and McGaven had encountered. They had handled a variety of cold cases and homicides, but this one had her spooked by the town, the people, and now the circumstances. In addition, they had to bring in more people they really didn't know and put them in official situations. These investigations were not only the hardest they'd had to investigate, but the twists and turns were both unusual and horrific. It was as if they were being dropped into a play with no script and didn't know what was going to happen next.

She walked to the back emergency entrance, where a headquarters for the hospital had been set up; here, everyone was given their duties and had to check in with McGaven and the chief.

After being briefed by Katie and McGaven, Officers Clark and Banning did a complete search of the hospital before the employees could have access to do an inventory to make sure that nothing was missing. The officers also searched the outside area.

Jack was working the crime scene in the women's bathroom and would soon have evidence and the chain of custody ready to go.

Katie entered the building and was stopped by Chief Cooper.

"Detective," he said. His mood seemed to be in good spirits, but his exhaustion was evident. There were worry lines and dark circles around his eyes and his mouth was slightly downturned.

"Chief, you really should be resting right now," she said.

"I can't."

"You can."

"We've never had homicides in our town and now there're five. That's not acceptable no matter how you look at it."

"I understand."

"You and your partner have handled this situation with strength and professionalism. I don't know how you do it."

Katie didn't feel like the strong professional the chief claimed she was. Since she had arrived, five people had been murdered. It was completely intolerable, but the worst part: they were no closer to finding the killer.

Katie glanced at a group of fire department volunteers who were standing in as security. She noticed that they seemed, at least to her, as if they'd had some military training. There were subtle mannerisms, their stances, and how they addressed authority.

"You've picked up the gauntlet," said the chief.

She looked at the chief, who seemed to be maneuvering well in the wheelchair. "It's what we do. I couldn't do this without my partner."

The chief smiled. "Somehow I think you could."

"Thank you."

"Now, everything is running smoothly and the crime scene is being processed. You and McGaven need to get back to what you do best and keep working the evidence." He studied her for a moment. "So... Detectives Scott and McGaven are cleared to leave."

"But..."

"No buts. It's an order not up for discussion." He raised an eyebrow watching Katie's reaction. "Go. Get some rest. Let us pick up the slack tonight and you'll have plenty to do tomorrow. Bright and early there will be more information and crime scene material."

Katie nodded. "Thank you, Chief."

She headed to McGaven who was briefing the two local police officers: Clark and Banning. The police radio was chattering with talk of routine crimes. They carried them in case there was a call they needed to take care of. The officers turned to go about their newly instructed duties. They nodded to Katie as they left.

"Hey," she said.

"You look beat," replied McGaven.

"That's an understatement. The chief has given us orders to leave and begin again first thing in the morning."

McGaven paused and looked around.

"He said that they can hold the fort."

Her partner smiled. "Everyone seems to be handling it."

"Where's Jack?" she said.

"He's still processing the scene. But the good news is that each victim has already been identified, at least informally."

"Who's the vic in the bathroom?" she said.

"Unfortunately, she was a young hospital aid, just started a week ago. Her name is Natalie Renaldo."

Katie thought about why the hospital had been a target.

Was Natalie the intended victim? Or was she an opportunity?

"Detectives," said the chief pointing at his watch. "Now."

McGaven waved and accompanied Katie outside to the Jeep.

"What do you think?" he said.

She turned to her partner. "What do I think?" She watched some of the volunteers take their posts around the hospital.

"I think we're in over our heads."

TWENTY-THREE

Friday 0745 hours

There was a soft knock at Katie's door.

Cisco jumped off the bed and padded to the door. His tail wagged.

The door opened a few inches.

"Katie?"

Katie rolled to her other side and moaned. She had heard the knock and knew it was McGaven and that they had tons of work to sift through. "Yeah," she said, her voice muffled.

The door opened wider.

"Hey, partner."

"So are you my new alarm clock?"

He chuckled. "I seem to sleep great here..."

"Good for you."

"We have a ton of paperwork to go through and I have a surprise for you," he said.

"I don't like surprises."

"C'mon. Everyone likes surprises."

Katie sat up looking at the clock. It was nearing 8 a.m. and later than she thought. She flung the comforter back. "I'm coming, but I'm going for a half-hour run." She stood up, searching for her running gear. "If you could feed Cisco, I'll be back in a little bit."

"Sure, but—"

"Please close the door," she said.

McGaven and Cisco left her room and he quietly shut the door.

Katie didn't mean to sound rude, but she usually thought about the investigations by running. She could clear her head and be fresh and ready to go. It had been her usual routine and she needed more than ever to have a sense of habit with these cases.

Within ten minutes, Katie was running along the trails. She didn't see McGaven or Cisco as she rushed out the front door. There were sounds coming from the kitchen, but she didn't want to waste time and then have to postpone her run. She decided to head toward where her rental cabin was located.

She could feel the cool air with every breath. The sun was out, tricking you that it was warmer than it actually was. Katie pushed her run and now recognized the area; knew it was near the cabin. She pressed on, pumping her arms and taking longer strides. The events of last night consumed her.

Why kill the woman they found in the stall?

Did she fit the profile of the other victims?

Did she know something about the killer?

Or was she an opportunity and would throw off the inves-tigation?

And what about the other nurse and security guard who had been slain and left outside?

Katie pondered why there was a message this time and not a

totem. It suggested it was a different killer—or maybe that the killer didn't have time to prepare.

She passed the memorial bench with the plaque for Carol Ann Benedict.

Who was Carol Ann Benedict?

Katie stopped and took a closer look at the bench. Nothing seemed unusual, but there were some handmade letters scratched into the wood on the back.

I will love you forever, B.

Katie didn't know what to think and she didn't want to muddy her investigation by looking at things that didn't complement the homicide investigations. She kept running.

A strong breeze pushed along the trail; perfect timing as questions inundated Katie's mind. Before she reached the wider opening and before the trail continued to the cabin and first crime scene, she heard a sound. A soft pounding that resounded all around her. Knowing that sounds in the forest played tricks on the mind, she didn't take it too seriously.

Until... the sound turned into footsteps gaining speed from behind her. This was someone who was a runner or an athlete—she could tell by their stride and speed. But what was impossible to tell was if it was just someone who had the same idea as Katie to go on a run that morning—or if it was someone more threatening trying to catch up with her.

Katie decided not to ponder who it was any longer. Instead, she stepped aside and took cover behind one of the trees where there were plenty of rogue bushes to camouflage her.

The footsteps kept the same consistent speed and the person was just about to pass her. Katie waited in anticipation.

She saw black running pants and a green hoodie. Dark hair. Medium height. Definite athletic body type. And...

Katie emerged from the thicket.

"John?"

Immediately, the runner stopped and turned. John Blackburn was the amazing forensic supervisor at the Pine Valley Sheriff's Department, where she and McGaven worked.

"Were you hiding in the bushes?" he said, walking back toward Katie.

"What are you doing here?" Katie said, feeling incredible relief.

"Why do you think?" he said.

"I didn't know you were coming. Are you Gav's surprise?"

"The sheriff suggested I come down to help and act as backup."

"Who's watching over the forensic unit?"

"Eva is covering and she's doing fine. In fact, it will be good for her to run things for a while. She's such an asset. If there's something that needs me, I can drive back in a little over two hours." He smiled with a lingering gaze.

There were no doubts that Katie and John had an attraction to each other, but while she was engaged to Chad it had never been acted upon, and Katie hoped no one else had noticed this weakness of hers—not wanting to be vulnerable. She studied him as sweat trickled down his forehead. He had a way of smiling at her that made her feel as if he knew what she was thinking. They were good friends. In fact, they were close friends.

He pushed up his sleeves, revealing his tattoos from the Navy, where he had been a Seal. "So," he said. "Where were you heading in such a hurry? I could barely keep up with you."

"I like to clear my head first thing, but..."

"Somehow I have a feeling you're taking this route for a reason."

Katie smiled. She couldn't keep his gaze. "You know me so well. How much do you know about the current crime scenes?"

"I drove in around 5 a.m. and Gav was sleeping on the couch with paperwork spread across his chest. I woke him."

"That's Gav." Katie felt bad that she wasn't awake to help him sift through things.

"He briefly updated me and then I studied the board."

"I'm glad you're here because there are forensic questions we need answers to," she said and began walking toward her original destination.

"So where are we going?"

"I was staying at a cabin when a young girl, TJ, knocked on my door and took me to the first crime scene."

"Okay," he said.

"And I wanted to look at it again—I have some questions I want to try to answer."

"These homicides are full of questions, according to Gav."

Katie rubbed her face. She felt faint.

"Hey," said John. He stopped her and put his hand lightly on her arm.

Katie looked at him but didn't explain. She put it down to feeling overwhelmed by not getting answers she needed to solve the investigation.

"I know how hard the last case was for you—and that's why you were here to get away and rest. And now you've been thrown into these cases..."

"Yeah, that's part of it. I just..."

"Just what?" He still had his hand on her arm.

"Things are different this time. I don't think we're going to solve this one."

John smiled at her and took his hand away. "For as long as I've known you, you've never stepped back and hesitated about anything."

"Well, but these cases..."

"You need some coffee, food, and to regroup."

"Okay, but—"

"You're just having a moment when you're overthinking it. I know for a fact you're going to find the killer or killers."

"You think so? And what's your evidence?" she said, smiling back at him. She appreciated that he was supportive. She couldn't ask for a better team.

"Because that's what the universe says…"

Katie could barely tear her gaze away from his intense dark eyes.

"Show me this first crime scene area."

"Okay."

"Is it really true that a veterinarian worked the crime scenes?" he said.

"Yeah. It was definitely a first." Katie explained everything that had been going on as they walked the rest of the way, about the crime scenes, the first two victims having a striking resemblance to each other, Devin's cabin, and the town in general.

"Sounds interesting," said John. He paused and looked at Katie. "I have to say, as horrible as whatever's going on in this town is, it seems strange too."

"That's how I see it."

"That's why you feel you may not be able to get everyone rounded up?"

She chuckled. "After the scene at the hospital, I'm not so sure. Some things seem to indicate a serial killer, but then others seem more random… as a way to cause chaos and panic." Katie walked closer to the tree where the body of Theresa Jamison had been found. She stared at where the totem was set up.

"Is this the tree?" he said.

She nodded. "What do you know about totems?"

"Like amulets or talismans or putting a curse on someone?"

"I guess."

"I don't know much except there are some people who believe in spirits and that these types of representations ward off evil spirits… or send a message."

"Exactly." She studied the area, noticing the shape of the totem was still evident. "I get this sense someone is trying to send a message or warning and... The first two victims were found at basically the same type of crime scene, but the hospital scene showed a more desperate, spur-of-the-moment type of killing." Katie walked around the tree, noticing for the first time a narrow trail that ran parallel to the cabin she had been staying in.

John studied the marks on the tree left by the rope.

"John, take a look at this..." she said.

He joined her.

"Doesn't this look like a drag mark?" she said.

He bent down and studied the area more closely. "It could be."

"Look at how wide it is. It's not consistent with a person or even an animal sliding." She looked around at the low-lying scrubby brush. "Look at this." She pulled what looked to be tan fibers from the lower section of the trail. "What do you think? It's not from wildlife."

John looked closely, turning over the short pieces in his hand. "I can't tell for sure, but they definitely have the look and consistency of rug fibers."

Katie stepped back. She hadn't taken a thorough look at the area due to the weather and the fact that the crime scene was already being handled by the chief and Jack. "It's only been a few days. It's possible this could be from the killer, right?"

John nodded. "Let's photograph the area and collect these. Maybe we can find where it came from."

TWENTY-FOUR

Friday 1000 hours

Katie and John arrived back at the lodge to an active investigation. The fireplace was burning, making the room comfortable, and Cisco was on the couch watching over everything.

McGaven and Officer Clark were organizing crime scene information as well as making lists of interviews. There were more points indicated on a large overall map of the area that included the crime scenes with possible entrance and exit locations.

"Wow," said Katie as she studied the board. "What time did you get up?"

Cisco jumped off the couch and greeted Katie, sniffing her curiously, wondering where she had been without him.

"I couldn't sleep because I knew Clark would have reports and preliminary details of the hospital crime scenes," said McGaven.

"Next time, wake me up."

"You needed to sleep."

"I appreciate that, but this is more important," she said.

"Depends on how you look at it."

"Give me ten minutes and I'll be right back."

Katie hurried to her room to take a quick shower and change her clothes for the long day ahead. Cisco closely followed her.

She returned about fifteen minutes later completely refreshed and ready to work. The new information helped to breathe fresh life into the investigation.

"Where's Clark?" she said.

"He's back on patrol," said McGaven.

"What do you want me to do?" said John.

"By the way, where did you sleep last night?" she said to John.

"I crashed out on the couch for a couple of hours," he said.

Katie saw a leather duffel bag on the floor.

"Fresh coffee and toast," announced Jack as he emerged from the kitchen carrying a tray.

Katie was surprised to see him. There was a part of her that didn't like so many people coming and going; being in a place she didn't have one hundred percent control over. Back at the department, there weren't any surprises inside their cold-case office, but the lodge seemed to have a revolving door and there was no way of telling how many people had the combination for the front keypad. She wondered if Jack changed it when new people stayed there.

"You look surprised," said Jack as he handed her a cup of coffee.

"Thank you. This case has been quite the surprise on so many levels. We really appreciate you letting us stay here."

"My pleasure. Anything to help solve these crimes."

John didn't say anything and nodded his thanks when Jack gave him his cup. Jack then headed out. Katie wasn't sure if the men had met officially but decided not to worry about it and approached the board, munching on her toast. Noticing that the board had been previously covered by a sheet, she assumed McGaven was keeping things private from anyone who happened to be in the room.

Katie studied the two forest crime scenes and the hospital ones. The list of evidence collected seemed to connect, but the blood message with the warning was different. However, that warning was consistent with the other scenes on some level. The thought-out extravagant totems weren't an afterthought, but a clear warning—even if it only made sense to the killer."

John left the lodge and Katie assumed he was going to his truck.

"What do you have?" she said to McGaven.

"With Theresa Jamison, I remember you saying that Officer Clark's sister, Tami Clark, knew her."

"And?"

"I found out from Clark that Tami's in town and we can interview her."

Katie nodded. "Maybe get some background on Theresa."

"I also spoke with Theresa's mother. She didn't have anything to say about her daughter except that she was a good person and was working hard to become a nurse. She's an only child and has two cousins living in New York as well as the one in Pine Valley. And... her dad is deceased. He died two years ago. Everything seems to check out."

"Did her mother know about Devin?" she said.

"That's a firm no."

"Really?"

"Her mom told me that Theresa wasn't dating because she was concentrating on her studies."

"Okay, we'll have to see what her friend says." Katie put her hands on her hips and studied photos and the list from Theresa's crime scene.

"What's up?" said McGaven. He knew his partner well.

"The way everything came about... bothers me."

"Meaning?"

"So this young woman who called herself TJ came to my cabin door and brought me to Theresa's crime scene. No one knows her or has ever seen her before—at least that's what they're saying. How did she even find Theresa? What's her connection?"

John returned with a couple of boxes.

"What's that?" said McGaven.

John put the boxes on the table. "These are my on-the-road microscopes and goodies." He pulled everything out and organized them on the dining room table.

"Cool, a portable forensic lab," said McGaven.

"I can compare prints and look at any evidence up close for basic comparison."

Katie was pleased they would not have to wait for the forensic lab to return their reports.

"There hasn't been any word on the identity of TJ?" she said.

"Nothing."

"If she came to Echo Forest for whatever reason and doesn't live here—she had to have stayed somewhere," she said.

"Friend?" said McGaven.

"Just spending the day?" said John.

"No, I don't think so. It's so remote. I think she would have stayed at a motel, most likely, for a couple of days," said Katie.

McGaven keyed up searches for motels nearby or the closest to Echo Forest. "Good news. There're not a lot of places to stay."

"Except here," said John.

"I would think that TJ would have stayed somewhere that no one would notice."

"The closest motel is Valley Motel. There's nothing swanky

about it. It looks old and is on the outskirts of town. The next closest is about twenty miles away."

"Any B and Bs?" she said.

"There are two, believe it or not. Echo Forest Bed-and-Breakfast and Valley Inn are small boutique types. Both are not cheap and offer several amenities."

"And wouldn't really compete with this lodge," she said. Katie wondered how Jack perceived the bed-and-breakfast spots.

"Different type of lodging."

John pulled out one of the four large binders. "Just as I thought."

"What?" said Katie.

"This fiber appears to come from a carpet, based on its characteristics." John went back to his microscope and studied the fiber further. "It appears to be a green low-pile that has been looped into a backing—even though we don't have the backing, it has a slight curl."

"Can you tell where this fiber came from?" she said.

"I can only tell it's most likely synthetic—like polyester or nylon. If I had to guess, it would be poly."

"Like from a house or car?" said McGaven.

"It's a lower-end type of carpet I've seen over the years, but it's difficult at this magnification level to be able to tell if it's for house or car. It could be both."

"Wait a minute," said Katie. She went directly to the reports from the laboratory from Theresa's crime scene. "It says here there were carpet fragments in Theresa's hair."

"Color?" said John.

"It says olive-green synthetic polyester."

"It's something," said McGaven.

"Yes and no," she said, looking at the board. "What's the preliminary at the hospital?"

"The victim, nurse in training Natalie Renaldo, was

working the late shift along with nurse Patty Brown. They were taking care of the chief. Nelson Gonzalez was the security guard. He had some defensive wounds, which means he saw the killer," said McGaven. "All victims were strangled."

"Is there at this point any connection with the nurse to Theresa or TJ?" she said.

McGaven shook his head. "No, we haven't connected anything yet. But Clark and Banning are still questioning people and we should hear from them soon. But, one thing they did say was that Natalie was new to town and she went to the café quite a bit."

"I think most of the town goes there. But that would mean the killer does too," she said.

"So what was the killer doing at the hospital last night?" McGaven said.

"Maybe they were there for the chief?"

"Why?"

Katie shrugged. "Maybe to shut the investigation down? Maybe the killer knows the chief? Or has been watching him and the other officers. But why didn't they kill him while they had the chance?"

"Then he brutally murders the nurse and takes out the other nurse on duty and the security guard in case they saw him?" said McGaven.

She shrugged again. "What about the security cameras?"

"There's only footage up to 8:30 p.m. The rest is completely blank."

"So by the time we got there around 10 p.m. the killer was already there." Katie was frustrated. Just when she thought they were making some headway they were hit with setbacks.

"More than likely. The killer was most likely the one who locked us into the bathroom."

Katie ran all the hospital events through her mind. "Three down... more to go..." she whispered.

"What?"

"The message on the wall. Three down... more to go..."

"What about it?"

"The killer highlighted the murders of the three young women, but didn't acknowledge the other nurse and security guard. That would make it five down. Or he could have been referring to the nurses and security guard as the three down... What is the killer trying to tell us? We need to retrieve an employee list for the hospital, including volunteers, and find out their whereabouts last night."

"You think the killer works at the hospital?"

"They must have some connection," she said. "Not sure what yet, but it's the first time they have been almost caught—and their MO changed. They were rushed. Or it's possible they don't have anything to do with the two previous murders—but that would be some coincidence."

McGaven added to his notes. "You got it."

"Let's get started. We need to find out if TJ stayed at a local motel... and we need to talk to Tami Clark," said Katie.

"Copy that," said McGaven.

"John, you up for a short jaunt?"

"You bet. What do you need?" he said.

"I know you don't usually work the investigative part of a homicide or cold case, but we need the help... and... I know you're the best at what you do," she said and smiled. "Can you check out places that sell and install carpets... including ones that have remnants? If I'm correct about the evidence from the first crime scene, the killer seems to have transported Theresa rolled in a rug. See what you can find."

John nodded. "I'll check it out."

Katie and McGaven grabbed a few files.

"Let's go, Cisco," Katie called.

"Road trip," said McGaven.

TWENTY-FIVE

Friday 1145 hours

Katie and McGaven headed to the small motel on the edge of town. It was difficult to find as it didn't have proper signage.

"Are you sure this is the right way?" said Katie as she looked around. It appeared they were heading into nowhere but a dense forest.

"Yes. Keep going."

Katie slowed her speed and couldn't believe people could find the place. Then she got her answer. They had come upon what was once a nice little motel, but now it was clearly abandoned and ready for demolition.

"It doesn't look like the photos that were on the internet," he said and began to search more. "It looks like they closed about two years ago... and it opened in 1974. Sorry, I didn't catch that."

Katie parked next to an old oak tree. The branches had since drooped, making it appear hunched over with its limbs dangling.

"You don't think TJ was here, do you?" said McGaven looking around.

"What I do know is that we're here, so let's take a quick look," she said and got out. She decided to keep Cisco in the car. They weren't sure what they were going to find. She had her remote for the door popper if they needed him.

Katie paused and made sure her weapon was secured. There was no indication that anyone had been here in years. There were no tire tracks or footprints, but it was difficult to see through all the overgrowth. She could hear the sound of water indicating that a small creek was nearby, but it was difficult to ascertain in which direction with the way sound bounced in the forest.

"Okay, let's go check it out," she said beginning to walk through weeds and dead underlying brush.

McGaven slowed his pace behind Katie as he kept watch behind them.

The old motel was one story with eight rooms and a small office located in the middle. The paint had long since peeled and flaked away. All the exterior doors were intact, which seemed out of place. Usually buildings that had been abandoned and were deteriorating had some indication of vandalism or tagging, but there was none. It was as if a generation had moved forward and forgotten this motel was even here.

Katie stopped.

McGaven followed suit, not saying anything.

Not only was the site excessively overgrown, but Katie had a feeling of being watched and she didn't want to get ambushed. Her fears were rational with her past experience in the military and previous police investigations.

Looking from left to right and back again, Katie thought it was best to begin from the left.

"Let's start over there," said McGaven indicating the left as if he had read her thoughts. His voice was low and his focus was intense.

Katie nodded. She loved it when her partner was thinking the same things she was. Usually they would break up and individually search, but she felt more secure searching each room together.

At the first room, a faint outline of a number "1" was still visible on the door. Katie tried it, but it was stuck. She looked to her partner and moved aside.

McGaven took a step and kicked the door open, causing it to smash back against the wall. The door was still on its old hinges. The room was empty. A bed frame leaned against the wall, the carpet had been torn out, and there were no fixtures in the bathroom. It was empty.

Katie looked at McGaven. "Let's check them all."

The detectives systematically checked each room. Most were empty with remnants of what had been inside, but nothing that suggested someone had been staying there. They closed each door after they left.

Katie and McGaven stood at the seventh room.

"Look at this," said Katie. "That's a new doorknob." It resembled the others, but it was clear it hadn't stood the ravages of time out in the open. It was clean. Katie tried the knob and it turned in her hand. She glanced at McGaven. He readied himself with his gun drawn. Katie nodded and then pushed the door open. McGaven rushed in and made sure there was no one hiding in the closet or bathroom. It was vacant.

Standing at the threshold, the room had clearly been occupied —recently. It had been cleaned and there was a broom leaning in the corner. A mattress with a sleeping bag had been pushed to the right, where it was neatly folded with a pillow. Two cardboard boxes were in the other corner as well as a duffel bag. The bathroom contained some toiletries and two neatly folded towels.

Katie kept a watchful eye at the doorway, but knew that if anyone were to try to sneak up, Cisco would bark.

The detectives pulled on gloves—just in case.

McGaven came back near the entrance.

Katie knelt down and looked through the first box.

"Anything?" he said.

"It looks like... newspaper clippings," she said. "They're dated about twenty years ago." There were copies of birth certificates, death certificates, printouts from websites of genealogy, and other miscellaneous papers someone would use to track down someone.

"Looks like she was researching," he said.

Katie quickly moved to the duffel bag and unzipped it. She flipped through clothing and personal items, and then looking into a zippered area, she revealed a driver's license. "Got it." She stood up.

McGaven was quickly at her side.

"Tamara Jane Lambert, nineteen years old, with an address in Springfield, Missouri. There's no other identification, no credit cards, nothing except for two hundred in cash."

"No cell phone or tablet?" he said.

"Nothing." Looking at the photo, she said, "But we found TJ."

"I wonder how long she had been staying here?"

"Looks like for a while. It appears she wasn't leaving until she found what she was looking for," said Katie.

McGaven went back to the boxes and quickly rifled through them.

"Anything else?"

"No. More newspaper clippings and government paperwork. Wait..." he said. "Here's an old photo."

Katie looked at the worn snapshot of two little blonde girls around seven or eight years old, standing in a yard somewhere holding hands. She flipped it over but there was nothing notated.

"Is that TJ and a relative, I wonder?" McGaven said.

"Could be. Look at how they resemble each other. They definitely look related."

"And close."

"Like sisters," said Katie.

McGaven stopped what he was doing and stared at his partner. "Sisters resembling each other."

"Like TJ and Theresa. Just as I first thought. No wonder no one had seen TJ before. She had never been in town and was staying out here, secretly looking for Theresa." Katie looked around the room. "C'mon, let's bag everything up besides the boxes and bring it all back."

"What are you thinking?"

"I'm thinking we can run DNA to find out if the girls were related. We need to get this information to the county morgue so they can officially identify TJ."

"So these killings must have had something to do with these two girls' relationship," said McGaven.

"I don't know how, but we're going to find out." Katie headed to the Jeep to grab some bags. She stopped at the doorway. "The Woodsman... of course," she said. "We've been overlooking it because it didn't make any sense and there was no direct correlation to it so..."

"What about it?" he said.

"This is just a working theory... but I think the Woodsman is the key."

"How?"

"I think it means something to both TJ and Theresa. TJ was terrified by the thought of him."

"Like a belief... meaning... or something with the totems?" he said.

"No, like there really is a boogeyman out there."

Three down... more to go...

TWENTY-SIX

Friday 1400 hours

Katie and McGaven packed the Jeep carefully with the belongings of TJ from the Valley Motel. Now they had an identity and a name—Tamara Lambert—but they still had to put all the pieces together in order to see how the murders were connected.

They had coordinated a time to chat with Theresa's friend, Tami. As they drove over to a small coffeehouse, One Cup, to talk to Officer Clark's sister, McGaven put a call in to Chief Cooper. No answer. He decided to send a text instead about the motel, what they had found, and where they were going.

"No answer?" said Katie.

McGaven shook his head. "He doesn't seem to be available —even after last night. I tried a couple of times this morning. It's odd."

"Think he might be overwhelmed?"

"I don't know. I haven't been around him enough to get a strong sense of his personality."

Katie figured she had about ten minutes before they got to

the coffee place. "Can I let you in on something that's bothering me?" she said, gripping the steering wheel tighter.

Cisco whined and pushed his head toward Katie.

"Is it bad?"

"No," she said slowly. "But it has bothered me for a while."

"My breath?"

"What?"

"I know with all that beef I eat..."

"No." She laughed. "I know you're trying to make light of this, but..."

"Is this to stay between us?"

"Yes."

"Shoot."

"I can't seem to get my head around Jack. He's been amazingly accommodating, but there's something amiss."

"Why do you think that?" McGaven eyed her curiously.

"How many vets do you know who can run a crime scene? And he's pretty efficient at it when he does, which is unexpected when there hasn't been a murder here for fifteen years."

"Have you asked him where he learned how to be so *efficient*?"

"He told me he trained at the police academy a long time ago before he switched to veterinary science, but that wouldn't account for it. I've asked about his past in a friendly manner, but he always finds a way to divert the question."

"You mean he's cagey?" he said.

"A little bit." Katie found a parking space along the street and pulled in. "Maybe it's his private business, but..."

"But what?"

"He seems too involved in these cases while claiming to know nothing about them."

"And?"

"Can you do a background on him?" When Katie said it aloud it did sound a bit crazy, but they had no idea who they were really dealing with in Echo Forest. He wasn't law enforcement, but the town vet. Still...

McGaven turned his gaze out the window watching a few people walk by wearing heavy coats. "Katie, you know I respect you and I would have your back in any situation. But are you sure?"

She nodded. "Yes."

"Okay, but I don't want to see it blow up in our faces."

"It's on the down-low, just between us. No bringing the chief or the officers into this," she said.

"Of course. I haven't been around him very much, but what I've seen is a very skilled crime scene technician and nice guy. But if something bothers you... then I'll get to the bottom of it." McGaven pet Cisco and the dog's tail thumped against the back seat. "Don't worry, we'll get you a treat, or maybe a pup cup?"

Cisco gave a low bark.

The detectives exited the vehicle and walked to One Cup. The coffee aroma was strong; the small business must be roasting its beans. The front façade was festive with a creative design revolving around drinking coffee. There were several outdoor tables, but it was too cold to stay outside.

McGaven opened the door and a hanging set of bells jingled to alert the baristas someone had arrived. Katie felt the warm air hit her body, along with the smell of coffee and pastries. She felt the calmest she had since she arrived.

A young woman sat in the corner already enjoying a hot coffee drink with whipped cream swirled on top. Her short bob haircut and dark hair made her stand out, and there was a resemblance to Officer Clark. She was wearing jeans and fur-lined boots and was still dressed in her bright red coat. She busily slid her index finger over her cell phone and didn't immediately see the detectives enter.

Katie approached the table. "Tami Clark?"

The young woman looked up. "Yes?"

"We're Detectives Scott and McGaven," she said. "We wanted to speak with you."

"Oh, yes. Bobby told me to meet you," she said as her eyes lit up.

Katie pulled out a chair and sat down.

"I'll be back," said McGaven as he headed to order some coffee. The detectives commonly split up when interviewing someone. It made people feel more at ease, so it was McGaven's turn to head off.

"Is it true there's a serial killer on the loose?" said Tami as her eyes opened wide with curiosity.

"We're working on the cases but that hasn't been established yet."

"Still, it's scary," she said, sipping her drink.

"You knew Theresa Jamison?"

She nodded. "We went to school together ever since kindergarten."

"So you knew her well?"

She shrugged. "Kinda."

"What do you mean?"

"We weren't besties, but we knew each other."

"When was the last time you saw her?" said Katie.

Tami thought for a moment. "It was a couple of weeks ago. I think it was the day before she was murdered... but I'm not sure."

"What do you mean?"

"I saw her in here two weeks ago, but she was in a hurry, so we just said hi."

"And?"

"Then I think I saw her riding in a truck a little later, which I thought was weird. It drove by just up the street. I remember thinking that she looked really upset and wondered who was driving."

"Where was the truck heading?"

"I don't know."

"What direction was it heading?"

"Oh. It was going north, uptown, you know, heading out toward the fields."

"Did Theresa have any sisters?" Katie was testing Tami to see what she would say.

"No. She was an only child."

Katie reached into her pocket and pulled out her cell phone. She showed the driver's license photograph of TJ. "Have you ever seen her?"

Tami really looked at the photograph. Then she shook her head. "No, I don't think so. But... she kinda looks like Theresa."

"What about Theresa's boyfriend Devin?"

"He's a loser. Sorry, I don't want to sound mean, but he is. He used to get into trouble all the time. He lived with his dad for a while... I think he was in construction."

"I see," said Katie.

Tami leaned forward. "I heard Devin was living alone because his parents disappeared."

"What do you mean, disappeared?"

"I don't know... just talk maybe. There's a lot of talk in this town." Tami's phone dinged with text alert. "I've got to go. I'm meeting someone." She stood up. "You need anything more?"

"Do you know the nurse who was murdered at the hospital last night? Natalie Renaldo?"

"Umm. No. Anything else?" She seemed bored and had her mind on other things.

"Oh, one more thing," said Katie.

Tami took her eyes away from her phone.

"Does the Woodsman mean anything to you?"

"Woodsman?" she repeated.

"Yes."

She shrugged, but her eyes and the expression on her face seemed to change. "Nope. Unless you mean some reality show where guys chop down really big trees?" She made a half smile. "Is that it?"

"I think we're good for now. Thanks."

"Text me anytime." Tami left.

Katie leaned back in her chair and thought about what Tami had told her. The young woman didn't seem to be hiding anything, but her body language changed when Katie had brought up the Woodsman.

"Hey," said McGaven sitting down. "Anything?"

"One of those for me?" she said referring to the two coffee drinks.

"Here." McGaven slid one over to his partner.

"What's in the bag?"

"Nothing."

Katie gave him the look that she didn't believe him.

"All right. I'll share my cinnamon roll, but it's under protest." He tore off a piece for her.

"Thank you."

"So, anything new?" he said.

"Not really, but she did say that she'd never seen TJ before... and she stated that TJ looked like Theresa."

"Interesting," he said munching on the cinnamon bun.

"She thought Devin was a loser. And mentioned that she thought she saw Theresa riding in the passenger seat of a pickup truck the day before she was murdered—not looking very happy."

"Don't know what to think about that. Think it was the last person she was with before being killed?"

"It's possible."

"Here's your pup cup," said the barista and set it down. It was a small cup with whipped cream.

"Thank you."

"You're going to spoil Cisco," she said smiling.

"It's the least I could do since he's got to hang out in the car while we interview people and check out places. Was there anything else from Tami?"

"A strange thing... when I asked her about the Woodsman, she seemed to be a little frightened."

"What's with this Woodsman?"

"The fear on TJ's face every time she said it spooked even me," Katie said. "I did some searches but nothing much came up."

"I'll see what I can do."

A text came into Katie's cell. She looked at it.

"Chief?" said McGaven.

"No, it's John. He's back at the lodge and has some things to tell us."

McGaven stood up. "Let's go."

"I was thinking that Cisco needs a crime scene search before we return," she said. "There's still daylight."

"Let me guess... the second victim in the park?"

She nodded. "I was thinking since it was so dark when we were there, even though we had lighting... I want to go look around before going back to the lodge."

"Anything specific you're looking for?"

"Drag marks and tire impressions. We can grab a quick bite before going out there."

"I'm in."

TWENTY-SEVEN

Friday 1500 hours

Katie drove into the old park where Mountain Trail Pass and TJ's crime scene were located. It was easier to navigate since it was still light, but the uneven gravel and large boulders were still a road hazard.

"Geez," said McGaven as he held on to the handle above the door.

"I'm trying to make it less bumpy."

"I don't think the killer came this way to dump the body." McGaven grimaced after the last chuckhole in the parking area.

"I think you're right," she said. "But why this location?"

"Why the tree next to your cabin?"

"For someone to have these totems and messages, and then to stage the scenes in a particular location, no doubt it meant something specific to the killer. Maybe something the killer wants us to believe or know." Katie glanced to her partner. "Whenever we've worked a case where the killer leaves a victim in a rural setting, what has it meant?"

"Well... some of these killers think they're smarter than the cops, so they display their crime scenes in a shocking or theatrical way to show the cops that they have an advantage. They aren't opportunistic, that's for sure. They were all sending us a message," he said.

Katie parked close to the area she did two nights previous.

"And the last message we had was that they're not going to stop. Right?" she said. "I think Theresa and TJ were planned victims and meant something to the killer. But I'm still trying to figure out why the killer went to hospital and killed the new nurse in training... There's got to be something about the hospital that connects the three young victims."

"I'll do a deep dive on all three women and see what pops," he said.

"It may be nothing, but there's one or maybe two big chunks of the puzzle we're missing." She sighed and turned her attention to the park and the entrance to the trail. Feeling a bit of anxious energy trying to rear its ugly head, Katie took a deep breath to slow down her racing thoughts about the cases and set her focus on TJ's crime scene. There had been so many things happening, it seemed like a tidal wave of events. She had to keep her concentration on one thing at a time.

"Ready?" said McGaven.

"I want to look around first before bringing Cisco out."

He nodded.

Both detectives got out of the Jeep. Cisco spun in excitement in the back seat because he seemed to know this setting was going to include him.

Katie looked in the opposite direction of the crime scene area. It had a different overall feeling. It was clearer today that the park had been neglected. She wasn't sure why, but she guessed budgets weren't allocated—maybe it wasn't as popular as the others. But with the two bed-and-breakfast inns along with Jack's lodge, it seemed the area would grow as a tourist attraction.

Katie looked at the panoramic view and hoped Echo Forest wasn't going to become known for a murder rampage.

She turned and walked toward the open space where TJ's body had lain from left to right between two large trees. It reminded Katie of a play where the stage was set between pulled-back curtains—which began to tell a story.

"Katie," said McGaven.

She turned to see her partner standing between the large dense set of trees on the left side.

"Check this out," he said.

Katie hurried to his location.

"Slow down," he instructed.

She studied the ground around her partner. It appeared there were branches piled on top of one another. Upon first glance, the downed branches blended into their surroundings. But the more Katie studied it, the more she realized they had been put there recently. The broken ends still looked new, light with a greenish hue, and not darkened as if they had been there for years.

"Why didn't we see these two nights ago?" she said.

"We concentrated on the immediate area and around the trash cans."

"Maybe this is what happens when we don't have an experienced crime scene technician and more uniformed officers to assist with the search," she said, frustrated.

"The point is we've discovered it now."

"We need to systematically remove them."

"Documenting each layer?"

Katie nodded. She took a step to the right side, mirroring her partner. "It's better to have too many photos than not enough."

The detectives began removing the fresh pine branches, taking a photo after each one was discarded. They carefully inspected the layers.

Katie began to think they weren't going to find anything until after removing the ninth branch they revealed what appeared to be a makeshift trail. It had the same drag marks as Theresa's crime scene.

McGaven took several photos. He retrieved a dollar bill and set it beside the deepest impression to give perspective and size. "Wouldn't this take time?"

"Yes, it would, which means it was planned and the killer felt at home," she said.

Katie's phone chimed with a text message from John.

Recvd prelim reports from hospital. No fingerprints unaccounted for. Getting list of everyone who had access...

Katie replied:

Thanks. See ya soon.

"What's up?" said McGaven.

"The hospital isn't turning up any leads. No fingerprints. No video during those hours leading up to and after the murders." Katie frowned and stepped back.

"Katie?"

"I can't get it out of my mind."

"The crime scenes?"

"They seem too planned for..."

"For what?"

"For one person to accomplish in that close of a timeline."

"Two killers?"

"Not necessarily. But I think there might be someone either coordinating or helping with the props."

"Based on?"

Katie paused before she answered him. "There's quite a bit of detail at these crime scenes. And the hospital scene needed to be well coordinated. It would have been much easier to pull off with assistance. I just still can't see how the hospital murders are connected to Theresa's and TJ's."

"Things aren't adding up."

"Exactly. But it's possible that we're supposed to think that."

Once McGaven took several more photos, the detectives cautiously followed the trail they'd uncovered. It wasn't a steep trail, but it had obviously been carefully cleared and not just trampled into existence. Once at the bottom, it was obvious a vehicle had been parked there recently.

"Those are definitely tire impressions," said Katie.

McGaven took several photos, again using a dollar bill for reference.

Katie's mind spun. Things were falling together as to how, but the why and who were still foggy in her mind. The crime scenes said a lot about the killer, their preparation, their skill, the timing, a message, and the end result.

"Maybe John can research the tire, make, and model of the vehicle?" she said.

"I bet he can."

They took a few more minutes documenting the overall area.

"I'm sending these to my computer and to John as well," McGaven said.

"Great."

"Do you still want to use Cisco?"

"Yes, I don't want to miss anything. The weather looks as if it's going to storm again and then if there is anything to find—it will be lost forever."

"On it," he said.

. . .

Katie geared up Cisco just as if it were a serious priority or search. She made sure his vest was secure and his eyes were protected. She also changed her shoes to more appropriate tactical outdoor boots.

"Cisco ready?" said McGaven.

"Yep." Katie put a shorter leash on the dog due to the thick sections of the forest. That way she could keep control and not have him get tangled. "Cisco, let's go," she said.

"Want me just behind you?" Gav asked.

"That works. The wind is very calm."

Once they reached the area and headed to the right, Katie said, "*Such*," meaning to search.

There were piles of leaves, some cleared spaces animals had used as trails, and underbrush just like most places this time of year. Cisco took off at a fast pace, much quicker than what was usual for him. He seemed to have caught the scent of something strong and was going to make his way there in a hurry. It definitely wasn't his regular moderated speed and sweeping search on a grid pattern.

"What's up?" said McGaven trying to keep up with Katie and the dog.

"I don't know. He's on scent." She tried to slow down Cisco, then made the decision to let him off leash.

Cisco's big paws moved through the leaves and it became clear that he was heading toward something big. Katie kept a running pace, keeping her eye on the black dog gaining speed.

Then she couldn't see him anymore and her heart skipped a beat.

"Where did he go?" said McGaven, breathless, running a few feet behind his partner.

Katie didn't answer, she was thinking of the worst-case scenario—and couldn't help it. Her thoughts were interrupted by Cisco's barking. It wasn't a rapid bark like danger was near, but rather he was alerting her to something important.

Katie followed the dog's barking and accidentally turned left before realizing the barking came from another area. Echo Forest was living up to its name, so she stopped and waited to regain her bearings. Turning around expecting to see McGaven, he was not there.

She turned to retrace her steps. The forest was quiet— jarringly silent. If there ever was a situation where you could actually hear a pin drop, this was it.

Katie stepped lightly as if her footsteps would make too much noise.

"Katie?" came a whisper.

She turned and no one was there. As far as she could tell, she was alone.

Why couldn't she hear Cisco barking anymore?
Where was McGaven?

Suddenly she had a strong headache, causing her to put her hands to her forehead and squeeze her eyes shut. When she finally opened them, she heard McGaven calling her name. Katie quickly ran toward his voice. She could hear Cisco continuing to bark.

Katie caught up with her partner.

"Where did you go?" said McGaven.

"I just went the wrong way," she said, still a bit shook up about what had happened. She didn't want to explain to her partner because she felt like she might be going crazy. "Sorry."

McGaven gave her a curious look. "This way," he said and led her to where Cisco was.

The barking had stopped and Cisco was sitting down facing them when they approached. He was in alert mode with his ears straight up, leaning slightly forward. His yellowish wolf eyes kept watch as he waited for his handler. He resembled a beautiful statue with his shiny black coat reflecting the light. He began to lightly pant.

"Cisco," said Katie, slowly moving toward the dog. As she

got nearer she saw something sticking out of a pile of dried leaves about a foot away from Cisco.

Her heart stopped.

"What is it?" said McGaven. His voice sounded strange, as if he was in another room.

"I don't know..." Her voice faded as she moved closer. "Good boy," she said to the dog while he remained in his position, waiting for Katie to give the command to release.

Katie turned her attention completely on what Cisco had alerted to and knelt down... Sticking out of the pile of leaves was a fur-trimmed boot. She kept her breathing calm, but she wanted to cry out. She remembered instantly that Tami Clark had worn the exact same pair at the coffee shop.

Katie turned and saw McGaven standing over her with a look of shock on his face.

"Tami Clark?" she barely whispered.

TWENTY-EIGHT

Friday 1645 hours

The longer Katie stared at the fur-lined boot sticking out from underneath a pile of leaves, the more she felt her heart skip a beat and an extreme heaviness overcome her body. How was she going to be able to tell Officer Clark they had found his sister's body?

"Tami..." she whispered. Katie began to slowly brush away the leaves. She expected to see a leg and the rest of the body, including the other boot, but she didn't. With meticulous care, she kept digging the leaves until she found there wasn't a body, or any body parts. It was just a boot.

"What the...?" said McGaven.

"There must be human scent on the boot, otherwise Cisco wouldn't have alerted to it. And it must've been strong."

"Is that really Tami's boot?" he said.

"Don't know for sure, but it looks like it. I haven't touched it, so let's bag it."

"If the scent was strong, could the killer have been here?"

"That would mean the killer is following us or knows our

schedule. Why else would this fur-lined boot happen to look just like the one Tami was wearing?" she said.

"That was only two hours ago that we met with her."

"It could mean two things. The killer is toying with us—like telling us we're never going to find him. Or the killer is sending us a message."

"Like?"

"Like he could kill Tami Clark at any time and there's nothing we can do about it." Katie looked around them. "We need to warn Officer Clark that his sister's boot was found."

McGaven took out his phone and left a message for Clark to call them immediately.

Katie looked at her phone. "I think the signal is becoming spotty again."

McGaven studied the area and the weather. "It's getting colder and I would guess that storm is coming in tonight."

"Let's hurry," she said.

Katie and Cisco started a grid search, making sure they weren't missing anything important. After twenty minutes, Cisco didn't show any behavioral change and hadn't alerted on anything. Meanwhile, McGaven had documented and collected potential evidence.

The detectives packed the Jeep to drive back to the Echo Forest Lodge.

"You're quiet," said McGaven. "I know it's not because you have nothing to say."

Katie concentrated on the roads. It started to snow, making traction slippery. She made sure her four-wheel drive was enabled.

"Well, if I were Detective Katie Scott, I would be thinking that there are more things being thrown at us... and we need more people to help with the investigation. We owe it to the family and friends of the victims to solve these investigations," he said. "Am I close?"

Katie had been thinking about needing more people, but what she was really thinking about was her name being said in the forest and how uneasy she felt about it. It was somewhat unusual for her. She knew what it felt like to be in danger and to have difficult cases—but this rare perception had been how she had felt since she got to Echo Forest.

"You know I'm not making fun of you, but did I get it right?"

"You did. But I think it goes deeper than that." Katie slowed her speed. "This weather isn't going to help. It looks bad."

"From what I'm seeing on the forecast," he said, looking at the next twenty-four hours of weather on his phone, "the storm will be heavy and cold, but it will clear back to like today in a day's time."

"A day?"

"Sorry we can't arrest the weather."

Katie smiled. "I wish we could."

"The high point of the storm won't be for another six to eight hours. It gives us time to prepare," he said.

Katie pulled into a parking place in front of the veterinary office next to Jack's truck. She saw John's and McGaven's trucks as well, but there weren't any other vehicles.

The detectives, followed closely by Cisco, hurried up the stairs to the entrance of the lodge. As they walked in, they found John busily working at a desktop computer and microscope. A stack of printed papers was neatly sitting next to him.

He looked up. "Hey, thought you got lost."

McGaven shut the door and Katie carried the bagged boot to the dining table. Cisco went into the kitchen where his bowl of water sat and drank noisily.

Katie was exhausted and wanted to sit down on the couch

for a few minutes, but she was drawn to what John had uncovered.

"What do we have?" she said.

"It's interesting."

"Wait," called McGaven from the kitchen. He had grabbed a bottle of water and hurried back to the living area.

"Have you seen or heard from the chief or Officers Clark and Banning?" said Katie.

"No. It's been quiet, which is great. But not hearing from them is a bit worrisome."

"I agree," said McGaven.

"We have to keep trying to get ahold of them," she said. Katie leaned against the table as Cisco padded by, dripping water along the floor. "I don't know what else to do. They all know we're here working on these cases."

"We need some updates and more results from the lab and medical examiner's office," said McGaven.

"The only thing we can do is keep working with what we have... and Katie needs to add to her criminal profile," said John. "We have most of the forensics from the crime scenes, autopsy reports, and of course the behavioral evidence left at the scenes."

"You're right." Looking at a small piece of paper, she said, "What's this?"

"A list of items we need," said John. "I have most of the technology things in case we lose electricity, but you can't be too careful."

Katie read down the list, "Batteries, compact chargers for phones and computers, firewood stocked inside, printer paper... I saw firewood on the other side near the downstairs entrance."

"Good idea, John," said McGaven. "We need more food supplies too."

"Who wants to go?" Katie said. "No sense two or three of us going."

"I'll go," said McGaven.

"You sure?" she said.

"You guys will just slow me down... besides, it's not far. I'll go now before the weather gets worse," he said.

Katie looked at the growing amount of information and something inside made her feel as if she were trying to hold tight to a sinking ship. She stood at the board.

"I'll be back," said McGaven with a silly voice from a famous movie. He shut the door behind him.

Cisco ran up to the door and then turned back.

"Do you want to hear what I found or wait for McGaven?" said John.

"I'll update him. We need to move forward and I get a feeling the weather is going to be a problem for us."

John nodded. His solemn demeanor and neutral facial expression made it difficult to read him sometimes. "I looked at the weather report too. The owner of the carpet and flooring store said not to worry—it can be bad, but it'll be short lived."

Katie pulled up a chair next to John. "What do we have?" She remained hopeful.

"I went to a couple of flooring stores, one in town and another heading into Walnut Creek. Both places said the same things... that this particular rug and color has been discontinued."

Katie listened and felt her body get colder.

"But the store here in Echo Forest, Crane Flooring, said they have an old remnant pile out back that they give away for free."

"Free?"

"This isn't choice stuff but lower end, like colors weren't popular and weird sizing. They're just castoffs."

Katie got up and stoked the fire, trying to bring more heat into the room.

"But the manager, Stu Jenkins, said that about a week ago he noticed that a large amount of these castoffs was missing when he came into work."

This caught Katie's attention. "I'm guessing the remnants were similar if not identical to the fibers we found."

"If I were in my lab, I would be able to confirm that but here I can optimistically say that it's ninety percent positive," he said.

Katie sat back down. "So we know the killer must've used these old pieces of carpet to move the bodies to the crime scene areas. That would mean they had to know what this business did this with its offcuts."

John nodded. "You can't see them from the street or near the building."

"So who would know about it? Customers? Carpet delivery personnel and installers?"

"Well, I can make this easy. Crane Flooring gets almost all their carpeting and flooring from a distributor, ATC Floors, out of Southern California. They've been doing business with them for more than twenty years. But they have only one installer locally and his name is Bill Westin."

Katie stood up and went to the board. She had a renewal of energy. "We have another lead. We've got to chase this guy down. I'll have Gav do a background when he gets back."

"I'm sending the address and cell number to your phone," John said. "And the manager said Bill would be dropping off some unused carpet pieces in the morning before noon."

"Just because he has access to the carpet that left fibers at the crime scene doesn't make him the killer... but it does make him someone we need to talk to. Great work, John."

"I do what I can," he said and smiled.

The lights flickered, but remained on.

"Is there a generator here?" said John.

"I'm sure Jack has one, but if not, we need to make sure everything is charged one hundred percent and there's wood stockpiled for the fireplace."

"That's why I wanted Gav to get whatever battery chargers that he could."

Katie began updating the lists, highlighting important information to include the new evidence and locations. She wanted to see if there were links or a consistent connection with their other clues.

Victims/Crime Scenes:

#1 Theresa Jamison

Nineteen years old. Good health. Found in woods near vacation cabin, **hung** *in tree, cause of death* **strangulation***, manner of death homicide,* **totem** *left at scene,* **drag marks** *behind tree indicating how she was brought to the location.* **Her face was covered** *with a* **burlap bag***. She was a* **resident of Echo Forest** *working at the* **Sunrise Café** *and going to go to nursing school.* **Boyfriend, Devin Bradley. Friend, Tami Clark. TJ (Tamara Jane Lambert)** *found body and came to the cabin to ask Katie for help—then TJ disappeared. Striking resemblance to TJ (related?).*

#2 Tamara Jane Lambert (TJ)

Twenty years old. Found **near the Mountain Trail Pass***.* **Posed in field area***.* **Face covered with fabric** *similar to Theresa's burlap. Cause of death* **strangulation** *(haven't received official autopsy report), manner of death homicide,* **totem left at scene***,* **clothes bagged and left in trash can***, drag marks indicating she was brought there and where* the killer entered the area. **From out of town. Staying at the abandoned Valley Motel**. *No one seems to know her or have seen her from people questioned.*

#3 Natalie Renaldo

Twenty-one years old. **Nurse** *in training.* **Found at hospital. Posed in ladies' restroom. Strangulation.** *Message in blood written on the wall:* **Three down... More to go...** *Waiting for more information. Crime scene appeared rushed, cutting things close.*

Hospital Murders: Preliminary report, waiting for official reports

Nurse Patty Brown (throat slashed)

Security Guard Nelson Gonzalez (throat slashed)

Persons of Interest and Others Interviewed:

Devin Bradley (boyfriend of Theresa Jamison, lives alone out on thirty acres) POI

Gladys Miner (owner of Sunrise Café) Interviewed

Tami Clark (friend of Theresa, sister of Officer Clark, found boot near TJ's crime scene) Interviewed.

Jack Thomas (local veterinarian, crime scene tech for the police department) Interviewed

Stu Jenkins (Manager at Crane Flooring) Interviewed

Bill Westin (Installer at Crane Flooring) POI Not interviewed yet.

Police:

Chief Beryl Cooper

Officer Bobby Clark

Officer Terrance Banning

Katie had also noted a few other things they were in the dark about:

Woodsman (*In reference to what?*)

The name on the bench along one of the nearby trails: **Carol Ann Benedict** (*Who was she?*)

Katie stepped back and studied the lists. The first thing she noticed was that there was still little to go on as they waited for reports from other sources. But she knew they had to move forward with what they had and act accordingly. The bloody, written words found on the bathroom wall resonated in her mind.

Three down... more to go...

"What are you thinking?" said John.

"We don't have enough information and we're supposed to wait for other agencies to respond. The medical examiner's office and the crime laboratory," said Katie. She was sure John sensed her frustration.

"Tell me what your gut says."

Katie thought a moment. She hated giving open theories because that's not how she worked cases, but under the circumstances there wasn't much of a choice. "Honestly?"

"Just throw it out. You're not being tested," he said.

"It's that easy?"

"Yeah, just do it. Tell me what you really think and don't worry about the facts."

"I think this town has some old wounds and secrets. I think the cold case of a woman who was murdered fifteen years ago may be the key. I couldn't find any information on her, not even a name. But I have a suspicion that the name on the bench along the park trail—Carol Ann Benedict—could be her." She took a breath and stared at the fire.

John watched her. He never pushed her, always gave her space. "Okay, we can work with that."

"I also think a good portion of the town is keeping things from us. When I first met Chief Cooper at Theresa's crime scene, he definitely didn't trust me and didn't want my help. But then, like overnight, he's been helpful and appreciative."

"So you think he's working with you to distract you from something else?"

"Maybe? I don't know," she said. "I don't have enough to work with to make a constructive approach and move forward."

"So tell me, where *is* the chief now?"

"I don't know. We can't get ahold of the two officers, Clark and Banning, either." She began to pace the large room, making Cisco sit up and stare at her. "I tried calling the police department, where they have an assistant, Libby, and there's no answer there either. Just a way to leave a voicemail."

"So can the town call nine-one-one?"

"I don't know. It probably goes to the county sheriff's department and they'll dispatch accordingly."

John stood up and stopped her from pacing. "Katie. This is

what we've been given right now. There's plenty to work on. Give yourself a break."

Katie met John's gaze. She could tell he cared about her. Perhaps he cared more than he let on. "I'm sorry."

"For what?"

"Whining." She forced a smile.

"Katie Scott a whiner... I don't think so." John averted his eyes. "We'll get to the bottom of it. Gav should be back soon and we'll plan on working through the storm."

The front door slammed open and McGaven rushed in carrying bags.

"Is there more?" said John.

"Yeah, two bags in the truck," he said, winded.

Katie grabbed the food and headed for the kitchen to sort things. She tried to keep optimistic and not to replay everything until the overthinking became relentless.

"Hey," said McGaven. "You okay?"

"Yeah. John has made some great connections. We'll update you."

He studied his partner closely. He could probably tell her stress levels were heightened, but he didn't push. "Cool."

Cisco nudged in between them.

"Not yet, Cisco," she said, referring to the dog's dinner.

"It's cold and there's some light snow flurries out there," said McGaven.

"That's not good."

"We'll be okay. John went to bring up some more wood for the fire." McGaven's cell phone rang. "Wow, I haven't heard that for a while." He looked at the caller ID. "It's the chief. McGaven," he said answering the phone. He put it on speaker so Katie could hear.

"You and Detective Scott need to get over here," Chief Cooper said. They could barely make out the words.

"Where are you, Chief?" McGaven asked.

"At the hospital." His voice was strained and had a strange breathless quality that made it sound as if he'd been running.

"Isn't it closed down?" said McGaven.

"I know what's been going on and I'm sorry that... If you both could please—"

The line disconnected.

McGaven look at Katie. "We have to go now."

"Wait. What if it's a trap?"

"What do you mean?"

"I just... I've been thinking about everything. We need to be smart about this before we go charging in there."

"Katie, we need to go."

"What about Officer Clark?"

"The chief asked specifically for us."

"Call Officer Clark and Banning to give them a heads-up."

"Fine." McGaven tried both officers and the calls went straight to voicemail. "We need to go now." The tone of his voice was urgent.

The detectives rushed out of the kitchen and grabbed their coats, gear, and weapons.

"Where are you two going?" said John.

"The chief just called and said we need to come to the hospital ASAP," said McGaven. "And then the connection went dead."

"You're going to need backup," said John gathering his coat and taking his weapon. Since he was a Navy Seal, he could easily handle himself and would be the best possible backup for them. "You two need to take Katie's Jeep in case the roads get dicey. I'll follow in my truck."

"Let's go," said Katie opening the door, letting Cisco out and the cold inside.

TWENTY-NINE

Friday 1800 hours

The temperature had dropped since they had been out at Mountain Trail Pass. The roads were almost deserted as most people were staying inside to wait out the storm, and with no traffic, Katie increased speed as much as she dared. At the moment, the roads were fairly clear, but if the flurries turned into heavier snow, there was going to be a problem.

Katie turned up the heater and glanced in the rearview mirror, where she could see John following in his white truck. What she hadn't seen back at the lodge was Jack's truck. She wondered where he'd gone while they'd been talking. Obviously, being a resident here most of his life, he would know how to keep himself safe. A storm wasn't any problem for him.

Cisco seemed to know they were going to something official. Instead of whining and turning circles in the back seat, he sat concentrating straight ahead at the road.

"Do you really think we're walking right into a trap?" said McGaven.

"It's a possibility," she said gritting her teeth. Her gut also said so. "We need to be aware."

"Okay. But the chief seems on the up-and-up to me. Once you take away this weird town and the tight-lipped residents... I think he's okay."

Katie didn't think about it like that, but her partner had a point. "The other side to that equation is... what has he really given us? Haven't you noticed that it's just enough information and reports to give the appearance of transparency?"

McGaven remained quiet; he seemed to be lost in thought.

"We need a plan," she said. She called John from the vehicle's Bluetooth.

"What's up?" said John.

"How do you want to handle this?" she said.

"I was thinking that you two enter from the front and I'll go around to the ambulance entry—and then we'll meet up."

Katie thought that seemed a good idea. She looked to her partner.

McGaven nodded.

"What about Cisco?" said John.

"He'll be fine in the car with the K9 heating system. I have the remote for the door popper... just in case."

"Copy that," said John.

The silence was almost deafening between the detectives. Katie didn't know exactly what McGaven was thinking, but she knew what most cops would be. Stay alive, stay vigilant, assess the situation, have your partner's back, and get to the chief safely.

Katie saw the entrance to the hospital. It looked so different from the other night. Since they had closed this smaller medical center due to the ongoing investigation, it was now dark, strangely shadowy, and out of place. No activity. Normally there would be lighting on the building leading to the emergency entrance, but now it almost resembled an abandoned building.

Katie pulled into the parking lot. She opted not to park up front, but pulled to one side out of the way in a darkened area where the Jeep would still be easily accessible and Cisco would be able to deploy from the car with ease—if the situation came down to that.

"There," said McGaven. "The chief's police vehicle."

Katie studied it in the darkness. "No officers?" She took a minute to set up motion video on the dash cameras facing the side and front entrances. She wasn't taking any chances. She quickly checked her cell phone and the cameras were working.

McGaven looked at his partner. "You ready?"

"Affirmative."

"Keep your eyes and head on swivel."

"I've got your back," she said. "It looks like John had other ideas about where he was parking. I don't see him," she said.

"That's who he is... you won't see him coming." McGaven gave a sly smile.

Katie always felt a twinge of uncertainty leaving Cisco alone in the car, but it was better than leaving him at the lodge. Too many people had access to that. The town was proving to be deeply disturbing. It was as if the detectives were in some kind of maze, never knowing what was going to happen next.

Katie dismissed her thoughts and put in her tech earplug and attached the microphone to her collar. McGaven did the same. Using their cell phones as walkie-talkies was a risk—they could lose the signal or it could be jammed by an outside source —but it was the best they had.

As Katie checked her firearm, made sure she had another magazine, and attached a flashlight on her gun belt, McGaven did the same. This time Katie also carried another smaller gun in her ankle holster. It may have been overkill, but they were walking into something virtually unknown.

They were both quiet as they prepped themselves. Even Cisco was quiet. It was as if they all knew something was about to go down.

"You know we don't have to do this," she said. "It's just us and John... no backup if it goes sideways. We could call and wait for the county sheriff's department to arrive first."

"It's our duty as police officers, on or off duty, to act if someone needs help no matter what—especially when it's one of us."

Katie nodded. There was no way she was going to leave the chief in distress, or anyone else for that matter. "Copy that."

The detectives got out of the car and shut the doors, barely making a sound.

They headed to the front entrance where there were double glass doors. Normally a red neon "open" sign would be brightening the door area, but there was nothing tonight. It was as if they had cut the electricity completely.

Katie gently pushed the door and, to her surprise, it opened. That made her pause. There was no reasonable explanation for that unless it had been Chief Cooper who had unlocked and entered through that door.

Katie turned to her partner.

He nodded.

She pulled her weapon and entered first. Her boots made a soft whisper on the smooth floor. She replayed when they had come through here to visit the chief. There was a reception area straight ahead and turning right led you down a long hallway with doors on both sides.

Katie decided not to talk if she could help it, so she made a gesture with her hand that she was going down the hallway.

McGaven nodded and kept pace six feet behind his partner.

Katie stopped and listened. Her heart was racing. Her right hand slightly shook, holding her Glock. No, she thought, anticipating her anxiety and military flashbacks returning.

She stared ahead, expecting to see some light and not just the reflection from hospital equipment, carts, and outlines of the nurses' stations. It was quiet too without any sound of the indoor air system or equipment. If Katie didn't know better, she would have thought she had gone deaf. With very little light coming in from outside, it was difficult to tell if you were indoors or out. The air was stuffy and surprisingly warm.

Katie didn't turn to look at McGaven, but she knew he was close. Moving forward, her instinct seemed to tell her to go straight to the hospital room the chief had been recovering in. Pulling the flashlight from her belt, Katie switched it on and kept the beam low. It was enough to illuminate the area and give surrounding items shape. The area was just the same, except the bed had been changed and remade with perfect corners. There was no indication of anyone having been there recently.

"What do you think?" whispered McGaven.

"I'm not sure."

"We don't know if the chief is here."

"What if he's hurt or had another heart incident?"

They left the room and began to systematically try each door off the corridor, including storage closets, offices, and patient rooms. There was nothing.

Katie could feel her frustration rising. She turned to McGaven. "We don't know for sure if the chief was calling from here, even though his police vehicle is here," she said. Cold shivers and prickly bumps attacked her spine, but her face felt flushed and hot.

"Wait," he said. Using his cell phone, he was able to partially pinpoint where the chief's call originated from. It wasn't exact, but gave a fairly accurate reading. He looked up. "The chief was actually calling from the area near the cabin."

"What? The cabin I rented?" she said. "Why?"

McGaven looked concerned and his face appeared to turn white.

"Gav?"

He didn't say anything or acknowledge her.

There was a light tapping sound up ahead and it started to echo around them.

"Is that John?" said Katie.

McGaven sent John a text message.

The detectives were relieved to hear a chime back meaning that John was still in the hospital.

Katie leaned close to McGaven and said, "Let's finish the search to see if anything has changed. I don't want to run around like we're on a scavenger hunt."

McGaven nodded.

Katie decided to search on the left, leaving McGaven to examine the right. She crept along looking to see if anything appeared out of place. There were some indications of the cleanup from the other night. Moving more into the interior, wheelchairs, carts, and rolling equipment for IV bags and a kidney machine were out of place and skewed. There were canisters of all sizes and heights in one spot. The detectives had a difficult time not running into various things in their way.

Everything was telling Katie they needed to get out, but her cop instincts told her they also needed to find out what was going on. Even though things looked messy, there didn't seem to have been an altercation or anything out of the ordinary since the murders.

So why was the front door unlocked, showing no signs of a break-in?

Where was the chief?

Why did the chief have them come to the hospital?

These questions and more swirled through her mind, but she moved forward quickly to where the emergency entrance was located, waiting to run into John.

The darkness ahead felt endless. Finally they were close enough to see outlines. John appeared like a ghost emerging from the darkness, a warrior apparition by the way he walked.

There was the sound of something hitting metal again, but it seemed louder.

Katie stopped. She thought she smelled something out of place. Maybe some type of cleaning fluid. Maybe the crew had cleaned or sanitized an area? Or maybe—

Several gunshots fired at the group, pinging off the equipment and taking out sections of the walls.

Katie and McGaven immediately hit the floor, while John dove over a nurses' station, disappearing over the other side.

Katie immediately wondered if someone had come into the medical facility looking for drugs. But as she took cover behind one of carts, she realized she was completely wrong. There had been no warnings. No sounds or sights that anyone was there besides them.

It was a trap—*for them*.

Katie looked to McGaven, who had hidden himself; most likely trying to assess the situation.

There were no sounds in the facility. No more bullets. No movement.

Katie ran several scenarios in her mind, but nothing seemed to surface that was credible. If the person wanted to kill them, they would have already done so. No one would have witnessed it.

She could feel the cold floor and could still smell some type of disinfectant. There was a hissing sound...

Two more shots fired over their heads, hitting the ceiling tiles and causing pieces to shower down on them. Whoever was shooting wasn't aiming for them.

McGaven and John returned fire.

Katie remained in her position so she could go over everything through her mind. Contemplating. Running situations.

Going through all possible setups and ambushes. Why the hospital setting?

The hissing continued, as did the pungent smell.

She kept running through ideas and factors...

Cleaning materials...

Hospital chemicals...

Nitrous oxide...

Anesthetic gases...

Oxygen...

Ethyl alcohol...

And...

Gunfire rounds...

"We need to get out now!" she yelled. "Now!" Her heart skipped several beats. Katie began to crawl back to where they had come from. She turned and could see McGaven and John following her lead. "Now!"

One... Two... Gunshots...

Katie stood up and began to run. She heard footsteps behind her right before the last gunshot rang out at the same time as the explosion.

THIRTY

Friday 2130 hours

Katie wasn't sure what was worse: the deafening noise, blinding bright light, or the feeling that her insides had been moved around in her body. She had been thrown to the floor and she could feel the icy air mixing with the heat from the fire. It was a strange combination, feeling more like a nightmare than real life.

Smoke filled the air but was quickly siphoned out through the broken front windows. Katie's arms and legs seemed cemented to the floor. She began to move her hands and feet as the feeling in them began to return. She couldn't understand why she didn't hear McGaven and John. The only thing she heard was the loud pounding of her heart and the throbbing of her head. Face down, she pushed her body up with her hands and then slowly got her balance with her feet on the ground.

Smoke filtered around the area, and scattered everywhere were broken pieces and shards of what were once useful hospital supplies.

Katie looked down and saw her gun was gone. There was

blood trickling down her arms. Stunned and unable to move right away, she couldn't see well and her eyes stung. She raised her hand and gently touched her face. It was covered in blood. Wiping the blood away from her forehead, her vision began to clear. She could see an outline of McGaven lying on the floor, not moving. There was what was left of a rolling cart lying sideways across his chest. Her heart seemed to stop and she couldn't breathe.

"Gav." She could barely whisper. Her throat hurt and felt so dry she wasn't sure if she could speak again.

"Katie? Gav," said John.

Katie looked up and saw John climbing over shattered pieces of metal and ceramics.

"Katie," he said, moving toward her. "You okay?"

"I... think so..."

John was immediately at her side. "You saved our lives. If you hadn't warned us..."

"But it wasn't in time..." She could barely keep herself together. She pushed past John and dropped to the floor. "Gav... Gav... can you hear me?" She pushed away the cart and examined his body. He had blood on his face and hands. She made sure his neck was okay. "Gav... *please* talk to me..."

Katie was in shock and didn't notice John at her side examining McGaven.

"He's breathing. But we need to get him out of here. It's too volatile," he said glancing around.

Katie took hold of McGaven's hand and squeezed it. There was no response.

"I think he's knocked out, which means..."

Katie couldn't stop the tears... and immediately blaming herself. They should not have rushed here when there was such a strong chance that it wasn't safe...

"Katie, did you hear me?" said John.

She turned to him.

"Katie, pull yourself together. We need to get him out of here. Understand?"

She nodded. "Yes."

"I'm going to see if I can get a gurney I saw at the other entrance. I'll be right back," he said.

Katie grabbed his arm. "Please be careful."

John glanced at her one more time and left through the front entrance. Katie was relieved to see he still had his weapon.

"Hey, partner," said McGaven weakly.

Katie sucked in a breath. "Gav... you're okay."

"It was like getting kicked in the gut in an explosion at the hospital..." He forced a smile and squeezed Katie's hand. Then he slowly sat up and winced. "Nope, can't do that."

Katie kept a watchful eye, making sure they weren't going to be surprised. The small fires at numerous locations were winding down... but there was a fire gaining momentum toward the back of the building.

"Where's John?" McGaven asked.

"He went to get a gurney to move you outside," she said, glancing at the growing fire and the smoke building momentum.

"No, I can get..." McGaven grabbed his chest.

"What?" Katie down and could see blood seeping through his shirt and jacket. Pulling gently at his shirt, she revealed a piece of metal. "Gav," she said, "you have a shard stuck in your chest."

"Get it out."

"No." She stopped him from touching it. "We don't know how deep it is, just leave it alone."

"Then what?"

"A doctor needs to assess it."

"If you haven't noticed, they're all gone." He was trying to get up.

"Stop. Let me help you." Katie saw McGaven's gun and she picked it up and stuck it in her holster. "C'mon."

Katie helped pull McGaven to his feet. She wrapped her right arm around his waist as he leaned on her. They began to move slowly toward the front door. Katie's head pounded like a raw migraine and now she could feel every cut on her body stinging and hurting. Her body felt as if it had gone through a meat grinder.

The sound of screechy wheels neared. There was a creepy vibe until Katie could see John moving toward them.

"What took you?" said McGaven. His voice was weak and he could barely move legs.

John immediately helped Katie get McGaven on the gurney. He looked almost white as a sheet and he dozed intermittently.

"I tried nine-one-one, but there's a recording that all circuits are busy," said John.

"How are we going to get medical attention?"

"I don't know. The snow is really getting heavy outside. There's no way we can drive to the nearest hospital. It's nearly thirty miles away."

"We can't take the chance we'd get stranded on the side of the road," she said. Katie was beside herself. Her partner needed medical attention. He could have internal injuries. She stood at the entrance considering what to do.

"Katie?" said John as he studied her.

"We go back to the lodge. We have a doctor and medical supplies downstairs."

John looked surprised, but then said, "Jack is a doctor. An animal doctor is a doctor."

"Let's go," she said.

They decided to load McGaven into John's truck, where there was more room, causing less discomfort. The snowstorm was indeed building force and soon the roads would be completely impassable. There was no way to contact emergency resources in Echo Forest.

The hospital fire was slowing down, though intense smoke escaped every crevice, blown window, and entrance. Katie hoped it wouldn't spread, but there weren't any buildings or trees near. The snow would help to smother the fire.

Katie jumped in her Jeep with an anxious Cisco waiting. The dog kept trying to lick her wounds and sit next to her. She watched as John pulled his truck out onto the main road with her partner hurt and bleeding in the back seat. The pain she felt at not being able to get him to a hospital would forever gnaw at her soul.

As she pulled out into the snow, for some reason, an obsessive thought kept running through her mind.

Three down... more to go...

THIRTY-ONE

Saturday 0000 hours

Katie was relieved when they finally reached the Echo Forest Lodge and Jack's truck was parked out front. There had been a few risky moments as they drove back from the burning hospital. She hastily parked and leaped out in the snow followed closely by Cisco. Once her boots sunk down in the cold her legs froze. For as long as it took to drive back to the lodge, it must've dropped another ten degrees. Katie reached the truck to help John with McGaven. They made their way to the entrance of the veterinary clinic. Before they got there, Jack opened the door.

"What's happened?"

"We need your help. We were ambushed at the hospital and there was an explosion," she said.

"What?" said Jack in disbelief. He didn't waste any time and hurried them inside. "Please, take him to the main examination room."

Cisco trotted inside.

Katie and John helped McGaven to the room, which was

designed for domestic animals and so had a short examination table. Nevertheless, they were able to wrangle McGaven onto the stainless table and lay him down. His lower legs and feet hung over the end, but the detective didn't seem to mind. Katie found some clean towels and improvised a pillow, gently positioning it under his head.

Jack entered carrying a stainless-steel bowl with emergency supplies of gauze, bandages, various ointments, and other necessities.

"He's got some shattered pieces in his chest," she said. "We didn't know how deep they were, so we left them there."

"You did right." Jack began assessing the wounds on McGaven's head and hands before he got help to remove his jacket and shirt.

Katie felt herself losing it—there was much more to do but McGaven's injuries took precedence. She fought back the tears and stood strong, watching Jack sanitize the wounds and dress them.

The vet put on glasses that were extra magnified, studying the area around McGaven's chest where the pieces were imbedded. He carefully moved one piece back and forth, trying to determine the deepness of the shrapnel, then he stood up.

McGaven grimaced. "That's painful."

"The good news is that it isn't as deep as I first thought."

"That's good." He let out a breath.

"I'm going to have to numb the area with a mild antiseptic, remove the pieces, and... I think you might need a few other stitches."

"Cool," said McGaven.

Katie smiled mostly out of relief, but also because her partner could still crack jokes even when things seemed almost impossible. "Can I do anything?" she said.

Jack looked up at her and smiled. "No, it's routine."

"You mean your local dogs and cats get shrapnel in the chest?" said McGaven.

"No, but they get bites and complications from all kinds of injuries," said the vet. "Detective, I'm sure you're exhausted. Go up to the lodge."

"I think I'm going to wait here," she said.

"I'll wait too," said John.

"There's some coffee in the kitchenette. Help yourself."

Cisco whined.

"And there's all types of dog food for this guy," said Jack.

Katie looked at her partner and he gave her a thumbs up sign.

"You look beat," said John.

Katie poured herself a cup of coffee after she gave Cisco some dog food.

"You just went through the same thing I did."

"You've been investigating these homicides longer than I have."

"We're both tired," she said.

"You should have the doc look at those." He stood close to her and gently ran his fingers near her cut forehead. "I'll be right back."

Katie forced herself out of enjoying the physical attention from John, and went and sat down on one of the sofas near the reception area. She let out a long cleansing sigh. It felt good to sit down on a comfortable cushion. It wouldn't take much for her to fall asleep, but she wasn't going upstairs until McGaven was definitely all right. She would wait.

"Okay," said John as he sat down next to her. He gave her a blanket and held some antiseptic, gauze, and small bandages. Without asking, he helped to clean her cuts and bandaged them.

Cisco stayed close to Katie, trying to get in between them.

Katie fought her urge to sleep as she pet the dog. She wanted to keep working the cases because there was no room to slack or sleep. The only thing that was potentially keeping the killer at bay was the storm. He wouldn't be able to stage a scene in a snowstorm.

"Hey," said a groggy McGaven. Jack steadied him as they walked down the hallway.

Katie stood up. "Gav, how are you feeling?"

"Like I've been put through a wood chipper, but other than that I'm great."

"I gave him a mild sedative so he can rest. His bandages will need to be changed every few hours," said the vet. "I was able to get through to fire and rescue and let them know about the hospital. And I also said that Chief Cooper was missing."

Katie was relieved the hospital was going to be monitored and the fire put out. Something still struck her about Jack, but she had to ignore it for now. "Thank you," she said.

"Oh, and they are forecasting the storm to last another day as well."

Katie felt defeated, not to mention sore and tired. How were they going to find out what happened to the chief and whether he was somehow involved in the ambush?

"We're going upstairs," said Katie.

"I should take a look at you two as well," said Jack.

"We'll be fine."

"If you need anything don't hesitate to let me know," he said.

Katie and John assisted McGaven as they left the vet's office. The storm had built more momentum and the freezing temperature slammed into them as they climbed the stairs. Cisco easily navigated the icy steps and waited at the top for the others.

Katie wondered why Jack hadn't offered for them to climb

the inside secret staircase to the kitchen. It only added to her list of questions about the veterinarian, but she had to remind herself it was just a feeling and that wasn't proof of anything.

They got to the top landing, all breathing hard. Katie opened the front door to the lodge and they made their way inside. With sighs of relief, McGaven and John sat down on the couch. Katie grabbed a beanie and a warm scarf and gloves. She also took a large flashlight.

"Where are you going?" said John. He eyed her suspiciously.

"Taking Cisco out," she said flatly. "We'll be right back." She went out the front door with Cisco, not waiting for any more questions. She carefully walked back down the stairs. The dog went about his business but still seemed as if he kept an eye on Katie the whole time.

The snowfall had stopped momentarily and the air was clear but exceptionally cold. Snow had drifted into the corners of the patio and clustered into the branches of the trees. There was something quite magical about it—the scent, the view, and the feeling difficult to fully describe.

Katie stood in the quiet night alone, gathering her thoughts. She had never been in such a position before. Was the chief missing? Or was he at home waiting the storm out just as the others? What was with his cryptic phone call? Katie knew he was in trouble one way or the other.

The sketchy and unreliable cell signal and the storm for the next forty-eight hours made for an impossible situation. There wasn't anyone they could turn to for advice. It was just the three of them—four if you included Jack. She needed reinforcements. These homicides were the tip of the iceberg; something was going to break.

Cisco returned to Katie, pushing his nose against her hand and then looking up at her with that curious gorgeous face.

"I know," she said softly. "What are we going to do?"

A noise in the forest broke the silence. It was coming from the hiking trails. Or was it? Sounds were unpredictable and unnatural in Echo Forest, which made the exact identification of where they were actually coming from difficult. Katie knew she had heard the sound and so did Cisco. The dog froze, staring at the location the noise seemed to have come from. He resembled a statue, unmoving until there was a low growl and the fur along his backbone rippled.

"Cisco, *bleib*," Katie said, making him stay in position. She retrieved her holstered gun and directed the flashlight accordingly.

As she walked toward the trail entrance, there was a flurry of sounds much too big for forest creatures. Most wild animals would stay hidden, out of sight, during the storm.

At the trail, Katie panned the flashlight beam. There were no more sounds. She thought for a moment she saw the outline of a person in the deep shadows, but then it was gone. It was unclear if her eyes were playing tricks on her or if it was wishful thinking—she wanted to get the killer off the streets.

Katie and Cisco returned to the lodge and shut out the storm. She began peeling the layers from her body and could instantly feel the warmth from the fireplace.

"Thought I was going to have to send out a search party. Did you find anything interesting?" said John with some sarcasm in his tone. His stare read anything but lighthearted as he looked up from the computer he was seated in front of.

"No. Everything is fine. Cisco just had a lot of smelling to do."

"I see."

"Where's McGaven?"

"He went to crash out for a while."

"Oh, good. He's been through a lot."

"We all have. You should get some rest."

"I think I'm going to stay up for a while. I'll check on Gav first."

Katie walked to the suite her partner was staying in. She quietly opened the door where she was greeted by his soft snoring. The room was cool. He was lying on top of the comforter, so Katie found two warm blankets from the closet and covered him. She took one last look at her partner before shutting the door behind her.

John appeared to have been waiting for her in the living room.

"What's up?" she said. She couldn't meet his gaze.

"I may be the forensic supervisor, but I know a few things about people and investigations."

"Of course. Your point?" she said, feeling found out. It took every ounce of strength to not show her emotions, but after the past few days it was becoming more and more difficult.

"Katie, how many cases have I seen you work? I know your motivation here."

"And?" Katie knew John could almost read her mind when it pertained to investigations—it was unnerving at times. And she knew now that he knew, or at least suspected, that she was planning to get the answers she needed to solve this case no matter what.

"C'mon, Katie. You're driven, but know you're up against the weather, an injured partner, and a missing police force... not to mention what just happened at the hospital."

As she watched John make his point, reciting the investigation checklist, which she already knew, he seemed to be more than annoyed. Katie had never seen him like this.

"You're right."

John kept serious eye contact on her.

"I do have an idea that might help the case," she said.

"When were you going to let us in on it?"

"Actually, I wasn't," she said.

"You haven't learned anything," he said. "You're not a one-woman army. This isn't how police investigations work."

"I... it's because—"

"No, you can't just go out on your own without telling anyone. We have your back."

"I know," she said sitting down.

"Look, you know I'm your friend and I have your back no matter what—just as you do Gav's."

Katie had never had anyone from the department be so blunt with her, even McGaven trod lightly. "You're right. You're completely right."

"We all care about you and what you've been through. We don't want to see anything happen to you," he said, sitting next to her.

"I do have a plan and I'll understand if you don't want to come with me," she said.

"Go on."

"As with anything, you need to start at the beginning. And... well... I want to go to the police station," she said.

"You don't think anyone will be there, do you?"

"I'm counting on it."

Katie took Cisco and put him in McGaven's suite. Immediately the dog took a comfortable spot in an overstuffed reading chair. She then left a note for Gav to say where she and John were going and when they left.

She watched McGaven comfortably sleep and wished she could take back everything about the hospital explosion. Shutting the door quietly, she planned her next move with John.

THIRTY-TWO

Saturday 0300 hours

Katie and John decided to take the Jeep. It was more reliable with four-wheel drive, and it was a smaller, narrower vehicle that could maneuver in tight places if necessary.

"You sure you know where the police station is?" said John.

"Yes. Gav and I drove by it a few times. And, by the way, it's not a police station like you think... it's more like a small place of business." Katie wasn't entirely sure that what they were doing was the right thing to do, but since the police force was missing something had to be done. She slowed her speed and skillfully maneuvered around large snowdrifts. "It's down that alley."

She then drove by.

"I thought you said we were going there?"

"On second thought, it would be easier and not to mention more legal if we had the keys."

John smiled and nodded, knowing what she had in mind.

The roads were definitely more difficult to drive. There were times Katie had to veer off the main road and take short-cuts along sidewalk and parking areas, which had less snow. As she drove closer to the hospital, they saw a couple of emergency fire vehicles.

"Where is it?" she said.

The chief's vehicle was gone.

"Wasn't it parked out front?"

"Yes. Definitely." Katie found a place where she could safely turn around and headed back to the station.

"That's not good," said John. "Do you think the chief is behind this?"

"I don't know. But we have to get to the bottom of it while the storm works in our favor."

John remained quiet as he watched the road. The falling snow increased, making it difficult to see even with the windshield wipers.

"Our window is about thirty minutes until it gets too difficult to drive back to the lodge," he said.

Katie agreed.

They returned to the police station and made their way down the back alley. There was no use trying to hide the Jeep. The alley was narrow, mostly used as a walkway, so the car doors wouldn't open all the way.

The cold attacked her body and her face was close to being almost completely numb. She ran her gloved hands over her cheeks, trying to warm her skin. She fought the urge to let her teeth chatter and pushed through the discomfort.

They approached the front door from the main street. She did the normal thing and knocked. When there was no answer she knocked again, trying the door, but it was locked. There was still no answer. There was a small window next to the door and it was obvious the lights were out inside. She stood on her tiptoes, but she didn't see much except for a couple of desks.

"What do you want to do now?" said John.

Katie looked directly at him and said, "We're going to have to find another way inside."

"You mean break in."

"You have a better idea?" she said, but knowing the answer.

"Finding the key?"

"I would say these are exigent circumstances, wouldn't you?" she said.

John slowly smiled. "I would say so."

"Okay then." Katie viewed the window. "Do you think we can break this?"

John went back to the Jeep, opened the back hatch, and found a crowbar. He returned to Katie. "I'm not going to ask why you have this in the back. Most people have this with their spare."

"It pays to be prepared."

Katie stepped back and let John smash the window and then he used his sleeve to clear off the broken glass at the bottom. The window was smaller than the average and it was clear Katie would have to be the one to climb through. They waited a moment, expecting to hear an alarm, but since the patrolling cops were missing, probably no one would investigate even if there was one. But it remained quiet. The only sound was the moderate wind accompanied by the light snowflakes carried along by the breeze.

"A little help," she said, wiping away the cold particles on her face.

John gave Katie a leg-up to the window, where she was able to balance herself and push her petite body into the small building. She hit the floor harder than she had anticipated and scrambled to her feet. She made her way almost blindly to the entrance, unlocking the door.

John quickly slipped inside. "You okay?"

"Yeah, fine."

John wiped the snow from his jacket sleeves and stomped his boots.

"I can't find the light switches. They don't seem to be in the usual places," she said.

Katie moved to one of the desks where there was a lamp. She fumbled a bit, but managed to switch the light on. The low light bulb shined a yellowish glow around the room. She thought it was better to keep the lights to a minimum in case someone did see them, even though it was highly unlikely.

"What are you looking for?" said John.

"Notes, reports, something about the homicides."

The office was small, just one room. Three desks, four filing cabinets, two large floor-to-ceiling bookshelves. Surprisingly, things were organized, but definitely squeezed due to the small space. The first desk had some personal items, a framed photograph of a couple and their large husky dog. It was clear it was the assistant who answered the phone. Katie remembered talking to a Libby and assumed it was her desk.

Katie could hear John looking through filing cabinets with his flashlight. The beam moved from drawer to drawer.

The second desk was almost clear, but there were blank incident forms, a notepad, a couple of phone messages, and a cup with various pens and pencils. Katie supposed that Officers Clark and Banning shared the desk. Interesting. She opened the drawers and there wasn't anything suspicious or out of place. The last desk was larger and had many drawers and small cubbyholes. Upon closer inspection, even in the insufficient lighting, it seemed to be an antique mahogany desk. Perhaps one that had been here for decades or something the chief owned that was sentimental.

"Anything?" said John. His voice sounded stressed.

"Not yet."

"There's definitely not a lot of serious crime here. These murders must've overtaxed the cops and the chief. Maybe they ran."

Katie stopped and turned to John. "You mean abandoned their posts?"

"I don't know, something like that. It'd be a perfect time during this storm."

The thought had never occurred to Katie.

"Some of these cases... a Mrs. Arnold filed against a neighbor for stealing her chickens... a man exposing himself to children... someone skipping out and not paying for their breakfast... it's all stuff like that."

"What would make the entire police force, granted it's small, disappear?" she said.

"It could be anything."

Katie shook her head. "It's one of two things: They skipped just like you said or they're involved somehow in these cases. I'm not saying all of them, but I'm betting at least one of them."

"Here's something curious," John said, pulling a file out of the bottom cabinet drawer.

Katie joined him.

"It's dated a little over fifteen years ago... Carol Ann Benedict."

"That's the name on the memorial bench on the hiking trail."

"You sure?"

"Yes, I'm definitely sure." Katie's curiosity heightened.

"It says she was found murdered, strangled, on a remote trail," he said. "Looks like after an exhaustive investigation, where there were no suspects or forensics of use, the case stopped and is officially a cold case until new evidence comes to light." John studied the report. "Look at this."

Katie read the page John was referring to. She didn't see anything to grab her attention until she saw the victim was referred to as Carol Ann Benedict-Cooper. "Cooper?"

"Think it's a coincidence? Do you think she was married to the chief—well before he was appointed to his position?"

Katie looked at the chief's desk to find a date. "It looks like he was sworn in six months after Carol's death."

"That would make sense. He became chief to solve his wife's murder. In a small town it wouldn't be difficult to get put in that position," John said.

"How sad that this case hasn't been solved. And there haven't been any homicides in Echo Forest since."

"Until now." John studied Katie's face. "What are you thinking?"

"It's hard not to think that maybe all these cases, including the one from fifteen years ago, could be connected somehow." Her mind was on overload. The crime scenes, the hospital, and now this made her more convinced that they all had something in common. And right now, the common denominator was Chief Cooper.

"The chief seems to be a part of all these cases," John said, as if reading her mind.

"And he called us to the hospital before we were attacked, and now he's gone missing."

"He could be a victim too in all this."

"It's possible, but we need more. Grab everything pertaining to the recent cases and the old homicide. As well as who was the mayor and part of the town council fifteen years ago. It will be easier to comb through the reports back at the lodge."

They systematically began pulling files that would be helpful.

"Get your hands up!"

Both Katie and John immediately reacted, pulling their guns.

THIRTY-THREE

Saturday 0435hours

Katie kept her aim on the intruder. A person stood in the doorway in a shooter's stance wearing a puffy coat with the hood pulled up. The dim lighting made it difficult to see the person's face, though it was definitely a woman by the sound of her voice. Several questions crossed Katie's mind. Who would be out in this kind of weather? And why would they care about someone at the police station?

"I would suggest lowering your weapon," said Katie. "Now!"

"You're not supposed to be in here," the woman insisted.

"Put your weapon down!" said Katie.

"Who are you?" the woman said, her voice not sounding as intense as before.

"Detective Katie Scott and you're not authorized to be here," said Katie.

"I am."

"What do you mean?"

"I... I'm Libby Castel, Chief Cooper's administrative assistant."

Katie blinked. She glanced at the photo on the admin's desk then slowly lowered her weapon. "What are you doing here?"

John followed suit and lowered his weapon too. He looked to Katie with a question in his eyes.

Libby lowered her gun. "I'm sorry. I've been trying to contact the chief but haven't been able to find him or Officers Clark or Banning. Have you seen them?"

Everyone put away the guns as the atmosphere lightened.

Libby sat down at her desk and looked as if she might faint. "I don't feel well."

"Take some slow breaths and try to relax," said Katie.

"Okay..." Libby took several breaths.

"We came here because we haven't heard from anyone since the homicides at the hospital," Katie said.

"That was so horrible."

Katie was careful with how much information she shared. They didn't really know Libby or what her motives were.

"Tell us, why are you here?" said Katie.

"I couldn't sleep. I've been so worried. They've never just vanished. They always left a message or have been in contact before, so I came into the office," said Libby.

"What were you trying to find?"

"A note. A clue that one of them had been here. I don't know—something."

Katie could understand her concerns, but she still didn't trust her. If there was one thing about the town she had learned it was to not trust easily. "Can you fill us in on some things?"

"Uh... sure."

"Was there more information to the first two homicides that the chief was either investigating or holding on to?"

Libby looked confused. "What do you mean? Aren't you investigating the cases?"

"Yes. But we don't have the forensic lab and the medical examiner's reports..." Katie watched her closely.

Libby fidgeted in her seat and played unconsciously with her long brown hair. It was clear she knew more than she was telling.

Katie glanced at John, who remained quiet and let Katie keep taking the lead on the questions.

"Who is Carol Ann Benedict?"

Libby's face looked confused and surprised. "I don't know..."

"Yes, you do, Libby."

"No."

"I thought we were on the same page here. You do want to find the chief and the officers, right?"

"Of course."

"Who is Carol Ann Benedict?" Katie kept her hard stare on the woman.

The storm outside made more noise against the broken window and partially open door as the wind howled.

"She was well known to the community..."

"Go on."

"She was... the chief's..."

"What?"

Libby seemed to be fighting her conscience, unsure what to do.

"Libby, she was chief's wife, wasn't she?"

Libby nodded.

"There's very little information in the news articles and on the internet. What happened?"

"I can only tell you what I know."

"Go on," Katie encouraged.

"There had been a big argument between Beryl and Carol. This was before he was the chief." She paused. "One morning about fifteen years ago a hiker found her body and an investigation was carried out. But there were no witnesses. No leads. There was next to nothing in forensics. There was nothing anyone could do. The murderer was never found. Beryl managed to get the town, including the mayor and town counsel, to appoint him sheriff a few months later."

"So he could continue the investigation officially into Carol's death?"

Libby nodded.

"When did you start working for him?"

"About eight years ago."

"Do you know anything more about Carol's death?"

"No, I swear. Just that she was the chief's wife and the case became cold." Libby began to cry.

Katie was frustrated. They had already figured all that out about Carol. There had to be more. Something that would blow the case wide open, that had to do with the murders. Katie knew this was a big piece of the puzzle but didn't know how it fit.

"Is there anything we need to know about the recent homicides? Something the chief would want kept quiet?"

"No, nothing. This is all I know."

Katie retrieved her business card and handed it to Libby. "You call me if you hear anything about the chief and his officers. I mean anything. Understand?"

Libby nodded.

"Go home and wait the storm out."

Libby got up, looked at Katie and John before leaving out the door.

Katie gathered the information she thought they would need.

"You let her go too easily."

Katie smiled. "No. I squeezed her for information she really didn't want to give up. We'll let her go and see what she does.

Once the storm loses some strength she'll be the first person to keep under surveillance."

John nodded. "Good idea."

"She's not the only one I want to watch."

"Who else?"

"Bill Westin, the carpet installer."

THIRTY-FOUR

Saturday 0815 hours

Laughter erupted from the other room, along with loud voices. Katie looked at her cell phone. It was only a little after 8 a.m. Her room was dark and she couldn't see any morning light shining through her window. She'd had only three hours of sleep.

More laughter came from the living room. Katie put her pillow over her head and groaned. She wanted to push her exhaustion and Echo Forest out of her mind—even for another hour.

What was so funny?

Now she was awake, there was no way she could go back to sleep with the investigation whirring in her mind. There was work to be done and she wondered if Chief Cooper had been located or heard from.

Katie got out of bed with some mild protest, showered and dressed in clean clothes. Taking a quick look out the window, she could see it was overcast, dreary, and there was deep snow. Even though it had stopped falling, what there was on the ground would be an inconvenience. She sat on the bench at the end of the bed and put on her boots. She was ready for what the day had in store for her.

She opened her bedroom door and could hear the men's voices even louder. She paused a moment and listened, curious. They weren't discussing the investigation, from what she could ascertain; they were sharing experiences and funny stories.

Katie walked into the room.

"Hey, partner," said McGaven. He looked rested and you wouldn't have been able to tell he had been in an explosion and been struck with shrapnel yesterday.

"Good morning," she said. "You look like you're feeling much better."

"Jack here gave me some great pills," he said and they all laughed.

"There's some eggs and bacon in the kitchen in the warmer," said Jack. "And coffee."

Cisco bounced around in the middle of the group, wanting to be part of the fun.

"Thank you," she said and headed to the kitchen.

Katie poured herself a cup and immediately took two sips, letting the heat warm her body. She thought she would have more energy this morning, but she was still beat. Her dreams had been vivid and disturbing, which didn't help. And now, she was concerned, worried, and not feeling on top of her game. She wasn't so sure about having Jack around the investigation. It wasn't because she was pointing fingers at him; she didn't trust anyone who wasn't McGaven or John. She couldn't take the chance that someone might disclose their work and case information—it was possible one of the people they had met in Echo Forest was the killer.

"How did you sleep?" said Jack as he joined her in the kitchen.

"A little restless," she said.

"Get some food and... a few more cups of coffee." He smiled.

"It all smells great."

"There are some bagels and fruit as well."

"Thank you."

Jack looked at her hand. "You need to make sure your bandages are changed periodically too."

Katie grabbed a plate from the cupboard. "I will."

Jack left the kitchen as Katie made a plate for herself. She didn't want to seem rude—after all, Jack was allowing them to stay at the lodge and he had been nothing but nice and helpful.

She noticed Cisco's bowl at the end of the counter where he had been fed his dry and wet food. She smiled, knowing McGaven had fed and cared for him. If anything ever happened to her, she knew her partner would take care of Cisco.

Katie, McGaven, and John sat around the large dining table, each with files and paperwork. Katie was relieved Jack had gone back to his veterinary office. Katie and John updated McGaven about what they had found out last night.

"I tried to call the chief and officers again but there was no answer, so I sent each one of them a text message," said McGaven. "But still nothing."

"We're at a point now that we need to decide what to do. Do we call in county or even the state law enforcement agency? I'm sure the roads aren't passable yet, they probably won't be for a while," said Katie.

She watched their reactions. It was difficult to read John, but she could tell McGaven was leaning toward calling in backup, even though they might not be able to reach them for a while.

"I think we at least need to call Sheriff Scott and bring him up to speed," said McGaven. "I know you've been hesitating for personal reasons, but I think it's time."

John nodded. "I agree. He has no idea what's been going on here."

Katie knew they were right. In the back of her mind she was deeply concerned about another victim being targeted. If the killer had been prepared to blow up the hospital and injure or kill them, they wouldn't stop at anything if they had further murderous plans.

"Let's get him on conference," she said, knowing a regular phone call wasn't good enough.

McGaven set up a laptop so that he and Katie could squeeze together to see the video.

Cisco made his way to Katie and decided to rest at her feet.

McGaven sent the sheriff a link and message. He pulled up the conference screen waiting for the sheriff to answer the call. As the crew waited, they gathered the files they'd borrowed from the station and began systematically going through them to see what they could glean.

The laptop chimed and everyone was ready. Sheriff Scott's authoritative demeanor filled the screen. He was dressed in his police uniform, his five identifying stars gleaming, distinguished with his cropped grayish hair. It was difficult to read his expression. Katie couldn't tell if he was annoyed or relieved to be talking with them.

"Good morning," she said.

Still keeping his stern expression, the sheriff nodded. "It's been interesting reading your first few reports, but I haven't heard anything else from you. However, I'm aware of the storm that has hit Echo Forest."

"Yes, sir, we're basically snowed in here. The roads are closed," said McGaven.

"I see," he said. "Then why don't you tell me about the

hospital explosion?" His expression changed slightly to a more worried appearance.

"How did you hear about that?" said Katie, treading carefully. Even though the sheriff was her uncle and only family, there were many emotions vying for her attention. She kept calm and focused.

The screen blurred in and out a couple of times.

"When I didn't hear from you and the cell phone connection was interrupted, I made some calls to emergency services in that area. I also heard about the third homicide victim and the deaths of two hospital workers."

Katie could feel his intensity even through the computer screen. "We've been bombarded with a serious situation, multiple homicides, and no backup."

"What do you propose?" he said.

"We haven't seen or heard from the police chief or his two officers for more than twenty-four hours," said McGaven.

Katie glanced at her partner. When he said those words aloud, it sounded bad—really bad.

"What have you uncovered?" said the sheriff, taking a breath as if to calm his growing irritation.

Katie was worried he was going to pull them and order the state police and investigators to take over. She couldn't blame him, but they'd started this and she wanted to finish it.

"We have a couple of new leads as well as some suspicions that we wanted to pursue, sir," said McGaven.

"Which are?"

"Which are... a forensic lead we need to run down. A piece of carpet fiber that was found at the crime scene. And there's a trail. And there is a connection to a cold case here from fifteen years ago," she said, flinching slightly because she'd made it all sound too trivial.

"And you think this will solidify your case?"

"Yes, sir. There are town secrets and it's been difficult to get people to open up, but we are slowly breaking down barriers."

Sheriff Scott took a moment, never averting his gaze from his detectives. "I'll give you forty-eight hours to produce a suspect or an arrest. Not a minute longer. I will have the backup agencies on standby," he said. "I hope I won't regret this because by all accounts I should be pulling you out and letting state authorities take over right now. I need to hear from you any way you see fit—text, email, phone call—every six to eight hours. No exceptions. If I don't hear from you, I'll be calling in reinforcements immediately."

The signal on the conference blurred again as if on cue for the magnitude of the situation.

Katie was relieved they had more time, but she also knew it was a big risk. "Thank you, sir," she said.

"Be careful," he said and then looked at Katie directly. "Take care of each other."

The call disconnected.

Katie sat there staring at a blank screen. She'd noted the tone of his voice when he told them to take care of one another.

"You heard the boss, forty-eight hours," said McGaven.

"And not a minute more," she said.

"Wow, that was intense," said John.

"He's tough, I know, but he cares about all his officers and detectives," she said. "How do you want to do this? We need to find out about Bill Westin and a few others."

"I'm getting closer to finding out the make and model of the tire impressions. It's a bit more complicated when I don't have my lab to work in," said John.

"I'll look up background and addresses for both work and home on some of these persons of interest," said McGaven.

Katie glanced at the time. It was prudent to research before they left. It would allow the snow to melt and perhaps recede from roadways. Turning to McGaven, she said, "Are you okay to go out and conduct surveillance? Maybe even investigate?"

"I'm fine. My chest still hurts once in a while, but really, I'm fine," he said.

"When you're done with the searches, I want you to change bandages."

"Look who's talking?" he said.

Katie let out a loud breath. "I will change mine too."

While McGaven and John searched and examined their assignments, Katie decided to take the time to concentrate on the killer who had set out to murder Theresa, TJ, and Natalie. It looked as though the other nurse and security guard had unfortunately been collateral damage, helping to set the stage and leaving no witnesses.

Katie uncovered the murder board and stood for a moment studying it. They didn't have all the information they should, so she had to work with what they had. Katie turned and watched McGaven and John for a moment. Through all the unusual, strange, and terrifying moments in Echo Forest, she wouldn't want any other team with her. Under difficult situations, sometimes we forget to be thankful and mindful for what we have.

Looking at each crime scene and victim, Katie could see a transformation in the killer. It was clear from the behavioral evidence that they were evolving. The how and why the killer conducted himself was like a behavioral fingerprint. How they chose to murder. The level of force used—low level to overkill. How they set the scene. Why they did what they did. If you looked close enough and scrutinized every clue and surrounding area, a story began to develop.

Katie made notes for herself. Theresa's murder appeared to be carefully planned and her body left in a shocking display. The totem was unusual, but telling as well. It was made up with items from the victim, but it didn't seem cohesive. There was possibly some deception in the staging. Her face being covered either meant the killer knew her or they didn't want to look at their victim. It showed some remorse and that the killer knew the depth of the act they had committed.

TJ's murder seemed to try to replicate Theresa's, but it didn't quite make it. The clothes in the garbage can indicated that the killer had hurried and didn't plan as thoroughly as the first murder. This could mark a clue about his behavior with the psychological process of pausing, deciding, or taking an action. Was the killer lingering to make sure everything was in place at the crime scenes?

Natalie's crime scene was the most forced. Strangled, no totem, and the sinister words on the wall—it was completely different. She had cuts on her arm and chest. And what was the meaning behind the hospital? Was it important to him? Or was it a way to try to cover up the horror and deaths?

Katie pondered each crime scene and how the behavioral evidence seemed to waver and become forced. It was an unusual combination of homicides.

Crime Scene #1 Theresa Jamison

The first crime scene in Echo Forest seemed to have the most organization. It was thought out down to the details. The body was clean and had a little clothing, indicating that there was some modesty involved. The killer didn't want the body to be naked. Her face being covered usually meant that they knew the victim or they didn't want the victim to watch them. Strangulation is a means of death that's up close and personal, usually indicating the killer knew them in some way—from as a casual acquaintance to someone they had a close relationship with. Hanging the victim is often thought to represent sacrifice. The totem left was the most telling and the most difficult because all the items meant something just to the killer and what they were trying to convey. It wasn't random, it was very specific.

Spiritual significance.

Symbolic.

Warning.

Pine cones have been known to represent fertility, resurrection, and even enlightenment.

Sticks were sourced from the vast and dense forest.

Wild berries were often seen as sustenance or life.

A rock was something heavy or final. Did that pertain to the Woodsman? Was that the final end?

Crime Scene #2 Tamara Jane Lambert, "TJ"

Although this crime scene was organized and planned, it seemed to be less terrifying when you first saw it. It had all the same elements as Theresa's, but it seemed more hurried and forced. Not something that had been planned down to the last detail. The clothes in the trash appeared as an afterthought, as did the cloth over the head. The area in the field was manipulated to compete with the first scene. The killer was trying to recreate the same thing.

Crime Scene #3 Natalie Renaldo

This crime scene was completely different. Inside a hospital women's restroom with a message on the wall written in blood: Three down... more to go... The message was ominous but lacked the earlier drama of the first two crime scenes. There was no totem or other clues besides Natalie had been strangled with a written message on the wall next to her.

Katie stepped back and contemplated the three crime scenes.

The hospital seemed to be an important clue, but how? Natalie was a nurse in training. Theresa was getting ready to go nursing school once she saved up enough money. They didn't know much about TJ except that she had come to Echo Forest looking for Theresa.

Katie turned to McGaven. "We need to find out if Theresa and Natalie knew each other in nursing school. Is there a way to see if they were registered for classes at the same time?"

"On it," he said. "I can have John oversee the searches when we leave if I haven't found out."

"No problem," said John.

"And we need to have the medical examiner run Theresa's and TJ's DNA to know whether or not they are related."

McGaven looked at his partner. "That could explain a lot."

"Another important thing, we need more background on Chief Beryl Cooper and his wife Carol Ann Benedict-Cooper. I need to find out about her previous life—anything, family, when they married. *Anything*," she said.

Katie had some theories but needed absolute facts before going down that road. Time was of the essence. They had forty-eight hours and counting before the cavalry would descend upon Echo Forest and things got complicated very quickly.

THIRTY-FIVE

Saturday 1100 hours

Katie drove into the driveway at Crane Flooring. What should have taken ten minutes at the most to get there took almost twice as long. It was located in the industrial area, so it was highly unlikely anyone would see them. There were no cars in the parking lot and the building looked dark. She continued to drive around to the back.

There was a large area with leftover carpeting, tiles, and wood planks, which had a plastic tarp acting as a roof. They were behind chain-link fencing. Next to the back door were stacks of garbage and several high stacks of wooden pallets.

"I don't think we can say there are exigent circumstances for entry," said McGaven.

"Perhaps not," she said smiling. "But there's no lock on the door." Katie pointed to the entry for the remnants.

"Let's check it out. John was here talking with the owner. We're following up."

Katie grabbed two sets of gloves, and the detectives got out of the Jeep. Katie shuddered. She wasn't enjoying the cold weather, but it could've been worse. The air was cold, but not as bad as last night. She pushed through her uncomfortable feelings and glanced over to McGaven as he walked toward the storage area. She noticed he walked stiffly, slowly, and every so often he put his left hand on the side of his chest. It was clear he was still hurting from the aftermath of the hospital explosion.

"Gav, you okay?" she said.

"Fine. Why?"

"Well, I don't know, we were nearly blown up last night."

He stopped and turned to face Katie. "It's uncomfortable, I'll admit, but it's healing. When we get back, I'll have the doc take a look and change the bandages."

Katie was relieved to hear that. "Good."

They looked around again, ascertaining that the store was indeed vacant. McGaven flipped the metal gate lever up and pulled the door open. It was fairly organized with like things piled together. There were many piles of carpet remnants that probably wouldn't sell even at a high discount.

Katie immediately spotted the green carpeting. It wasn't the typical medium or dark green; it was a lighter version, more yellowish green. She pulled out the larger pieces and worked her way to small remnants that had been cut off from corners, and trimming lengths and widths.

"This is what John checked out," she said. "But I'm wondering how long they keep these pieces here."

"There's probably a trash area or recycling," he said.

Katie exited the enclosed area and walked farther to the back of the property. That was where she saw a van that was obviously used for deliveries. Her first thought was... could the van's tire impressions have been found at the crime scene?

"Gav," she said.

He joined her.

"Didn't John say that the tire impressions from the crime scene were from a truck or van?"

McGaven nodded.

"We need to dig more up on the owner, employees, and Bill Westin so we can clear them of being suspects."

McGaven made notes in his phone.

"Do you have a dollar bill?" she said.

McGaven handed one to her and she went to the area where the old van was parked. Katie took photos of it and the license plate. She tried the doors, but they were locked.

"Anything?"

"Not yet." Katie scrutinized the van, especially the side sliding doors. Not seeing anything suspicious, she took close-up photos of the tires and then of the tire impression leading out the back entrance—even with the snow the tracks were discernible, which meant it had been used not long ago. Using the dollar bill to give the size and dimension of the tire treads, Katie finished with a couple more photographs for John to compare to the crime scene impressions.

The detectives were just about ready to go when Katie spotted a large dumpster along the alleyway.

"Wait a minute," she said.

McGaven looked toward the alley. "Oh no, not another dumpster," he said with sarcasm.

"Why not? It's not on their property, so it's open season."

"It's freezing out here."

"So?" Her thought was that they needed to follow every lead and make sure to be thorough.

"So?"

"You can wait in the car with Cisco." She smiled and walked to the dumpster. It was an extra-large one and it didn't have a lock. She wrestled with the lid and finally flipped it up. Immediately, the horrendous smell hit her in the face and she retreated.

"What's up?" said McGaven hurrying to her. "Yikes, that's horrible." He covered his nose and stepped away.

Katie didn't want to say it, but there was no other choice. "Something's dead in there."

"Oh man. You think?" said McGaven. "You're not going in there."

"Just give me a leg-up so I can see."

McGaven shot her an "I don't think so" expression.

"C'mon, let me just check it out. What if it's something worse?" she said. Katie had all sorts of notions running through her mind.

"Fine." He walked up to Katie as she was putting on her gloves.

The snow had become icy around the dumpster and made it difficult for the detectives not to slide or fall down. Katie steadied herself with McGaven and placed her hands on the dumpster rim.

She peered inside. "Don't drop me."

"I won't," he said, with stress, trying not to inhale the stench.

At first Katie thought it was a dead dog, but upon closer inspection she saw that it was a possum someone had tossed in there—likely from being run over on the street. "It's a dead possum."

"Okay, mystery solved."

"But wait, wait a minute." Katie hoisted her body closer to the other side of the dumpster and grabbed the edge of a rolled piece of carpet with heavy plastic scraps attached. It wasn't huge, she estimated, maybe three feet wide and four feet tall.

"What are you doing?" McGaven was losing patience.

"I've just about got it," she replied and yanked the carpet piece out. She jumped down.

"Is that...?"

"Without testing we can only speculate," she said. "But it looks like there are some small blood smears on this green carpet."

"It wasn't near the possum, was it?"

"Nope."

"We need to take this back," he said.

"We can cut out a small piece for testing. I saw some plastic rolls and a carpet cutter in the storage area."

Katie took photos first and then ran to get the cutter and plastic. She was now so focused that she didn't feel as cold anymore. The snowfall had taken a break and it should be out of the freezing temperatures tomorrow.

They retrieved the evidence. The find gave Katie instant energy and her focus cleared. If they could test not only the carpet fibers, but the blood and match it to either Theresa or TJ, it would be a huge piece of the puzzle.

But as Katie drove back to the lodge, she began to lose hope about the evidence.

"Okay," said McGaven. "What's wrong?"

"Matching the fiber and blood is great, but it doesn't mean that anyone from Crane Flooring is the killer."

"But it could."

"Maybe the killer wants it to look like someone from Crane Flooring is the killer. Remember, the crime scenes, especially Theresa's and TJ's, seemed to be well planned out. We don't know how long all this has been set in motion."

McGaven sighed. "True. But we still need to verify the evidence."

"I think it's possible there were more than one person involved."

"More than one killer?"

"No. Just one killer, but more than one person involved."

Katie, McGaven, and Cisco were driving slowly to get to 2710 Cedar Oak Street, the house of Bill Westin. The day was overcast, but it wasn't snowing, and the town was extremely quiet.

There were no cars on the road and no snowplows either, which meant that most people wouldn't be out. Driveways weren't cleared. There was just a huge vision of white everywhere. It was a little unsettling.

Katie had no trouble navigating through and around deep snow. She left tire impressions behind, which would make it easy for someone to follow them.

"How do you want to handle this?" said McGaven. He had been looking up background information on Westin.

"I don't think we should go up to his door and knock."

"Then what?"

"We need to sit back and watch, for now," she said.

McGaven looked at the digital map on his iPad. "It looks like his house is at the end of the street and there are adjacent roads, which would be good places to park and not be noticed."

"Sounds good," she said.

"There's also an empty lot across the street."

"Even better."

Katie weaved the Jeep around difficult places, up and around where the sidewalks were buried by the storm.

"I've kept calling Chief Cooper and his officers," said McGaven.

"And?"

"Nothing. Clark's and Banning's just go to voicemail. And voicemail for the chief too."

"Do we have the capability to ping their phones?" she said.

"I've tried to use the software on my laptop, but I haven't had much luck."

"These might just be their work phones. Maybe they have personal cell phones?"

"It's worth a try."

"Ugh," said Katie frustrated. "We don't have all the information and we don't have access to our working stuff."

"Hey, I get it. But we are making progress and we will figure this out. I know you, partner, you will find a way." He smiled.

Katie nodded. She hated showing her annoyance. "That's only because I have you as a partner."

"Turn there," he said. "I think you can access the vacant lot."

"I see it. There are a lot of trees for cover." Katie managed to pull into the property and found a flat location where they could see in between the trees but no one should be able to see them parked there. "What do you think?"

McGaven craned his neck and looked in all directions. "It works."

Katie managed to retrieve some binoculars to see the house more clearly. There was a truck in the driveway, and by the looks of the snow in the back, it had been there for at least a day. It also appeared that someone had helped to clear the snow from their street.

"Looks like Westin had been jailed for theft and trespass, but nothing violent. He's single, but there could be a girlfriend," said McGaven.

The detectives waited for twenty minutes. There wasn't any movement until all of a sudden a blue sedan pulled up. A woman with short brown hair got out of the car and cautiously looked in both directions before continuing. She hurried to Westin's front door.

"Uh, we have an interesting visitor," said Katie, peering through the binoculars.

"Who is that?" said McGaven, squinting. "She looks familiar."

Katie gave McGaven the binoculars as Libby hugged Westin.

"Now that's interesting," he said. "Very interesting."

"I wonder what Libby is doing here. From the background

check we did, she has a husband and it's definitely not that guy."

"Nope."

"And wasn't she the one who said someone, anonymously, called in TJ's crime scene and she wasn't sure if it was a man or woman?"

"That's right."

"But how does she fit into all of this?" said Katie.

"Well, she's worked for the chief for a while."

"The more information we have, the more it has the chief in common," she said.

"I still don't see him as a killer, especially with this much crime scene orchestration."

Katie had an epiphany. "We've been approaching this all wrong."

Turning toward her, McGaven said, "How do you mean?"

"I think we've been a bit jaded. We've been working on serial killer cases too long. Even though I believe these homicides are connected, and there is only one killer—at least at this point. These murders have been made to *look like* a serial killer," she said. "To throw off the investigation and to potentially send us on a wild goose chase."

"So once we find the main links..."

"It will lead us to the killer," she said. "Let have a little chat with Westin." Katie started the Jeep and pulled out onto the street in front of Westin's house.

The detectives got out of the car and hurried to the door. Katie knocked.

The door immediately opened and Libby stood there. She recognized the detectives and looked both surprised and embarrassed.

"Detectives Scott and McGaven. We need to speak with Bill Westin. Official business," said Katie.

"Uh, he's not here," stammered Libby.

"Nice try. We saw you both barely twenty minutes ago," she said. "We just have a few questions."

"Okay," said Libby, shamefaced, and opened the door wider for the detectives to enter.

Westin emerged from the living room. "What can I do for you?" he said. His stiff body language and inability to keep eye contact with the detectives showed his nerves.

"Where were you on Tuesday morning around 6 a.m.?" said Katie.

Westin shrugged. "Sleeping. My alarm goes off at seven. What's this about?"

"What time did you go to bed Monday night?"

"I dunno, around eleven, I guess."

"You slept the entire night?"

"Yeah."

"I see. You work for Crane Flooring?"

"Yes."

"For how long?"

"About ten years. What's this about?"

"When was the last time you used their van?" she said.

McGaven casually looked around the small home, moving away from his partner.

"I'm not sure."

"That's not an answer."

"Wait," he said and went to the kitchen where his cell phone was lying on the table. He opened an application. "Here, see."

Katie took the cell phone and saw the app was a type of spreadsheet for checking the van in and out.

"You can't get the keys for the truck unless you sign in to the app. It will give you the digital combination to get the keys. It changes every day," he said.

McGaven joined his partner. "That's interesting."

"Yeah, my boss is very protective and tries to keep misuse down. Our installers have their own vehicle."

Katie saw that Westin's last sign-in was ten days ago and the notation said "dump run." But there was a sign-out on Monday evening with no name. "What's this?"

Westin looked at the log. "I don't know. It could be my boss, but I swear to you I haven't used the van in more than a week."

"Do you know anything about green carpet remnants?" she said.

"I saw some in the cage out back, but I don't know anything about it. There's all kinds of carpet pieces and I don't pay much attention." He paced and realized what the detectives were there about. "Wait, is this about that girl who was killed? I had nothing to do with it."

Katie studied Westin for a moment and she glanced at Libby. They both didn't seem like they were hiding anything. "So what's the connection between you two?"

Westin shrugged. "It's personal."

Katie remained quiet and decided that was enough—for now. "Thank you both for your time," she said. "If we need anything else, we'll be in touch."

The detectives walked back to the front door.

"Detective," said Libby. "Anything about my boss?" Her eyes were glassy and it was clear she was genuinely worried.

"Not yet," said Katie.

Katie and McGaven walked back to the Jeep.

"What do you think?" said McGaven.

"I think he's telling the truth, but there's more to this. The van was taken out the night before we found Theresa's body... We need to figure out by who."

THIRTY-SIX

Katie, McGaven, and John compared notes.

"I was able to get through to the medical examiner's office and they were able to confirm DNA from both Theresa and TJ," said John. "And you were right, Katie, they are sisters."

"How did you get results so fast?" she said.

"Well apparently it was already requested as a priority."

"From who?"

"Chief Cooper," said John.

"Why?" said McGaven.

"I don't know, that's all they told me. They will be emailing the results soon."

"Okay, so TJ came to Echo Forest because she somehow tracked down her sister. We will never truly know how and why. But why all the secrecy?" she said. "When she came to my cabin, she acted like she didn't know it was Theresa hanging in the tree. And how did she find her?"

"Maybe she didn't know," said McGaven. "She would have had to remove the burlap sack."

"Unless she already knew that Theresa was dead," said John.

"I don't think so," said Katie. "Everything seems to read like a soap opera and not a crazed killer taking victims. There are too many moving parts to this case. People who aren't who they say they are. People not telling us the truth."

"This may help," said John. "Apparently Chief Cooper's wife Carol Ann Benedict had two children, girls."

"The chief never mentioned children," she said.

"That's because Benedict gave them up for adoption right around the time she married the chief. They weren't his biological girls. They were five and six years old."

"How did you find that out?" she said.

"Once I searched for her birth, death, and marriage records, there was mention of a husband, Brent Benedict, who died in a construction accident, and it was noted they had two children."

"Wow," said McGaven. "It looks like the big town secret has been broken wide open."

What they were saying made sense to Katie, but it certainly made things more complicated. "So if you wanted to keep a big secret like that, you would have to have others to help you, right?"

"That's right," said John. "There would be no way to bury this without help."

Katie walked to the board. "But not long after the chief and Carol were married, she died. When I tried to find out more information about the cold case I couldn't find much." Katie turned to her team. "Maybe we're looking at this all wrong?"

"How?" said McGaven.

"Follow me for a minute. Maybe Chief Cooper didn't ask for favors and pull strings to be appointed police chief. What if his motive was to bury the cold case and not solve it?"

"That would mean..." said McGaven.

Katie nodded. "The chief killed Carol."

"What's the motive?" said John.

"It could be anything. Crime of passion, accident." Katie thought more about it. "Before the chief married Carol, he had to have known about her two girls... and known them. So why did she give them up for adoption? Something must have been awry in that relationship."

"That could be a big motive for murder," said John.

"But all this doesn't answer certain questions," she said.

"You said it looks like there's more than one person involved in the murders. What if they wanted it to look as if a serial killer murdered the young women to give everyone an explanation for their deaths? But then of course they wouldn't find him," said McGaven.

"Okay," she said and began writing on the board. "Say the chief did kill Carol. Who would be the logical person to help keep such a secret? Libby? She seemed really protective. Not to mention she appears to be stepping out on her husband with Westin. Right now Westin has some serious explaining to do about the carpet and van. Officers Clark and Banning could be in a position of keeping the secret, but I'm not sure it would be both of them."

"I think I get where you're going with this," said McGaven.

"I'm making it into a bigger mess than it needs to be. And it seems like such a big convoluted one, which is what I wanted to avoid. We need proof—rock-solid proof. Do you see how one person could orchestrate the murders and the hospital massacre and the explosion?"

"We have to keep digging," said John. "More background on the chief. Something doesn't make sense."

"The more I think about it, either way, there's one thing that stands out: Theresa and TJ were loose ends. And I think they knew the killer, or at least why their lives were in danger. If we find their killer, everything else will fall into place."

Katie went and picked up the contents of TJ's two boxes

from the Valley Motel and sat down at the large dining table to thoroughly go through it again. She had to put more pieces together. The time until Sheriff Scott told the backup law enforcement to take over was ticking away.

"There's one person you haven't mentioned in a while," said McGaven.

"Who?" she said.

McGaven got up and sat close to Katie and whispered in her ear, "Dr. Jack Thomas."

Katie looked at him.

"Don't forget," he whispered. "He's right downstairs and made this place available for us. And he could have *us* under surveillance."

Katie hadn't thought about that. She suddenly felt trapped.

THIRTY-SEVEN

Saturday 2005 hours

Katie, McGaven, and John went through the piles of information and began putting together timelines. There were holes in their investigation they couldn't fill, and it was tiring and frustrating. They had to break these cases wide open and they had to let the chips fall where they may. There were going to be suspects who had nothing to do with the murders, suspects who helped indirectly, and those who had carried out the murders.

Katie needed rest both physically and mentally. She was on a tight deadline and could feel the squeeze. She opted for bed and fell asleep as soon as her head hit the pillow.

A strange dream woke her and she couldn't get back to sleep, so she decided to get up and fix some tea, hoping it would help her to drift off again. She threw her covers off and got up. Spying Cisco sleeping quietly on the big chair in the corner of the room, she tiptoed out of her suite. The lodge was quiet and she figured everyone was asleep trying to rest up for a big day tomorrow.

Her bare feet felt the wooden floors and she could hear the crackling fire. The heat felt good. She saw that McGaven's door was closed and thought she could hear him snoring. She smiled and walked into the living room, where the flickering light of the fire gave a lovely glow. The tables, chairs, and the murder board were visible with all the work they had been completing. The board had been covered with a light sheet, even though no one else would see it. It was important to take a break from the investigation.

John was sleeping on one end of the huge couch. Katie paused and watched him sleep; he looked so peaceful under a couple of blankets. His face was relaxed and she wondered if he was having a nice dream.

She moved on and went into the kitchen, switching a light on. Seeing that dishes and glasses had been washed and sitting in the dish rack, she was surprised. Everything was organized and tidy. Not sure who cleaned up the kitchen, she was impressed. The coffee maker was set for the morning, which would make the lodge smell great before rising.

Katie grabbed a cup, filled it with water, and put it in the microwave. She went to the cupboard, where she picked out a non-caffeine tea bag.

She heard a thump sound just as the microwave beeped. Katie immediately turned around and looked into the living room, but all was quiet and John was still sleeping. Shaking off her uneasiness, she went back into the kitchen, where a rush of cold blew through the area, making Katie shiver. The door leading down the secret staircase was slightly ajar and she assumed that whatever had thumped or knocked against the building might have caused pressure to push it open.

Katie moved toward the door. The cold air continued to waft into the kitchen. There was no other explanation than a door was open downstairs. It could happen. The storm outside was building momentum again. She put her hand on the door; it felt more like a kitchen cabinet, even though the wood was rough and seemed old. Slowly opening the door, she was hit with the full force of the bitter wind. The light in the kitchen behind her lit the stairway and she could see that the door downstairs was open.

Katie let out a sigh because she knew the door needed to be shut, so she quickly padded down the freezing stairs, making it to the bottom in seconds. The upstairs door to the kitchen slammed shut from the air pressure.

Shivering, she quickly pulled the door shut, then fussed with the dead bolt. It wouldn't quite fit securely in the lock without some finagling.

Katie unexpectedly felt a presence, but before she could turn around a strong hand clamped over her nose and mouth. An arm held her firmly across her chest. She tried to fight the attacker, pushing backward, kicking, and trying to scratch them, but nothing worked. There was a sweet, sickly smell and her body strength dwindled. Her arms and legs weakened like jelly as her head felt mushy and clouded until... everything went black.

THIRTY-EIGHT

Saturday 2330 hours

Katie felt the sway of being on a boat during rough seas. She tried to do everything she could to stop the rocking motion. What seemed like hours she had been fighting were indeed only minutes. The faint weird sickly-sweet smell lingered.

Opening her eyes, Katie tried to focus, but everything around her seemed murky, discolored. She flailed her arms and fought to sit up. The light was too intense to look at, so she shut her eyes again. Using her hands, she felt a smooth fabric that made her think of something she had felt before.

With her bare feet touching the floor, she prepared herself to stand. But when she tried she almost plummeted with horrible dizziness that made her feel like she were upside-down. It was no use. She flopped back again and waited out the feeling of nausea and weird disorientation.

A few minutes later, Katie tried again, sitting up, her heart pounding, raising her pulse rate. Her body quickly weakened, but her vision had come back. Looking around the room she saw sofas, a check-in desk... she had a memory of this place. She stood up, a bit shaky, but she knew where she was and wondered why.

"Detective."

Katie spun around and faced the person who had addressed her.

"Are you feeling okay?" he said.

"What?" Katie focused on the man's face and remembered it was Jack, the veterinarian. Suddenly, she became wary of him. There were too many unanswered questions.

"Don't worry, it'll wear off and you'll be just fine." He smiled, but this time instead of being warm and inviting, it was sly. "Fluothane, which is similar to chloroform, but has some odd side effects that last from a few minutes up to an hour to dissipate. Don't believe everything you see."

"Why did you do this to me?" Katie could only think that if Jack had wanted to talk, why he didn't say so. "Ugh..." she said and sat down.

"Take a breath and try to relax. I'm not here to hurt you despite what your mind is telling you."

Katie couldn't make sense of the situation, but slowly, just like he'd said, thoughts became clearer and she remembered what had transpired. She'd woken and decided to make herself some hot tea...

"What do you want?" she said, sounding more like herself. She stood up to face Jack. "Who are you?"

"I don't want anything but to help you."

Katie's skin crawled and everything inside her was telling her to run. She had no other way to protect herself, no weapon, no backup, no plan. It was the worst possible scenario for her—a nightmare coming to life.

"I'm sorry, Katie. I really didn't mean to scare you," he said.

"You don't scare me."

Jack chuckled. "We got off on the wrong foot. Allow me to explain."

"Am I being held here against my will?"

"Of course not."

"Explain to me why you had to drug me then," she said, watching his every move. She contemplated if she could race up those secret stairs to alert John and McGaven before Jack could catch her.

"I wanted to get you alone."

"There are better ways to go about it."

"I guess in hindsight it wasn't such a great idea." He took a couple of steps toward her.

Katie backed away. She still couldn't get a solid read on the vet. Thinking about the time they had spent together, the hospitality, kindness, and him taking over as the forensic technician, all of it had seemed to be from a genuine person. Now she wasn't so sure.

"I will explain everything to you," he said. "I promise."

"I want McGaven here too."

"I thought about that, but no offense, I trust only you."

"Why is that?" Katie eyed the entrance to the staircase. Her feet were frozen without socks or slippers, making her entire body shiver.

"I've been watching you all, and I admit it, I've looked at your investigation board."

Katie felt exposed. "So you have cameras in the lodge?" She kept his gaze.

"Just in the main area. It is protocol for when I have guests and when the employees were present. I don't have them to spy," he said. "There are no cameras in the suites or other personal areas."

Katie didn't believe him.

Jack took a deep breath, as if he were deciding whether or not to tell Katie something.

"Why don't you just tell me?" she said.

"I get the feeling that you and the others are closing in on the killer. I think you've learned a lot in the past two days."

Katie didn't say anything, but she did think it was interesting that he referred to the *killer*—one, singular—rather than killers. She decided to just blurt it out. "Who killed Theresa Jamison, TJ, and Natalie?"

"Direct. I like that."

"Well?" she said. "If I don't get any answers, you're holding me against my will." Katie began to move toward the interior stairs.

"I said I didn't want to hurt you. I wanted to talk to you alone."

"I'm tired of talking in circles. You are holding a law enforcement officer against her will."

"I don't think so, but first—"

"I thought you could handle this, Jack," said a familiar voice coming from the examination rooms. "I'm sorry, Detective. I can only imagine what you're thinking."

Officer Bobby Clark, dressed in casual clothes without his firearm, came into the living room.

"Clark," said Katie. She was surprised, but not entirely. "Where's the chief?"

"Good question," said Clark. "I don't know. The last time I spoke with him was at the hospital."

"I don't believe you," she said, flatly.

"I'm telling you the truth. Whether you choose to believe me or not is on you."

"Look at all this from my perspective," she said. "I want answers. My partner and I both want answers." Katie walked toward the secret staircase. She wanted to retreat, reevaluate, and proceed accordingly. Since there wasn't any law enforcement in charge, Echo Forest was like a Wild West town. A literal free-for-all.

"Fine. Let's sit down," said Jack.

Clark nodded.

"I want to know who tried to kill us at the hospital. And where is the chief? Is he even alive? He called us saying he was at the hospital and that we needed to come. So why did you try to kill us?" she said.

Clark seemed genuine and calm. "I will tell you everything. We're not holding you here. Get your partner if you like."

Katie studied both men. She couldn't get a complete read on them. It was strange. She wasn't sure if it was the drug still in her system or not—but it made her reasoning skills a bit skewed. They appeared honest, but the fact that she had been drugged didn't sit right with her. She didn't respond but turned and headed to the stairway to get back to the second floor.

As Katie climbed the staircase, she half expected to hear gunfire at her back, but it remained quiet and the men remained where she had left them.

Katie reached the kitchen and ran into the living room. "Get up! Now!" she yelled to John, who leapt up.

"What?" he said groggily.

Katie made her way to McGaven's suite and burst through the door. "Get up!"

Cisco barked from her room and Katie let him out.

"Everybody get up!" She grabbed a pair of socks, shoes, and a sweater.

When McGaven and John met up with Katie in the living room area, she explained everything to them. They were quiet for a moment, digesting the new information.

McGaven seemed the most upset. "So you're saying Jack sedated you to bring you to his vet office. And Officer Clark is somehow his accomplice..."

"We don't know that for sure," she said.

"And it's not like we can call the cops because they're all missing except Clark. Who knows how much spying they've done on us? There's probably listening devices in our cars... and..."

"I know how you feel, Gav, but we need to hear them out," she said.

"You're crazy."

"Listen... whether they are the good guys or not we need to know," said Katie. "We need to know not only for this investigation, but for our safety too."

"You're quiet," said McGaven to John.

"Just processing it as if it were a mission. I think they're trying to figure out what we know. Sometimes you need to know your enemy in order to make a sound judgment... and then ultimately a battle plan."

McGaven looked at Katie. "You good with this?"

Katie nodded.

"You too?" he said to John.

"Yes. I'm with you both."

All three of them changed their clothes, made sure they had their weapons, and Cisco was going along as well. Katie was nervous because they could be walking into another trap like the hospital, but they didn't have many other choices. They were isolated and the two men downstairs seemed to be the only ones who knew what was going on.

Katie looked at the men and she knew they had her back. They all had each other's backs. Cisco included.

It wasn't like a typical investigation, or even a fight. No one was who they appeared to be and they were all alone. It was still hours before any backup arrived.

She stayed solemn. "C'mon, stay alert."

THIRTY-NINE

Sunday o145 hours

Katie led McGaven and John down the interior secret staircase. The sound of their footsteps was like an entire group of combat soldiers going into battle. No doubt Jack and Clark could hear them coming. Cisco weaved and padded down the staircase as if it were nothing. He too was alert and ready for anything, waiting at the bottom. They were a team of four and between all of them they would find out the killer's identity.

The group stood in the large waiting area—no one sat down. It was like a standoff. The storm was gaining strength outside and they could hear the thrashing winds slamming into the structure.

"So where is he?" said McGaven. It was clear he was annoyed and anxious at the same time, which was the opposite of his usually chill demeanor.

"Thank you all for coming down," said Jack.

"There really wasn't much of a choice," said Katie.

"Please let me explain." Turning to Katie, he said, "I apologize for the theatrics and not fully trusting all of you. I can see you are a great team. I did a little digging of my own and your Pine Valley case solve rate of one hundred percent is quite impressive."

"We're not here so you can tell us what we already know," she said.

Jack looked at all of them. "I've misjudged you."

"Where is the chief?" said McGaven. "Who are you protecting?"

"I told Katie I don't know where the chief is."

"Why do I find that hard to believe?" said McGaven.

"If I were in your shoes, I would think the same thing," said Clark.

"What kind of game are you both playing?" said McGaven.

"Look, I will answer your questions," said Clark. "I lost contact with the chief not long after the bodies were found at the hospital. And I've been looking for him ever since. When the storm hit yesterday I was going to be stranded, so I called Jack and he put me up until the storm passes."

Katie watched the officer as he began to explain himself. She didn't completely believe him. "Why didn't you answer our calls and text messages?"

"I'm sure you know the cell phone signals have been intermittent."

"Yes, but we were still able to make calls and access the internet."

"Here, look at my phone," he said, showing that he didn't have a signal.

"Better yet," said McGaven, "why didn't you just knock on the door upstairs and update us?"

"I thought I could find the chief and find out what's going on. I know you all were conducting interviews and working the case."

"I think this is a bad idea," said McGaven to Katie and John.

"We were pulled into this investigation because your police

force didn't have the experience to conduct such an investigation," she said. "I agree with my partner. This is a bad idea. We need know the truth and everything you know."

"That's what we've been trying to tell you," said Jack.

"No, I've only heard bits and pieces. I have not heard what I believe to be the truth," she said. "Let's go." She leaned toward John and spoke in a low voice. "What do you think?"

"I think you're right, but I also think you need to interrogate them to get any information that will help," said John.

Katie stopped at the staircase and looked to both men. "They're lying."

"You have the experience to know the truth and the lies," said John. "Use it."

They were put in a tough spot and had no backup until Sheriff Scott released the reinforcements to help them.

"Gav?" she said.

"I have doubts about this, but I have your back."

Katie took control of the situation and had everyone seated around a dining table. She didn't want to give Jack and Clark any of what she and her partners had found out or suspected. Her attitude was that of a police detective interrogator until they felt certain the vet and officer weren't part of everything that had been going on since Katie had arrived at Echo Forest.

Cisco paced around the room until he found his spot at Katie's feet. She liked having Cisco near her—it kept her grounded and focused. The dog could read her emotions well.

Katie took point in the interviews, which was what *she* did well. McGaven and John watched the men as they answered her questions.

"Do you know why the chief is missing?" she began.

Clark looked down for a moment. "I have some ideas."

"Like?"

"For the past six months or so, he's been different."

"Different how?"

Katie watched Clark. He appeared calm and was even-toned.

"Secretive. Paranoid. And that wasn't like him."

"Not at all," said Jack. He got up from the table. McGaven and John watched him closely.

"Did he know more information about the murders than he was saying?" asked Katie.

"I don't know. If he did, he didn't tell me."

"Where is Officer Banning?"

"He had a family emergency in Arizona and left shortly after the murders started."

"Didn't that seem like convenient timing?"

"I don't know... well, maybe."

Katie leaned back in her chair. There was something about Clark that made her want to believe him—but something was also off. "How long have you worked as an Echo Forest police officer?"

"I transferred from Redding about a year ago."

That surprised Katie, but she didn't show it. Merely glancing at McGaven, he seemed to pause at that too. "Why?" she said.

"Why come here? I got tired of my superiors in Redding. I wanted something more laid-back, where you feel like you're a part of a real community—not the notion of us and them."

Jack brought fresh coffee and mugs to the table. "It looks like it's going to be a long night, or morning, however you look at it."

Clark was the first to pour himself a cup and the others followed suit, taking their first sips.

"You do understand what an uncomfortable position we've been put in?" said Katie. "It's like we're rogue officers but we're here to help you."

"I understand... what... you're saying..." Clark appeared as if he was going to get sick.

"You okay?" said Katie. Her voice sounded strange in her own head. She looked to McGaven and John and they were rubbing their foreheads... The room spun in a nauseating motion... Everything around her faded away... Katie managed to pick up her mug and throw it across the room where it hit a wall, shattering. The coffee slowly rolled down the barrier. Katie tried to say something and stand up, but she passed out and dropped to the floor.

Two hours later

Katie felt a nudge and then a lick to her face. She opened her eyes, trying to focus, she had a pounding headache. Looking up, Cisco was standing over her. His nose in her face. Her memory was foggy, but she remembered everything leading up to passing out. With effort, she rolled to her side, where she saw McGaven lying face down on the floor eight feet away.

"Gav," she barely muttered.

He didn't move.

Katie pushed herself up into a sitting position as Cisco ran circles around her. She remembered firing questions at Clark. She grabbed the chair to pull herself up to a standing position. It was exhausting. She looked around and didn't see any sign of Clark, Jack, or John.

She was too weak to call out, so after steadying herself she moved to her partner. Dropping to her knees, she made sure McGaven was still breathing; he was, but very shallow. He seemed to be still under from whatever was in their coffee. Katie was angry that she had been drugged twice in one night. She was going to get to the bottom of things. No matter what.

Katie stood up as her head cleared. She retrieved her gun, which was thankfully still in her boot holster. There was a sound of drawers opening and paperwork shuffling nearby. It was coming from one of the open doors. Making a hand gesture, she conveyed to Cisco to down and stay.

She readied her weapon and quietly inched her way toward the sound. Once she reached the doorway, she saw Officer Clark rummaging in Jack's desk, pulling contents out of drawers and skimming through files. There were two bottles of water next to him.

"Stay right there," she said. "Show me your hands."

Clark froze and slowly turned his head toward Katie. "You don't understand."

"Don't I?"

"I couldn't say anything."

"Of course not, you just fed me more lies and conjecture." She moved closer, making sure he didn't have immediate access to a weapon. "Where is Jack? Where is John? They're both missing."

"I'm going to reach into my pocket."

"Stay right there!" When Katie yelled her head hurt worse than the worst hangover possible.

"Okay, let me stand up. In my back right pocket, pull out my wallet."

Katie thought it might be a trick.

"I'm going to get up slowly." Clark pushed back the chair and stood up, turning around facing away from her.

Katie approached, holding her ground and her weapon directed at him as she pulled the wallet. It revealed identification and an FBI badge. "FBI?" She was surprised. It was a legitimate badge.

She relaxed some as things began to fall into place and make more sense, but she was still a bit skeptical and didn't want to fall prey to something unsuspecting. She lowered her weapon but didn't holster it.

"Where's the chief?"

"I don't know."

"An educated guess?"

"I really don't know. That's what I'm trying to figure out."

"Convenient."

"I'm sorry I didn't tell you who I was sooner. I was under orders to keep my identity secret, even from you when you took over the investigations," he said.

"You knew we were at a loss for information and hitting walls, not to mention someone tried to kill us. Isn't that worth telling us the truth? Five people have been murdered."

"I know. And I'm sorry."

"I hate to tell you, sorry just isn't good enough." Katie had so many things running through her mind. "I need to check on my partner, he hasn't woken up yet." She eyed Clark one more time and then went to see McGaven.

"Ohh... my head," said McGaven as he sat up. "What the hell?"

Kate dropped to her knees. "Hey, you okay?"

"What's going on? Where is everybody?"

"Just sit a couple of minutes."

He nodded.

Katie found some bottled waters that didn't appear to be contaminated with anything foreign. She went back to her partner. "Here."

"Thanks," he said, immediately drinking.

Clark appeared. "I've searched the entire first floor. No one's here."

"Where's Jack? Is he a person of interest? He obviously drugged us," she said. "Is this some kind of criminal enterprise? You better start telling us the truth."

"What's up with him?" said McGaven looking at the officer.

Katie helped her partner to his feet, and Cisco came to investigate McGaven. Katie quickly explained what Clark had told her.

"What are we going to do now?" said McGaven.

"I would suggest that we hole up, for now, and get all the information we can," said Clark. "And then wait for rein-forcements."

For the first time Katie was conflicted on what to do, but John was missing. He had obviously been taken against his will for leverage and insurance. It seemed that Jack had gone rogue. But why? At that moment, everything pointed to Jack as the killer.

"We need to go upstairs. It will be easier to control and defend... in case..." said Clark.

"What do you mean, in case?" she said.

"Of what?" said McGaven.

"You know the killer *will* be coming for us, right?"

Katie hated to agree with him, but nothing about this inves-tigation had been typical. They had to prepare for anything and everything. She nodded reluctantly at the FBI agent. "Yes, I know."

FORTY

Katie had finished searching the vet's office for anything that would be helpful for them upstairs. She found video cameras still in their boxes, all types of tools, extra ammunition, and some miscellaneous items like surgical tools—scalpels, sharp scissors, and puncturing items—used in veterinary medicine that might prove to be helpful.

After making several trips, Katie stopped at the bottom of the secret stairs. "How's it going?" she said to McGaven, who was securing the outside doors. They would soon have motion cameras installed.

McGaven stopped and glanced upstairs. "You think we can trust him?"

"What choice do we have?" She paused. "He's from the FBI, but I'm not one hundred percent sure why he's here. He's been vague and a bit cagey, if you ask me. He says he's here to investigate the chief on misconduct and possible connection to his wife's murder."

"But we're talking about John being held and we don't even

know if he's still alive. I don't know if I want to put my trust into this man."

"Knowing John, he's still alive. With his training as a Navy Seal, they have no idea what they're up against."

"That's true, but when it's one of our team…"

"I know." Katie looked outside. The snow had piled quite high in areas and the weather report said another storm riding on the coattails of the last one was coming. It was going to be fierce, but not last as long.

Katie went up the stairs with Cisco, who kept his pace with hers. She was trying to show how strong she was, but she also had to face the fact that she didn't know for sure how to address this new situation. Her thoughts were on all the times John had been there for them working difficult cases and now he was in the hands of a killer—and they didn't know where. John was special, not only great at his job, but he had been there for her. He was patient, kind, and a true friend.

"Detective?" said Clark.

Katie turned.

"I really want you both to understand my job here."

"Did you know Jack was going to drug us?" she said.

"No."

"Really? Did you know that John was going to be taken?"

"No. I mean, I knew it was possible that one of you might be—"

"Kidnapped? Killed? The list goes on," she said. "Explain to me how you knew that we were working the homicides, and why when we found out about the chief and his murdered wife you can disappear and act like its business as usual."

"I knew all of you could take care of yourselves."

"Wrong answer."

"Look, Detective, I've been gathering intel on the chief."

"What about Dr. Jack Thomas? How is he involved? You can't tell me he's not."

"He's been good friends with the chief. They watch each other's backs. They know this town and they know how to divert your attention from things they don't want you to know."

"No, there's something you're not telling me." Katie walked to the board, skimmed the crime scenes and the connections between everyone. She sorted through reports until she found what she was looking for. McGaven had received a background report on Dr. Jack Thomas. "Are you sure you don't want to tell me about Jack?"

Katie watched the agent's actions. He was perspiring on his forehead and upper lip, even though it was rather cool as the fire burned down. He paced and anxiously ran his fingers through his short hair.

"Jack had a sister," he said.

"Okay. He told us that he grew up here and mentioned siblings."

"Just one sister, an older sister."

Katie began to knit pieces of the investigation together as she looked at timelines. "She died fifteen years ago and her maiden name was Benedict."

"No, it wasn't. It was Thomas," said the agent.

Katie didn't know what to believe. "First, if that's true—and we don't have any document that says so—"

"It's true."

"It could be true," said McGaven. "I ran several background checks that I haven't received yet. John was helping. There might be something here."

"We're at a standoff as far as I'm concerned," she said. Her anger and frustration were growing.

"What do you suggest we do?" said Clark.

"I can only answer for myself and my partner."

McGaven nodded. "I agree."

"I will make sure this place is safe with cameras, but that's where our involvement with you ends. You can continue to work your own investigation under your superior's orders. There are lives on the line and I'm not going to have another homicide on my watch. I'm going to look around in Jack's office and personal living quarters," she said. Everything was located conveniently on the first floor.

McGaven glared at the agent. "I'll stay up here securing our investigation."

"It's going to be light soon." Katie and Cisco headed down to the first floor.

FORTY-ONE

Sunday 0645 hours

The smells, sounds, and the feeling that was pressed against his skin had a familiarity to it. His head hurt and nausea tried to overcome his body, but he wasn't going to let it happen. It was dark, but his instincts knew it was becoming lighter outside. He knew that he was underground and that no one would ever find him.

He was partly alert when he was tossed into the hole—it was a long fall. Before the plunge, he heard two voices. One was apologizing and the other was giving orders. John didn't know who was who.

Using every muscle he had, John sat up and pressed his back against the cold wall. If he had to guess, it was made of rock and dirt. It was underground and wasn't extremely cold, though he knew full well that there was snow above.

From the distance of the fall, he was sure he had been thrown down a well—most likely old and abandoned many decades ago. There was no way someone would stumble upon him, not even the brilliant Katie Scott. His only chance to stay alive was to free himself from his restraints and find a way out.

Pushing his dire predicament and thoughts of dying away from his mind, he rested his thoughts on Katie. Remembering the first day he met her, she hadn't changed much. Always determined, focused, and willing to do whatever it took to find a killer and protect the innocent. She wore her strengths and weaknesses as a badge of honor. John asked himself, what would Katie do? She would fight, no matter what. He couldn't fixate on being at the bottom of an old well, he had to keep his attention with one thing at a time.

His wrists were secured behind his back with handcuffs. It was easy freeing yourself from cuffs even without having the key. It was just that it meant physical pain and the chance it might not work the first time.

John's training as a Navy Seal pushed him to the limits with not only difficult, almost impossible physical tasks, but also pushing his mind to work past anxiety and fear. It had been almost seven years since he was in the military, but all that training had been ingrained in him.

John used his breathing techniques to relax, to be in the moment, breathing in for four seconds, holding for four seconds, and exhaling for four seconds. Focusing on controlling his mind and steadying his pulse, loosening his muscles, and gaining the strength he needed was a challenge but it needed to be done. His thoughts rolled back to Echo Forest, the homicides, working with McGaven, and especially Katie. But mostly, he thought about Katie's beautiful face, long dark hair, how her eyes crinkled in the corners when she laughed, and her intensity when she was studying a killer's profile. He'd witnessed her running into the action and going rogue, alone, to protect her family and the people closest to her. She made no excuse for what she did to help John and McGaven because they were her family. Being around her and working with her over the past two years, it had been almost heartbreaking to not tell her how he felt about her.

It was time.

John's shoulder and left leg still hurt from the original fall. Rolling on his right side to give his bruises on the left a break, he managed to work his arms underneath his body and finally bring his hands underneath him—and then out front. There was very little light, but his eyes had become accustomed.

John paused, twisted and turned to retrieve anything from his pockets that could be used to pick the lock. He had a half-size writing pen that he used to make notes in the field. He used it carefully and after about ten minutes, it freed the handcuffs from his wrists. Now he was able to use his hands, fingers, and arms independently. A quick pain was better than the alternative.

With nothing in his pockets, no money, no wallet, no phone, and, unfortunately, no gun, John just had his wits, training, and determination. He braced his back against the well's wall, and he then pushed himself up to standing. Keeping his hands out front, he determined the space to be about six to seven feet wide.

Breathing hard, due to the lack of enough oxygen, John looked up and could see a faint outline of the morning light. It was a good thing. But he also recognized that the top of the well was more than twenty-five feet away—that was a bad thing.

"Hello! Can anyone hear me?" There was no response and he didn't expect there to be, but he had to try everything.

He would most likely die of dehydration and lack of food before anyone figured out where he was.

FORTY-TWO

Sunday 0750 hours

The more Katie searched Dr. Jack Thomas's vet office and his personal area, the more frustrated she became. They needed a plan—a solid one. She had searched the two bedrooms and a smaller one that was Jack's office. She walked back into the hallway as fear overtook her. It was her usual anxiety and fearfulness, but every minute they waited the more than likely scenario was that John was dead.

Katie and McGaven were on the same page about not trusting Clark. If he wasn't going to be transparent, then they didn't want to include him in their plans. But she knew McGaven was still hurting from his injuries and wasn't his usual one hundred percent. That was definitely a concern.

Cisco trotted around areas where dogs had been and then stopped near Jack's office. It suddenly hit Katie and she kept going over it in her mind: *Why wasn't Clark as drugged as her and McGaven? She saw him drink the coffee just like everyone else, but he seemed fairly clearheaded when she confronted him at Jack's desk.*

Clark thought he would find something in Jack's office. What was he looking for?

Katie went into the office again. She had already carefully searched the drawers and filing cabinets. There were two bankers' boxes in the corner that she looked through as well.

Cisco caught a scent and seemed interested in the desk around the drawers. It could be anything in a vet clinic. Probably all kinds of animals had been around. She remembered on one of her cases that people sometimes hid things in drawers, taped underneath, or in clever secret compartments. Thinking about the hidden staircase, she was guessing that maybe Jack liked secret places.

Katie pulled the middle drawer out and set it on the desk. There was nothing unusual, just typical stationery like notepads, pens, pencils, paperclips, and such. She emptied the drawer into one of the boxes and then turned it over revealing nothing but a smooth thin piece of wood. She ran her fingers along the bottom and it wasn't flat. Upon closer inspection, she could see that one edge looked different. Grabbing a letter opener, Katie pried the bottom, which easily came loose. It was false.

There was an eight-and-a-half-by-eleven single envelope with nothing written on it that had been taped securely. It didn't appear to have been removed and reset recently.

Katie didn't care. She ripped the envelope free. It wasn't a crime scene so she was finding evidence that would help them understand the connection of the chief, his wife, and the three homicides. They already knew that Theresa Jamison and TJ were sisters, and by the obvious findings they must've been put up for adoption and separated, never knowing what happened to the other. For whatever reason and however she had managed it, TJ was able to find Theresa but not before she had been murdered. The thought that they didn't quite reunite was heartbreaking. Everything that came after was murky.

Katie opened the envelope and pulled out several old newspaper articles that had been carefully cut out. Underneath, there were official copies of documents: birth, death, and marriage certificates. They were old and had begun to fade with age and some appeared to have been wet at one time because parts of them were bumpy and rough. In a small white envelope were two separate snippets of hair.

Katie began to read what she could around the damage. It seemed that Jack Thomas had had these papers for a while. There were articles about his parents, Mr. and Mrs. Thomas, owning this building along with their two children, Jack and Carol Ann. Later, his aunt and uncle renovated it.

Katie stopped reading and stood up. Cisco spun around, obviously feeling her energy.

"Jack's sister is Carol Ann?" she whispered.

Quickly searching through the records, Katie came across a name change for Carol Thomas. It seemed she changed her last name to her mother's maiden name of Benedict. There was a newspaper announcement for Beryl Cooper and Carol Ann Benedict. Another article was from the crime beat stating that a woman had been found dead in Echo Forest.

Katie retrieved her cell phone. There was a blip of a one bar signal. She sent McGaven a text message to come down ASAP.

It didn't take long before Katie could hear footsteps coming down the secret staircase and the wind howling against the office window. The storm was their nemesis as it built more power.

Cisco went out of the office with his tail wagging.

"Hey," McGaven said. "What's up?"

Katie explained what she had found and showed her partner the documents and where they had been hidden.

McGaven was just as shocked as Katie was. "So let me get this straight. The chief was married to Jack's sister, who had given birth to Theresa and TJ before meeting the chief. Carol Ann then ends up dead shortly after marrying the chief."

There were adoption papers for each girl and they went to different families—so their last names would be that of the adopting family.

"Well the chief wasn't the chief yet," she said.

"Then Carol Ann's case goes cold and no one talks about it?"

"Sounds like a story instead of facts."

"But does this mean that the chief is the killer or that Jack is the killer?"

She let out a sigh. "We can't connect these two without more information that we haven't been given."

"Jack took John," he said.

"We're assuming that. There are other things that could have happened."

"But honestly, we've all been drugged and then both Jack and John go missing."

"We have to assume that because we haven't heard from John. There's no evidence of a struggle. But..." she began.

"What's your gut?" he said. "I know you hate to base things on that when we have limited facts."

"There're more facts than you realize. But... there's a possibility that Jack may have killed his sister. For what reason, I don't know. There could be a lot of reasons: accident, jealousy, maybe inheriting this building so he wouldn't have to share it." She thought back to her encounters with him and their conversations, trying to string together something solid.

McGaven took a step back. "Who killed the girls? And why? Jack?"

"Could be. Maybe the chief killed his wife and Jack knew about it, so he was going to make him pay." Katie was frustrated. "But how does all this translate to the five homicides here? There's something we're missing..." She recalled what the chief had said on the phone the last time they had spoken to him. He'd seemed spooked before the phone disconnected and wanted them to know he was sorry.

I know what's been going on and I'm sorry that...

"What are you thinking?" McGaven said.

"Just that the chief seemed desperate to tell us something. I don't think he's the killer. Why would he kill his wife's children? No way, it doesn't fit."

Katie slowly went through the paperwork again. McGaven took a second look as well.

"I know we're missing something huge that hasn't been revealed yet," she said. "And it's always bothered me that Jack was doing forensic duties at crime scenes. Why?"

"Look at this crime beat from fifteen years ago. It mentioned there was a suspected serial killer and that Carol Ann might have been one of their victims. But there's no other information."

"Grasping at straws." Katie turned to her partner. "Can you do some searches on unsolved murders with the same MO and signature as the victims here?"

"I'll do what I can with the intermittent internet signal. What areas?"

"Here, and then fan out to nearby counties and then statewide if you get that far."

"On it," he said. "What are you going to do?"

"I'm going to search Jack's personal files. His taxes, business stuff, holdings, and so forth. Not sure what I'm looking for." Her expression was grim as she worried about John.

"We're going to find him," said McGaven as if he read his partner's thoughts.

"I know," she said. Although she wasn't so sure, and the thought of losing him hurt her soul, but it also pushed her forward.

McGaven left.

"C'mon, Cisco, let's go find you some doggie treats first." Katie went into one of the examination rooms looking for a jar of dog biscuits. "Here we go," she said and gave Cisco one.

In the corner, there were three stacked boxes labeled "Real Estate" and "Taxes." Katie moved them to the office and began going through them. There were taxes leading back ten years and file folders of the warehouse building, improvements, remodel paperwork, and two other real estate listings. Apparently Jack owned some property in Echo Forest. He owned twenty-five acres on the edge of town that had no improvements and he owned another twenty-five acres under development that was located right next to Devin Bradley's parents' ranch. Jack's property showed it was an old ranch of some kind. There were notations of structures. There appeared to be barns, some type of mill, and other structures she didn't recognize. Katie thought it would be a perfect location to hide out, hide a body, or get rid of a body.

Katie and McGaven needed to be prepared for anything and everything because the killer likely knew they would be coming to get John—no matter what. And that's what the killer wanted. They were going to be walking right into a trap with no backup.

FORTY-THREE

Sunday 1115 hours

John's strength was dwindling fast and the cold began to seep into his bones. He wore a warm hoodie with a shirt underneath, but it didn't begin to combat snow season. He noticed he was breathless a lot, which meant that his body was trying hard to stay warm at whatever cost.

Since it was daytime, he assumed late morning, it made the light better. He could see more detail of his surroundings. His mind flipped from one scenario to another of where he was located and why. Katie and McGaven had a difficult and complex investigation they'd been thrown into, but John had seen them survive the most dangerous situations and solve the most multifaceted chain of events. If anyone was able to find him, he would bet on them every time.

His stomach was past rumbling in hunger. He was famished and it began to affect his body and strength. No water made it even more desperate. He knew he had been thrown down the old well to kill him slowly. First it was hunger, then numbness, and finally beginning starvation, where the body takes what it needs in order to survive—until it can't anymore and starts to shut down all the major organs.

He'd read somewhere that these old wells in rural locations were often connected to help drive water to different areas on a working farm or ranch. One of his thoughts was that if he could get water to enter the well, then it would fill up, taking him to the top. Would it work? John had no idea.

He fought the urge to sit down but finally gave in. He leaned back with his head against the cold wall. He thought, if this were a test... how would he approach the problem with the highest odds of winning?

It was so quiet that he thought he had gone deaf, but there was something that caught his attention—a tiny sound, like someone had started a jackhammer far away. A burst of energy, no matter how small, propelled him to investigate.

John stayed on his knees as he began to touch the wall, as if he were using his fingertips to read it. He kept at it and realized that there were clay, brick, and sandy soil components. There were indications of various types of rock indigenous to the area. When John reached the other side, there was dampness and trickling water—most likely due to the snow. It smelled like river water, clean and pristine, and then he put his tongue on the droplets on his fingers. It was fresh.

John knew what he was going to do. He would begin to chip and claw until he could open a floodgate. The downside was that if he couldn't release enough water to get to the top or near it in an expedient manner, then he wouldn't have to worry about dying from lack of food and water—he would die from hypothermia.

FORTY-FOUR

Sunday 12 1 0 hours

Katie hurried and finished her search of Jack's veterinary practice and home as fast but as accurately as she could. She didn't want to miss anything as they weren't going to be able to backtrack once they sealed up the place. She gathered loose pieces of paper with notes, stuffing them into her pockets, and snapped photos of the rest as a point of origin: photographs, cut-out articles from the newspapers, and a list of documents that were missing.

One thing that struck Katie was that there wasn't anything about the place that read criminal mind, killer, or someone up to no good. Everything was quite normal personal belongings, and even items that Katie thought might be keepsakes, such as concert ticket stubs, matches from restaurants, and pens from various hotels he stayed at, nothing had a creepy aspect. These were objects many people kept as mementos or souvenirs.

Katie found a nine-millimeter gun and plenty of ammunition hidden in the bottom drawer of a bedroom nightstand. There wasn't anything else that would be a helpful weapon.

She knew they would be heading into the unknown and the culprit or culprits knew the area and would have the upper hand.

She looked at the time and calculated that the reinforcements would automatically be deployed in roughly six hours. They could wait it out, but she knew John didn't have the luxury of time.

"C'mon, Cisco," she said. They went up the secret staircase for the last time.

Katie, McGaven, and Cisco left the Echo Forest Lodge with the excuse that they were going to search the hospital using the dog. Clark wanted to join them, seeming to not fully trust them, but they declined. Trust worked both ways.

The detectives decided to take Katie's Jeep. They remained quiet as Katie drove and McGaven loaded bullets into extra magazines.

Katie knew that when they tracked down the chief and Jack, things would begin to make sense—at least that was what she hoped. Her thoughts wandered to John. They had put him in difficult positions before and he always had their backs. John's expertise with forensics made him indispensable. And she cared for him. She thought he cared for her too. Perhaps always had. But she'd had a fiancé and then had been dealing with that breakup. Timing hadn't been on their side.

"What are you thinking about? I mean, you should see the look on your face," said McGaven.

"Just everything."

"That doesn't sound like the Katie Scott I know."

"I'm not feeling like Katie Scott right now."

"What do you mean?" he said.

She ignored that. "We've been able to track down information about the chief and Jack, but I can't get those crime scenes out of my mind," she stated. "You didn't see Jack processing TJ's scene. It was clear he was horrified but he managed to stay professional and very competent the whole time."

"The staged crime scenes, posing, and the totems left behind, seem to come from another type of person. You know as well as I do that there's no one type—or two or three. These killers all have their motivation for doing what they're doing," said McGaven.

"I *am* rubbing off on you."

"What can I say? I've learned a few things. But can we just not be inside exploding buildings anymore?"

"I can't promise," she said.

The roads were still deserted though it had stopped snowing the past couple of hours. There was a frosty wind making the temperature drop even more. There were no signs of anyone using a snowplow, but some sidewalks and driveways had been cleared. It would take a few more days for the roads to be drivable for most.

"I just can't stop thinking about Theresa and TJ. They never got to find each other again and just be sisters." Katie shook her head. She would have loved having a sibling, a sister or a brother, but this was her life as an only child. "Both of them had their faces covered and that generally means the killer was someone who either had met them or knew them. They were strangled and there wasn't any sign of overkill. No other injuries like numerous stab wounds."

"But the placements of a hanging and one lying peacefully in the park..." he said.

"Every time I think about the killer, I get mixed feelings."

"You mean more than one killer? That would explain the difference in how they were displayed, and then Natalie at the hospital being different again, and the other nurse and security guard."

"No, I believe only one killer murdered all five victims," she said.

"And Carol Ann?"

"That murder doesn't have the same MO and signature as the three key homicides. Everything that we have points to a different killer."

"It's been fifteen years. Maybe the MO and signature have changed?" he said. "When I searched down homicides in the past two years with the same signature and MO, it was limited. Why? The internet signal was terrible and the search parameters I used were vague. But still... I did find two that might have, or could have, been committed by the same person."

"Where?"

"One was a county over in Eagle Brook and the other was in Davenport, near the coast."

"That's vague."

"I know. I would need more time to deep-dive back in our *real* office. This was all I could do right now."

"I don't think we've ever been this unprepared for a situation and investigations—ever."

McGaven was looking at the property lines between Jack's property and Devin's on his iPad. "It looks like there are areas that almost seem to merge between the properties."

"Let me guess. The wooded area where there were hunters."

"Yes, but there's also another area that might be good to enter from," he said.

"It's not certain we're going to find them at this property. But people running from the law and committing crimes feel more comfortable in areas they know well. Many criminals who commit crimes like burglary, home invasion, and rape stay within a certain number of blocks of where they live."

"We're going to be searching and having surveillance in the area?"

"Yes. With all the stuff you brought, did you bring any of those wildlife cameras?"

"I have two. We might not need them."

"Why is that?"

"We witnessed people hunting, right?" he said.

"Yes... so there will most likely be those types of cameras in place."

"Yep."

Katie wasn't sure if she felt good about the search. It felt like they were going to be entering a combat zone.

"It's hard not to think about John," he said.

"I know. But he's a survivor." Katie kept telling herself this, and her instincts told her he was still alive. But not for long if they didn't find him soon.

FORTY-FIVE

Sunday 1330 hours

John was past being hungry and he didn't think about it anymore, but his thirst was almost unbearable. If he could make it to the top, there would be plenty of water with the snow. There was one time when he was on a Navy Seal mission when the team was pinned down for days and the water was severely limited. He remembered how they had worked together and each had just the smallest amount of water to sustain them.

He had been using the handcuffs to scrape away at the wall. It hadn't been successful at first, so he kept trying different places. The brightness from midday helped to illuminate just enough light for him to see basic outlines, but not many details.

John had found an area that was loose, getting ready to give way. He focused on what he knew in the moment.

He knew that he was in a well, which meant he must be on some type of farm or ranch.

He knew that the well was old since it wasn't being used.

He knew that it wasn't a working well based on the dry and crumbling interior.

It was highly unlikely that anyone would find him and that his only chance to survive would be to get out and reorient himself as to his location.

The noise that echoed all around him was the sound of his heavy breathing.

He seemed to be making headway. The water was more than a trickle and becoming closer to a steady stream. He decided to start several holes in the same area and soon there were several small streams hitting the bottom of the well.

John sat down to recoup his energy. He rested his hands and arms. There was a warm sensation on his hands and he realized his wrists had been injured with the constant pounding and friction of the handcuffs. Blood trickled from his wrists down his hands and spotted his shoes and the well bottom.

John closed his eyes and concentrated on something else for a moment while he rested. Good memories flooded his mind. Then he rested his thoughts on Katie again, her smile, her tenacity, and her training sessions with Cisco. He remembered several searches she had done with the German shepherd. There were so many good times with friends and making new memories. He knew in his bones that it wasn't his time to go.

John abruptly opened his eyes and looked up. He estimated the daylight would dwindle in approximately four to five hours —and then he would be shrouded in darkness again, working only by touch. He wasn't ready to give up yet.

But then weakness and thirst overtook him, and his eyes slowly shut...

FORTY-SIX

Sunday 1330 hours

Katie drove to Devin's property with the cabin on Pine Cone Way and then made a sharp left leading to the adjoining property owned by Jack. The road, even though it was mostly dirt and light gravel, had less snow, making it easier for Katie to maneuver the Jeep.

"I want to make this completely clear," said Katie. "We're doing a recon to try and find Jack, the chief, and most importantly John."

McGaven nodded.

"But you know…"

"That we will do whatever it takes, no matter what," he said.

"Until our backup arrives." Katie clenched her teeth. Tension rose in her body. She wanted to catch the killer and demand answers. She thought about the article Jack had saved about a possible serial killer and that Carol Ann might have been a victim. Nothing in her experience indicated that Jack was a serial killer—she could see him performing a revenge killing or a crime of passion perhaps, but not the planned murder of young girls.

"Having second thoughts?" said McGaven.

"No. I'm just trying to make fit that Jack or the chief committed all these murders. But it just doesn't."

Katie decided to take a side road where they could hide the Jeep and continue on foot so no one would notice them or the car.

"Are we taking Cisco right away?" McGaven asked.

Cisco heard his name and whined. McGaven petted the large dog.

"Not right away."

"You ready?"

"Absolutely." Katie wasn't as sure as she should have been, but there was nothing she wouldn't do to save a friend.

The car was safely tucked in a wooded area. Katie prepared herself with layers of clothing, a big coat, gloves, and weapons. She made sure Cisco was fitted with his tactical vest, but he had to wait in the car until the door popped open. She also noticed that McGaven was moving slower than usual.

"Everything okay?" she said.

"Yeah, fine." He finished layering his clothes and coat. Pulling on his gloves, he said, "I think it might be a bit warmer and the winds have died down."

Katie nodded in agreement.

After looking at the map again, the detectives decided to sweep their search to the north, but first they wanted to walk the property line. Katie shut the doors and hatch. It always made her tense leaving Cisco behind, but he would be with them shortly. Her idea was to use the dog to search for the men, but they needed to know what they were up against first.

Katie took point and headed in the direction of the two property lines. Glancing at her phone, there was no cell signal. She trudged forward realizing the snow was more difficult to not only move quickly but move quietly, without making a crunching noise.

McGaven kept up easily behind her, constantly watching left, right, and behind.

Katie felt better once they had trees to camouflage them. She fitted her walkie-talkie and whispered to McGaven. "Can you hear me?"

"Affirmative."

It made Katie feel protected from anything or anyone sneaking up behind them as she kept her focus straight ahead. She moved deliberately and at a consistent pace.

Once in the trees, it was clear it would make a good hunter's spot. Katie stopped. Both detectives started scanning the immediate area for a wildlife camera. It took about ten minutes until Katie saw the brownish box affixed to a tree trunk with a black band. She retrieved it. There was some recorded video and a card. She showed it to her partner.

"I can read the SD card," he said. McGaven put down his backpack, which was filled with all types of tools, ropes, and technology, retrieved his small laptop, and inserted the card into a designated slot.

They scrolled through the photos that showed the camera had been active within the last twelve hours. It was just some of the native wildlife seeking out food, but then, there it was...

"Is that...?" said Katie.

"It sure looks like Jack walking through with a long gun. Look at his stance. He's on a mission," said McGaven.

"Does that mean that..."

"No, it doesn't mean that John is dead."

"What's the timestamp?"

"Looks like about three hours ago."

"Where's he going?" she said. Katie looked at the compass on her watch. Since they were heading north, then Jack was too.

"We're heading the right way. It must be toward one of those structures."

"Let's go."

Katie finally felt a jolt of energy and a feeling they were going in the right direction. She kept the path straight and continued.

"How far can you be from Cisco and still open the door?" he said.

"About two miles."

McGaven was impressed. "Wow."

After walking for about fifteen minutes, Katie saw some interesting changes in the snow. She veered slightly to the left. "Do you see this?"

McGaven walked near her to take a look. "What is that?"

Katie knelt down. "These are footprints and, by the looks, I think there are two sets. They appear to be stepped around several times and one set had the impression of slipping."

"You think there was a struggle maybe?" he said.

"I don't know but it's definitely human footprints."

Katie and McGaven continued on their trek in the same direction as the footprints. They stayed close to the property lines and continued north.

Katie estimated they had walked almost a half mile when she started to observe the landscape change from densely wooded to more spread out with light in between the trees. She became more observant and careful.

Along the boundary divider, there was one of the drainage ditches, just like on Devin's property. She still thought it strange. Looking back, she saw McGaven regarding it as well.

Katie decided to walk more left, but still north. It was partly cloudy, alternating between low lighting and then bright sun. She heard a strange sound. It seemed like footsteps but could be anything. It was crunching in the snow, but it wasn't coming from them.

Katie and McGaven stayed still, both listening, trying to figure out where the noise was coming from.

The sound stopped.

Katie motioned to McGaven to back away. She was just about to retrieve her weapon when they heard a man's voice yell.

"Show me your hands!"

FORTY-SEVEN

Sunday 1510 hours

Katie and McGaven froze. Half expecting Jack, they weren't going to drop their weapons under any circumstance, but there was something familiar about the person's voice.

"Who's there?" said Katie showing her hands. She couldn't see who was talking to them—they seemed to be hidden in the trees but extremely close.

"Detective?" said the voice.

This time Katie knew she had heard the voice before. "Who are you?" she said with authority.

Emerging from the tree line behind the drainage ditch, a figure appeared, slight build, wearing a heavy winter coat, carrying a long gun, and when he came into view—it was Devin Bradley. Standing there staring at the detectives, he looked like a person who lived off the grid.

"Devin?" she said. "What are you doing here?" Katie didn't feel threatened by him.

"I live over there," he said and pointed behind him.

"We know that."

"I know you know," he said and smiled a silly grin. "I have video of when you both visited."

Suddenly, Katie felt exposed. She walked up to Devin with McGaven closely behind. "But what are *you* doing here?" she insisted.

"Just holing up during the storm like everybody else." Devin kept his gun pointed down.

"That's not what it looks like," said McGaven.

"Is there something you're not telling us?" she said.

Devin seemed hesitant. "I want you to know that I loved Theresa and I planned on asking her to marry me when she graduated from nursing school. I supported her going to nursing school. That's all she talked about. I didn't kill her or anyone else."

Katie looked Devin straight in the eye and believed everything he was telling her. "Have you seen anybody around here today?"

"Uh..." he stammered.

"You need to tell us," she said.

Devin stared down at the ground. "I thought that doc was going to kill that guy."

"Dr. Jack Thomas?"

"Yeah."

"Who was he going to kill?"

"I don't know... honest, never saw him before."

"What did he look like?"

He shrugged. "Kinda like one of you. You know... a cop. Short hair, dark, medium build."

"And?"

"And I don't know what else to tell you. But he did seem like he was drunk."

Katie turned to McGaven. "He must've still been under the influence of the drug."

"Drugged?" said Devin.

"We need to find our friend John immediately, and the doc and the chief."

Devin turned and began to walk away.

"Hey, where are you going?" said McGaven.

"You know this is a hunting area by permission, right?" said Devin.

"Sure," she said. "I guess." Katie remembered the shots when they were at Devin's cabin.

"I have video. All kinds and people you wouldn't think, well, you know."

"Is there a cabin or any other structures like that here?" she said.

"There's more than that. Underground areas and an old graveyard. It's cool. C'mon."

Katie estimated the daylight remaining and when they could expect backup. She thought about Cisco. He would be within distance if they needed him. She didn't believe Devin had anything to do with the murders, but there was still something they were missing. That bothered Katie, when she almost knew, but couldn't quite find it.

Katie knew they would learn more about the property and that's exactly what they needed if they were going to find John. Otherwise they could be looking for hours or even days.

"Hurry," said Devin. There was a type of childlike joy in his voice.

Katie wondered if he knew more about the Echo Forest since his parent had always lived here. If he knew more than what he was telling them.

The detectives followed him across a field.

FORTY-EIGHT

Sunday 1600 hours

John dreamed that he was blind and deaf. It seemed more of a reality than a nightmare. His body suddenly jerked unconsciously, waking him. It was a strange feeling as he concentrated on staying awake.

He was lying on his back instead of leaning against the well wall. It was as if someone had spoken to him, but he realized that wasn't possible. John wondered if the coffee had had something else in it. He wondered if he was really down a well shaft or if he was hallucinating. The more he thought about it, the more his thoughts tangled.

"Stop it!" he yelled. No one would hear him, but it felt good to release some of the anger he was feeling. It felt like he had been down the well for days or even weeks. The solitary confinement was excruciating.

John forced himself to sit up and then he stood up tall. It was challenging due to the weakness of his limbs, but he had to do something.

He had been reliving everything and allowing his thoughts

to take over; instead, he should have been hyper-focused on getting out of his predicament. That's what the military taught him. Now he was just getting lazy.

John hadn't realized that water was now falling steadily from the wall. It looked clean and natural. He cupped his hands and began to drink. It was the most amazingly satisfying drink he had ever encountered. There wasn't much water in his hands, but he kept drinking for several minutes and then splashed his face. He could feel the chill from above and the water below was freezing, but it made him feel alive.

There was a strange sound. At first, he thought he had imagined it. No, he was sure. It sounded like heavy steps moving quickly. And then he heard voices in low tones. He thought about it and then listened hard. There were voices from above.

"Help! Down here!"

"Help!"

John realized that the voices he thought he heard were only his imagination.

The daylight was fading—soon it would be dark.

FORTY-NINE

Sunday 1630 hours

Katie and McGaven followed Devin to his cabin and the big barn where he had organized his tools to almost perfection. The young man ran into the cabin. His energy level was not winding down anytime soon. His enthusiasm was almost childlike.

"Do you think he's..." said McGaven breathing hard.

"No, he's not the killer. Eccentric. Maybe a little bit hyperactive. And even obsessive-compulsive, sure."

"Okay, I get your point," he said.

"Let's see what and who he has on video."

The detectives stepped inside the small cabin. When they had visited the property before they couldn't see every part of the home, but now they saw in one spot he had little boxes neatly stacked from floor to ceiling with perfectly printed lettering labeling each one. There were also even more decorative crystals like the ones that Theresa had.

"What's in the boxes?" said McGaven.

"Oh, I like to collect articles," said Devin.

"What kind of articles?" said Katie.

"Anything, but mostly crime. I thought I recognized your name, Detective Scott, and so I read some articles about you and Detective McGaven."

Katie hadn't expected that.

"You've solved all your cases. Do you know how unusual that is?" he said. "I mean, percentage-wise."

"I don't know..." she said. "Are you interested in serial killers?"

"Not really, but there's always something interesting about them revealed after they're caught."

"Like...?"

"Why they did it. So many blame someone else for their killing. Stuff like that."

Katie looked at McGaven, who gave her a raised-eyebrow expression.

"You know there was a serial killer here once," said Devin.

"When?"

"It was before I was born, but there was a guy who killed women and would leave weird stuff at the scene."

Katie studied Devin and recognized his enthusiasm for killers. It wasn't out of the ordinary, but it did raise some questions.

"I can find the articles if you like."

"Devin," said Katie. "Does 'the Woodsman' mean anything to you?"

"The Woodsman?"

"Yes."

He laughed. "Every kid in town was told the story of the Woodsman. It's been handed down forever."

"Why?"

"It was a way to scare kids to not go into the forest at night or without a buddy. It's stupid, but some kids believe it's real."

Katie thought about TJ's reaction to Theresa's murder

scene and that made some sense. "So it's just a story to keep kids from going out alone in the forest?"

"Pretty much. I think I can find some stuff on it."

"Thanks, Devin, but we really need to get everything about the videos."

"Sure. Oh, by the way, I'm sorry that I ran from you."

"It's okay, Devin," said McGaven.

Devin pulled out a laptop with an accessory on it that Katie had never seen before.

"What's that?"

"It's a type of booster that helps with cell signal. Haven't you noticed how bad the cell phone signal is..."

"Totally," said McGaven.

Katie shot him a look of amusement. She was impressed by Devin; she had misjudged him because he was quite the bundle of surprises—intelligent but in an unusual way. Those perfectly organized tools in the garage began to make more sense.

"Did you ever find those things you said came up missing?" she said.

"No. It's still an unsolved mystery." Devin keyed up twenty-four hours previous on the footage and then let it run from three different video cameras.

"You can run it faster," said Katie.

The detectives and Devin watched the videos on fast-forward.

They saw quite a bit of wildlife; even though there had been a snowstorm there were still animals both small and large foraging for food. There were deer, rabbits, birds, wild hogs, and other small creatures.

"There," said Devin.

Two hunters neither of the detectives recognized appeared. The footage was taken around eight-thirty this morning and it was breezy and cold. As they patiently waited to see Dr. Jack and John again, they finally came to the timeframe around

3 a.m., and there they were walking north through the snow, but the view was from a different angle to what they had seen before. John walked slowly and Jack pushed him with the end of the rifle.

Katie watched the body language of Jack and he seemed different. It was the way he carried himself, his stride was shorter even though there was snow, and his posture appeared more forward, like he was in hunting mode. It was as if they were watching a completely different person from the veterinarian who had allowed them to set up for the investigation in the lodge.

"It's..." began Katie. The images made her stomach churn seeing John being victimized.

"It's like watching two people who aren't them," said McGaven. "Does that make sense?"

Katie turned to Devin. "Do you know Dr. Jack Thomas?"

He shrugged. "Not really. I mean, I've seen him around town and at the Sunrise Café."

"Can you show me the property blueprints?" she said.

Devin went to his filings system, rummaging around for a bit until he found them. Katie and McGaven studied the plans. There were two small houses. Barns. And on this set of plans she could decipher more of the notations she had seen earlier. There were old farming areas, drainage areas, and wells. The more Katie thought about it, the more she realized they needed to search the entire property. There could be old buildings and drainage that might not be seen due to being buried.

"We need to search the area now," she said. Her anxiety rose exponentially.

"What are you thinking?" said McGaven.

"Play that video again," she said. "If I didn't know better, I wouldn't think that was Dr. Jack. But it is..."

After Katie watched the video, she was sure Jack had taken John somewhere. And she thought that the chief had been taken somewhere, but why? "John and the chief are somewhere on the property."

"Why?" said McGaven.

"I think the chief knows what's going on and Jack wanted to silence him," she said. "Remember what he said in the phone call, asking us to come to the hospital? I think he was trying to warn us, not kill us."

"You think Jack is the killer?"

"I'm not sure, but everything points to him. I just can't help but think there's still a big piece we're not seeing."

Devin listened to the detectives carefully and seemed to be taking everything in.

"You think the chief is dead?"

"I don't know, but if we don't find the chief and John soon, there's no question, they will both be dead."

Three down... more to go...

FIFTY

Sunday 1745 hours

Katie and McGaven hurried back to Jack's property, leaving Devin behind for his safety, but were disappointed that most of the daylight was almost gone. It posed a problem for the detectives due to the fact that they didn't know the area as well as the others, but it was also in their favor because they knew how to hunt down a person at night. And they had a secret weapon: Cisco.

Once Katie and McGaven reached a well-hidden area, they began to set their plan in motion. McGaven would hang back to cover Katie and Cisco while they tried to pick up the tracks of the chief and John. Katie had done some training in snow because cold filters scent differently than heat. The cold generally keeps the scent condensed and doesn't allow the specific trace of what is being looked for to waft and slowly spread for the dog's nose to pick up.

Katie and McGaven ironed out a few more details and made sure they had enough emergency items divided between their backpacks. Katie stopped her mind reeling from everything that had happened since she had arrived for her two-week vacation—and what would have happened if she had chosen another location. She wouldn't be working the homicides and John wouldn't be missing, taken against this will. She felt her eyes fill with tears, but she wasn't going to fall apart now.

McGaven touched her arm and said, "We got this."

She nodded, took a breath and pushed the remote for the door popper that would release Cisco. The remote made a high-pitch noise and flashed numerous times. Then they waited for Cisco to find her.

Neither detective moved or said a word. It was as if they were frozen in the moment and everything up to that point whizzed past them at the speed of light.

Katie hated waiting. It seemed like it was taking too much time. Maybe the door didn't open and she would have to backtrack to the Jeep. The longer it took, the more negative thoughts pressed her mind.

There was the sound of footsteps pressing through the snow, slowing, and then moving faster. Within a minute, a four-legged animal came into view, his black fur in contrast with the snow—closer and closer. The magnificent outline of the German shepherd exemplified everything about the breed— loyalty, athleticism, and love. With a few more steps, Cisco came to Katie's side.

"Wow, that's amazing," said McGaven.

"I'm going to start a search like a long grid north." Katie snapped a lead on Cisco's vest. She would probably have him loose in areas, but would make that decision on a location basis. Katie looked Cisco in the eye and memories of all their missions flooded her mind. She knew that if the chief and John were on the property, they would find them.

"Hey," said McGaven. "Looks like the sheriff is bringing in backup within the next hour. I sent a text telling him where we are and what our plans are."

"Even after they get to Echo Forest, it's still going to take some time," she said. The news was a big relief, but it still didn't alleviate her immediate concerns.

"But things are moving in the right direction."

Cisco slightly panted and took several spins, ready to go. A subtle wind had picked up, but they were moving downwind.

"Cisco, *such*," she commanded.

Cisco took off, his movement was controlled as he went forward, and then swept to the left and then over to the right. Katie glanced to the sides of their track, but mostly kept her attention on Cisco. If the dog showed a change of behavior, she would immediately see it.

Katie kept a good pace with Cisco, a jog, not quite a run. She thought the darkness would work in their favor unless there were cameras where they didn't expect. If anyone was getting close, the dog would alert.

"Good dog," she whispered, just loud enough for him to hear. Cisco's ears perked a little bit higher.

Katie glanced behind and saw McGaven keeping up but also keeping attention. She knew there were some small buildings coming up on the left.

Cisco suddenly stopped, which was unusual. His breathing shallow, ears forward, and his body still. Katie didn't say anything and she too stayed still and quiet. She knew McGaven was in the same mode, waiting and watching behind them.

The outdoor temperature had dipped and even the slight breeze froze her body.

Katie gave Cisco more leash, but he still remained in his position. You can't hurry when a dog's on scent; they know what they are doing. Katie struggled to remain quiet.

Cisco put his nose to the ground in the snow and pulled up, snorting. He put his nose down again, testing the area. It was something Katie had never seen him do before and she was mesmerized.

Another minute passed, Cisco then took a perfect left turn and went west in a straight line. Katie kept up, trying not to cause any pressure on the leash.

Cisco slowed his speed and bounded through the snow almost like a deer. He moved ahead and then turned around. The dog stopped next to a tree, but there was something that had interested him and he seemed to recheck his track. That, again, was new to Katie.

She turned to see where McGaven was behind them. She raised her hand to indicate that Cisco was on to something.

Cisco took two steps back then rushed forward, digging into the snow.

Katie dropped the leash and dropped down next to the dog. It was pure instinct, but she also knew Cisco and there was something important here. Her gloves were cumbersome but she continued to dig through the fresh snow until finally there appeared an old piece of wood, knotted and splintering. She tried to move it but couldn't, so she continued to dig.

McGaven was soon at her side. "What's up?"

"I don't know. Cisco wouldn't leave this area and he zeroed in on this spot. I can't move this..."

"What is it?"

"I have no clue."

Between the two of them, they managed to dig around the edges to move the wood and found that underneath was an opening.

Katie switched on her flashlight and directed the beam. At first she couldn't see anything. The large hole went into a deep void. "It's a well of some sort."

"Isn't that what Devin had said?" said McGaven. "Is there anything down there?"

"I don't see anything," she said. Leaning closer, she called, "Hello?"

They listened to her voice echo until it disappeared.

Cisco became agitated and pushed to an area next to them.

"Look," said McGaven. "There's some kind of entrance."

Katie got to her feet and investigated where Cisco had showed interest.

There was a snowdrift in between two trees and underneath she could see an outline of a small building about the size of a storage shed. There was a door.

Katie moved quickly, fighting the snow, which was now up to her thighs. It had stopped snowing a while ago, but there wouldn't have been any sunlight that could penetrate this section of the woods.

"Help me get this open," she said to McGaven.

They worked hard to get the door open, but it wouldn't budge. A small window was around the side. Katie hurried, followed by Cisco who seemed to push her in that direction. She tried to peer inside but couldn't see anything. She picked up a piece of branch and used it to smash the window. Sweeping her flashlight, she saw the outline of what appeared to be a body lying in the corner on their side.

"No, no, no," she kept saying. Katie pushed herself up and through the window. The floor was dirt mixed with a bit of snowy ice. She rushed blindly to the corner. She thought it was John, but when she turned the body over toward her she was staring into the face of Chief Cooper. His eyes were closed, but his body tepid.

"Chief," she said. "Can you hear me?" Katie felt for a pulse. It was weak.

Without warning, the chief opened his eyes wide and stared at her. It was the look of pure fear; he had an almost Halloween aspect to his expression. He tried to talk but his mouth only moved. Parts of his body and face seemed to be frozen and frostbite had set in.

"Hang in there, chief. We're going to get help," she said.

McGaven was at the window. "Is he...?"

"He's alive but suffering obviously from advanced hypothermia. We have to get him out of here and to a hospital."

"The hospital is thirty miles away," said McGaven.

"Devin is closer than my Jeep."

"I'm not leaving you here," he said.

"There's no time or choice. We need to get the chief out of here."

McGaven called Devin and luckily he answered the phone. He began to relay the emergency and requesting things they were going to need.

Katie tried to warm up the chief's hands, wishing they had blankets. "We're going to get you out of here."

The chief grabbed her arm and slightly nodded. He then mouthed, "I'm sorry."

"Don't worry about it now. We know that Jack is behind this."

The chief gripped her harder and shook his head, before becoming unresponsive again.

"Okay," said McGaven. "Devin is bringing something we can use to carry or drag the chief to his property and then he can take him to the hospital."

"Cisco and I are moving on," she said.

"No."

"Yes. There's no arguing about it. John is still missing." Katie could barely say it without a crack in her voice and bursting into tears.

"Katie, we don't know where Jack is. He could be tracking us and ready to ambush us at any time."

"John's life is more important." Katie couldn't look at McGaven. "Let's get this door open while waiting for Devin to get here."

With a bit of figuring, the detectives were able to open the door enough to be able to get the chief out.

"I have to go. We'll meet up with you back at the first big tree grove," she said.

McGaven obviously didn't want to admit it, but he knew Katie was right.

"I'll be back after we get the chief into some heat and sent on his way to the hospital. I'll be as fast as I can." He looked at his partner. They both knew how the other felt.

"I have to go now if John has any chance," Katie said.

"It should be less than an hour to and from Devin's house…"

They knew it would take longer.

"We'll be fine," she said. Katie couldn't look at McGaven as she and Cisco headed north.

FIFTY-ONE

Sunday 1950 hours

Katie felt more alone than at any time in her life. It was complete darkness now with only the subtle outline of trees and surroundings. There weren't any twinkling stars or a full moon to help light their path. She and Cisco stopped for a minute, camouflaged between trees to rest and recoup their strength. They both drank some water and had part of a natural energy bar. She wasn't going to use the flashlight unless absolutely necessary.

Katie readjusted her pack and made sure her layered clothing, beanie, heavy scarf, and gloves were doing their jobs. She felt warm enough right now, but didn't know what to expect.

She kept thinking about the chief shaking his head about Jack, as if to say he didn't do it, which didn't make any sense. He'd drugged them and taken the chief and John to die a slow death out here.

The question was... did Jack commit the murders, and if he didn't, why was he so intent on silencing the chief and John as some type of witnesses? Things still weren't adding up, but either way her first objective was to find John. She didn't want to admit it, but there was no other reason than Jack took John to lure her and McGaven out here. This type of behavior and the behavioral evidence at the crime scenes indicated two different types of people. Jack didn't exhibit a split personality, but Katie wasn't a doctor or psychiatrist. Perhaps it was just very well hidden.

Katie glanced at her watch, noticing that there was a solid hour before she would even think of meeting up with McGaven. Prepping herself was key to be able to make quick decisions and staying alert to everything around her.

She and Cisco began another track and this time it seemed to be different with Cisco's change of demeanor. She didn't know if that was a good thing or not. There wasn't any way of reading the dog at this stage, to know if he was reading scent for a live person—or deceased.

The team made its way around clusters of trees, past several small structures that were dilapidated and seemed empty. John was Katie's priority, but she had to remain vigilant of Jack's presence. She hoped he had gone back to his vet office to spin some kind of story of where John had gone.

Katie still kept Cisco on the long lead and the dog's pace started to accelerate, which was a good sign. She kept a jogging pace in the snow, which began to wear her energy down rapidly. The terrain was difficult and the snow made it even more challenging.

Cisco kept his nose down, seeming interested in a specific area. Katie's heart pounded as she followed him, and she began to perspire, sweat rolling down her forehead, the cold turning her skin icy and uncomfortable.

Cisco sat, alerting Katie to a section.

She ran up to the dog and dropped to her knees. Assuming it was another buried building or storage, she began to clear away the snow. The opening was completely covered as if it had been disguised recently and in a hurry.

Katie kept Cisco away from the opening, not knowing what to expect or if it was dangerous—or even a trap. She took a good three-hundred-sixty degree scan of the area; it was quiet and clear. There were a couple sets of trees on either side of her, which helped to protect them. About two hundred yards away were nothing but clusters of trees and it would be easy to hide among them. She kept that in mind.

"*Platz.*" She told the dog to down; it would keep him in a safer position.

Cisco obeyed and kept his sights on the area as well as Katie.

Katie eyed the round opening and could see scratches and broken spots. They could have been recent marks, but it was difficult to ascertain when they were made. She lay on her stomach and peered over the rim, sweeping her flashlight below. She saw an outline of a body lying on its side.

"John. John?"

There was no movement. No answer.

Katie could barely breathe.

"John?" she called. "Please, John, let me know you're okay." Her voice cracked with grief. She couldn't lose him. "John..."

"I'm here," came a voice that seemed to echo all around her.

Cisco sat up as he heard the voice.

"Are you okay?"

"Define okay..."

For some reason, under the extreme stress, that comment made her smile. John's dry humor was definitely his signature. "Can you move?"

"Some." John's voice was strained.

"Do you have any injuries?"

"No. But the drugs made me weak and nauseous."

"Did Jack push you down there?"

"Yes."

Katie examined every inch of the area, her mind retracing everything that had happened since she arrived at the Echo Forest Lodge.

"I'm going to get you out. Hang tight." She stood up and dropped her pack. Retrieving a fifty-foot rope with two carabiners, Katie got to work. She decided to secure the rope to one of the heavy branches nearby, so she tested it for strength and reliability with her body weight.

"John, can you pull yourself up?"

"I think so..."

"You can do this." She pulled the rope and lowered it so it wouldn't plunge down all at once and hit him. She hoped it was long enough. "Can you reach it?"

"Almost."

"C'mon, John, you can do this." Katie wasn't so sure, but she was going to give encouragement no matter what.

The rope pulled taut.

"Got it," he said.

Katie felt vulnerable and kept a keen watch all around them. She heard John grunt as he fell backward. "C'mon, John! You've got this. I know you do." She dropped to her stomach again, aiming the flashlight beam, and saw him trying to tie the rope around his waist.

Once he'd secured himself he began to dig his toes into the well walls.

Katie grabbed the rope with her gloved hand and began to help by pulling him up. Slowly, they were beginning to make some leeway. She flopped down in a sitting position with her feet secured against the lip of the well and pulled with everything she had. The muscles in her arms burned and she could feel her strength declining.

Cisco let out a low whine as if to say, "You can do it."

Katie slowly and steadily began to pull more rope toward her.

"Almost," came a raspy voice.

"Keep going. You can do this!" said Katie, gritting her teeth. Her muscles were on fire and her hands stung, but she continued. Her back cramped, but she breathed her way through the discomfort.

As soon as she saw John, she gasped at his condition. His face was pale and he appeared older. His anguish was clear as he got his arms up and over the lip of the well.

Katie crawled to him and grasped his arms and pulled until he was to safety. "John," she barely said.

He got to his knees and met Katie.

"John, you okay?"

He nodded. "I never thought..."

Katie hugged him tight. His body was cold, but he held her tight too, catching some of her warmth.

"I thought no one would ever find me..."

"It's okay. I prayed that we would find you. But it was all Cisco."

The dog got up and squeezed himself between them.

"Thanks, buddy," said John, slowly petting the dog.

"We need to get you warm." Katie shed her insulated coat to give him. Her two sweaters were still helpful, but she instantly felt the cold invade her space.

"No, you need it."

"Put it on. We need to warm you up. Are you hurt anywhere? Any injuries?" She pulled her coat around him tighter, zipping it up as they stared into each other's eyes intensely. "Oh, John, I'm so sorry. I wish I never took these cases and..." She hugged him tight, feeling him shiver next to her body.

He squeezed her harder. "I'm okay." He took his hand,

tracing her face. "Just when I think you can't amaze me anymore—you do something like this."

Katie wanted to stay in that moment, but she knew they were out in the open and needed to get moving toward Devin's place and meet up with McGaven.

"C'mon," she said. "Can you walk?"

He nodded.

Katie and Cisco guided him to an area to take a break while she updated him as best as she could. She used her right arm to steady him and help him walk.

They sat down on two tree stumps while Katie retrieved water and part of a natural energy bar from her pack.

"Stay here," she said. To Cisco, she instructed, "*Bleib.*"

Katie went back to the well and retrieved the rope and carabiners, rolling it all up and stuffing it into her pack. When she turned around to return to John and Cisco, Jack stood in the open area like an apparition with reflector strips down the sleeves of his coat, barely ten feet away from her.

She gasped.

Jack had a shotgun in his right hand.

FIFTY-TWO

"Jack," Katie managed to say, trying not to show her surprise.

"Just as I planned," he said with a broad smile, swinging the shotgun slightly.

Katie took a step forward.

"Not so fast," he said, aiming the gun at her.

She stopped. She hoped John and Cisco remained quiet and hidden.

"You found your friend, I see."

"No thanks to you."

"How did you find him?"

"Just luck."

"I'm sure you used your K9. Amazing animals they are."

Katie contemplated her shrinking options.

"Hmmm. Where is he?" Jack said.

"He's dead," she said flatly.

"I figured." He chuckled.

Now it was Katie's domain. She knew how to deal with unhinged criminal types. "You drugged us. Why?"

"Why not? I had to lay out the plan."

"What plan is that?" Katie wanted to keep him talking and his personality type seemed to like to talk—killers usually did—and listen to the sound of his own voice.

He chuckled. "As intelligent as you are, you haven't worked out anything about what's going on."

"Try me." Katie could feel the anger growing in her body. She despised this man.

"I bet you're thinking I'm responsible for the homicides."

"No. But you have killed."

That seemed to surprise him. Jack's smile vanished and he stared at her with disdain.

"That's right. You think we thought you were the serial killer," she said, testing her theory. "But we know."

"What do you mean?"

"What I mean is... you killed Chief Cooper's wife."

He stayed quiet.

"Your own sister. Now that's truly despicable. You hated her that much?"

"I loved my sister."

"You have a funny way of showing it." Katie took one more step. She had a weapon in each of her holsters: hip and ankle.

"You wouldn't understand. I did it for her own good and the overall better good. She married that idiot and she was going to try to steal my share of the property. That was part of the deal, we had to be married to inherit. Everything changed when she married Cooper. Everything. I couldn't let that happen and I would do everything to protect myself."

Katie could see how this one fact of not wanting his sister to take half of the warehouse and other property had festered inside of him, for years, and built up to the point of being homicidal. This was an example of a killer being made over a period of time.

"All this time, you watched the chief mourn and become a

police officer to find his wife's killer. And yet you passed yourself off as the friendly town vet with a really nice lodge. You didn't think the chief would figure it out—but when he eventually did, and when he tried to tell me, you made sure he would never tell anyone again... He's probably out here somewhere, presumably dead." Katie didn't want to alert Jack that they had already found Cooper and he was still alive. "That's why you had to clean up loose ends. The hospital explosion was a nice touch, but it didn't take care of the job, did it?" She wasn't sure who had set the explosion until now. But Jack's confidence in killing had kept growing; it was as if he were drunk on the power of it.

"Bravo, Detective."

"You can't kill all of us to keep your secret safe. And many more know. There's plenty of evidence... back at your office. How you drugged us. It'll be simple to put together. Was it all your idea?"

"No one will be able to put the pieces together."

"Did you kill your nieces as well?"

"What?"

"Oh, you didn't know? Theresa and TJ, the first two victims, were Carol Ann's girls. She gave them up before marrying Cooper. Must not have been very close if you didn't know that she had children."

Jack became agitated and Katie wasn't sure whether or not he would open fire. What she had told him seemed to scramble his mind. Her instinct told her that there was something else, something big that upset him.

He fidgeted and made low comments as if he were arguing with himself. His words scattered. "No, it's not true, everything was for her, nothing was ever for me... She didn't deserve... You're lying," he finally said.

"Afraid not. DNA and birth records don't lie." Katie eyed the weapon, trying to figure out how to take his attention away from it so she could make her move. Risky, but there wasn't much choice. She moved closer.

Jack fired a round near Katie. It blasted close to her ear, making it ring.

"Back up. You're going to join your friend."

Katie took another step. She thought she had heard her name whispered behind her. *Katie*. It made her take a step to her right. Cold shivers traveled down her spine.

"For such a good detective, you're not very smart."

"You don't know the half of it."

Just as Katie finished her sentence, a gunshot rang out and pierced Jack's chest, causing blood to splatter, much of it striking Katie. She instantly dropped to the ground and scrambled for cover, feeling the heat of Jack's blood on her face.

Jack's body had crumbled to the ground, still holding his shotgun, with a surprised expression frozen upon his face.

Katie thought somehow John had fired at Jack, but the shot had come from the south area, quite some distance away. If she hadn't moved to the right, she would have been in the bullet's path as well.

The echo of the blast still wafted through the trees. Everything became clear to her now. She knew who the serial killer was and why.

Another shot blasted and then another, which glanced off a tree just behind her. The killer was clocking her trail. She had gone from the hunter to being the hunted.

FIFTY-THREE

Sunday 2215 hours

Katie had an idea who killed Jack and now they wanted her and her team dead—it made sense, but she wouldn't know until she came face to face with them. Listening to and seeing Jack respond to why he killed his sister was incredibly depressing and depraved. What Jack had become almost stumped her, but she knew too well how killers operated and what drove them. Pain and abandonment in families could fester enough to drive someone to do the unthinkable. His hatred and actions had turned him into a body laid in the snow.

Katie continued to move north away from John and Cisco, hopefully keeping them safe. John was military trained and they had worked together on several high-stakes investigations, so he was going to know what to do. John and Cisco were safe and that's all she cared about.

Katie kept within as much camouflage as she could so it would be difficult to shoot her. Her exhaustion had set in and she wondered if she should wait it out by hiding. It seemed to be the most prudent maneuver.

Over the past two years and her time in the military with Cisco, she'd learned a few things about herself and stressful situations. She knew not to overthink things, to weigh all her options because you always had choices, and not to hesitate when you come to a decision. Quick and efficient. No matter how difficult it was.

Now, as she headed away from the site, Katie wondered if she should try and backtrack to come up behind the shooter, or stay put and hope that help arrived. She didn't want anyone walking into an ambush and she knew John would stay hidden.

Katie studied her surroundings and knew she would be able to make a big loop west and come around behind the shooter. Even though she didn't have her coat anymore, her body was handling the loss of it. Layering worked and she hoped this would be over soon.

She hustled on her route and took two minutes to pause every once in a while to let her muscles catch a break. Being cautious was her main concern, but she also filled her time thinking about the first crime scene of Theresa Jamison. She recalled everything from when TJ came to the cabin door, discovering Theresa's crime scene, and when the chief, officers, and Jack arrived. It was a flurry of events that singularly didn't make sense, but woven together revealed a frightening picture.

Katie had been taken off guard when Jack arrived to process the crime scene for the police department, but he hadn't seemed shaken up by it. If he had known it was one of nieces, more than likely his behavior would have changed.

So who killed the sisters and the young nurse, as well as the two staff members at the hospital?

The last time Katie and McGaven saw everyone involved was at the hospital scene. The chief, officers, and the rest of the emergency services were all there.

Jack must've lured or followed the chief to the hospital the night of the explosion and then removed his vehicle.

Officer Clark confessed he was an FBI agent working undercover to force out Chief Cooper, but that still didn't feel right, even after Katie saw the badge.

And Officer Banning wasn't seen after the hospital incident.

Katie knew the killer staged the scenes, but all three were different, two subtly and one very much so. It seemed to read that there was someone else—someone who possibly made Jack a pawn. The hospital workers found outside were collateral damage and witnesses to the crime. This person killed easily and whenever they had to.

Katie trudged onward as quietly as possible and began to make her big loop to try to bypass the shooter and be able to come up from behind them. That was her plan, anyway.

Her mind shuffled facts swiftly. She focused on the crime scenes, the totems, and how the victims were killed.

All strangled up close and personal...

Hung from a tree...

Faces covered...

Totem using some of the victim's things...

Laid out for everyone to see.

Posed...

Message written in blood for effect... indicating there would be more...

People aren't who they say they are... and some surprised her...

Victims were killed with moderate and selective force. Nothing personal but their belongings, which meant that the killer was trying too hard...

Her, McGaven's, and John's presence posed a big problem, which needed to be taken care of...

The murder of Carol Ann was separate from the three main victims...

The secrecy...

The rural area...

The weather...

Devin had been watching and didn't know it... He understood where people were located, the news, the hunters, and even was intrigued with serial killers...

There was a serial killer about fifteen years ago and victims were scattered around the county and not Echo Forest specifically...

Who would know this?

They wanted to create copycat killings. Why?

People who copycat kill are rare, but it happens. They are usually insecure and feel that their life hasn't met up to their expectations. Katie had read several articles about this type of killer. This type of killing would make them feel important doing something that can't be solved. Their ego would expand by watching people try to investigate the homicides and what the media was saying about it. It was what drove him and he would continue until he was stopped.

The killer was attracted to a certain type of victim and couldn't help but kill and sexually attack them postmortem. By the look of the first crime scene and behavioral evidence, it had been something that was committed by more of a seasoned killer honing his skills and feeding his need. The clues left on purpose, the display of the victims, and then the totems almost seemed overkill. Even though they didn't have all the information they would normally, the picture of the killer was becoming clearer... and clearer. It was someone who knew and understood law enforcement, who was intelligent, clever, and becoming more efficient with every scene. It could have taken months, but most likely years for this to happen.

Katie paused, letting her body relax before going on. "It couldn't be," she barely whispered.

She heard a noise in front of her. It was someone's steps in the snow and heavy breathing, as if the person had been walking for a long time.

Katie jetted into a heavily filled pine area in between an oversized sequoia tree. She could see the outline of a person, average height, primed for shooting as they stared through a scope. There were some gaps in linkage, but it was Katie's extreme reasoning and experienced inference that pointed to the only person who could be the killer. Upon first thought, it seemed unlikely but the more she thought about it—she knew who the killer was.

Now she stared at their back.

It was him. He could use his authority to cover up his murders as well as using whatever he could to commit his crimes, making it appear that Jack or the chief committed them.

He posed as one of the Echo Forest police officers.

FIFTY-FOUR

Sunday 2355 hours

Katie looked at her watch. It read almost exactly midnight, which seemed fitting for what she was about to do. The wind changed direction. The setting seemed to become even darker around her and there seemed to be whispers everywhere. She continued to inch forward until she could almost hear the killer breathing.

She slowly retrieved her weapon from her hip holster and cautiously aimed it at him.

"Put your hands up!" she yelled.

It caused him to freeze and slowly raise his hands.

"Drop your weapon, Officer Clark!"

He complied.

Katie moved in closer. She wanted to see his face and hear what he had to say before he was arrested and brought in. Still her Glock remained trained on him and she was prepared to use it if necessary.

Clark slowly turned. His face remained neutral and it was difficult to read him.

"How long have you been killing young women?" she said. "It will never feed your needs."

"You're the expert, Detective, you tell me." There was a snide tone to his voice.

"It's over. You're not going to hurt anyone else. And your game of playing Jack against the chief is over."

He chuckled. "You're so naïve."

"Tell me this. When you took the job here did you know about the chief's murdered wife?"

"Of course," he said. "I do my homework, to leave nothing to error. I would never immerse myself into a police department if I didn't know the dark secrets or the skeletons in the closet."

"I suspect that you don't have a sister either?" she said.

"You're correct, Detective. Tami Clark was just a girl I had met and was starving for any type of acting job."

"Her boot. Nice touch."

He laughed, never taking his eyes away from Katie.

Katie was suspicious that he was so completely calm. "You were going to use that murder to pit the chief and Jack against each other throwing suspicion—all the while the town thinks there's a serial killer on the loose."

"Something like that."

Katie despised the arrogance and high-mindedness of Clark. She had picked up on some of it when she worked with him. "Your mother didn't love you enough and your father thought you were worthless. That about sum it up?"

"You're like all the rest. Cops, detectives, psychologists, and the behavioral science unit all follow the same playbook: the serial killer recipe. There's never any deviation. Every person who kills is different from the next. Pathetic." He shook his head.

"You must've flunked out of the FBI Behavioral Science Unit."

Clark's face turned dark and his eyes remained fixated on Katie.

"I knew I would find your trigger. So the murder fifteen years ago must've been inspiring to you and you figured no one would be able to solve these crimes too."

"First, I didn't have a mother and father. I was an orphan. No one wanted to adopt me, so I spent my young life living in group homes—several, one right after the next. That was an education, watching behaviors and learning how to survive. Watching what made people tick. Their fears, dreams, and what someone would do or not do. I would continually see the beautiful children, especially pretty little girls, get adopted," he said. "As for me, I was brutalized, bullied by older girls who humiliated and laughed at me as they pulled off my pants leaving me vulnerable and alone for everyone to see. No to mention beaten, deprived of food, and ultimately forgotten. No one ever cared about me. This was my way of paying it forward, leveling the playing field, to the way it should be. Getting rid of every one of those bitches who think they're better than me... Everything about them was incorporated into my totems. It was like their calling card for everyone to see who they really were. It set everything straight. I will never be bullied or laughed at again... ever. My childhood was taken from me. And now I'm taking theirs."

As sad as Clark's story was and the fierce hatred in his eyes, it made Katie that much more determined to take him into custody, where they could potentially study him. If a police officer or FBI agent could become a serial killer, then some of the experts' hypotheses needed to be updated and studied further. "Put your hands behind your back," she said.

Clark didn't move.

"I'm not going to say it again."

Clark deliberately put his hands behind his back.

Katie had already taken handcuffs out of her pack and was

ready. She was cautious, but had to lower her weapon and return it briefly to her holster, which she didn't want to do. But there was no other choice, she didn't have backup and she wanted him restrained immediately. As she raised her hand with one side of the cuff, she was able to snap it on. But when she was about to secure the other hand, Clark made his move.

With a one-two approach, he used a martial arts or cage fighting technique to turn on Katie. He caught her arm and was able to easily toss her on her back as she let go of the handcuffs.

Katie was stunned, the wind temporarily knocked out of her. She couldn't quite get air to return to her lungs, wheezing in the process.

Her gun flew into a snow pile.

Clark snapped the handcuffs on her while she was still trying to recover from the assault. He obviously knew how to open the one cuff or had a key. Her breathing began to return, but her body was still exhausted and running only on adrenalin.

Clark made sure she was secured and couldn't move, even though her hands were handcuffed in front. He then flipped her over to restrain her even further. "So you're going to live out your last remaining breaths down one of those wells just like your buddy." He sniffed and then chuckled. It was clear he was absolutely enjoying this moment, gaining more power.

Katie was face down in the snow; she felt every inch of the cold pressed ice hard against her face and neck. Her cuffed hands were underneath her belly. She frantically worked them until she was able to push them to the side, allowing her to roll over and to use the heel of her hands to slam his face.

He pulled her up and shook her like a ragdoll.

Katie broke free and dove into the snow where she thought her gun had gone.

Clark then pushed his rifle into her face. "Stop right there."

Katie stopped moving.

"Get up," he said.

She struggled to get to her feet. Stunned and alone, she wanted to take him down in the worst way—no remorse. At first, she'd wanted to take him in but now she wanted him dead. He would never hurt anyone ever again.

"Move," he said, pointing the rifle in the direction he wanted her to go.

Katie didn't have any other choice. She walked west. The cold was beginning to take its toll on her, the blowing wind making her eyes water as her face stung relentlessly; she hurt and found it difficult to move forward.

She could see where she was going through her blurred watery vision. There looked to be something in the ground and she could only guess that it was another well or deep hole of some sort. Slowing down, she used the time to figure out what she was going to do.

"Keep going or I'll blow your head off," said Clark.

Katie knew he would. "You don't have to do this," she said. "They're going to find out about you and no one is going to think you're brave or special—only weak."

"I know what you're doing and it's not going to work."

"I bet some of those bullies you knew are now successful and respected."

"Stop!"

Got him...

When you get someone emotional, they become off balance and more likely to make mistakes.

"You don't know anything. You know I did a background on you the first day I saw you," he said.

"Yeah, so?"

"From what I gather you think pretty highly of your-self. Maybe I should make an example out of you? What do you think about that?" Clark spun her around to face him.

Just as he did, Katie swung her arms and clasped hands,

making contact with his face again. There was a cracking noise as she broke his noise.

Clark still held tight to the rifle but she'd made him pause briefly.

Katie didn't wait and ran as fast as she could with her hands handcuffed in front of her. It made it awkward and slowed her down, but she thought she was making progress, until she was yanked backward by her hair. She had failed. The pain was excruciating, causing her to fall, hitting something hard, a tree stump or another part of an old building.

Rolling to her side, she still wasn't giving up. She stood.

Katie switched from defense to offense, charging Clark and taking him down to the ground. When they landed hard there was a strange noise in the snow. It sounded like someone groaning, or a howling like the wind, but it was coming from underneath them.

Katie pushed herself upright and saw that the ground had buckled. Within seconds they crashed through to an underground bunker followed by snow and forest debris, which fell on top of them.

Katie heard Clark mumble in pain.

She saw cement markers, some tall, some short and wide. Taking a breath and blinking her eyes to clear them, she saw they were surrounded by gravestones. One of the dates was 1862. This was a historical gravesite, often part of a large ranch, most likely a family plot of generations who had been buried there.

Katie didn't waste any time and tried to find a way to climb out. It was only about six feet to the ground above. She scrambled to find anything she could use as a step. But when she was about out the top, she was pulled back down, landing hard.

Lying on her back again, Katie looked up and saw Clark, his face bleeding, his arms above her head holding a piece of stone. He was intent on smashing her head.

Before Katie could move, a shotgun blast ripped by her ears once again, and she lost her breath for a moment. It was deafening and she thought she had been shot, but she saw Clark try to stand again with blood seeping from his right shoulder. He couldn't fight it. He dropped to the ground.

Katie looked up and saw John standing with Clark's rifle. He staggered, dropped the gun, before he also fell to the ground.

"John," said Katie as she scrambled to try to get to the top. Pulling herself up, she crawled in the snow to him. He was lying on his back.

Katie managed to push the door popper again for Cisco. It wasn't usually used that way, but his collar would beep when she pushed it and she hoped it would alert him to find them. "John," she said. "You saved my life." Her relief was overwhelming and a flood of feelings swarmed her.

"Sorry," he said breathlessly, "it took me so long..."

Katie leaned over him. "You were right on time," she said slowly and then kissed him softly on the lips.

He returned her kiss and something happened between them that changed everything.

"Um, what's going on?" said McGaven standing over them with a smile on his face.

Cisco ran up and took turns greeting Katie, then John, and then over to McGaven. Then the dog spun a few more times.

"Nothing," Katie said, hiding her embarrassment.

McGaven moved carefully to the edge and looked down in the graveyard bunker at Officer Clark. "He's the serial killer, isn't he?"

"Is he dead?" she said.

"No, he's moving and covered in blood." McGaven looked at Katie and John. "I told you I'd be back in about an hour. But... this... I knew would happen one day." He pointed at Katie and John, trying to make light of everything, but it was clear he was relieved that everyone was okay—the ones who mattered.

"I will fill you in later," she said. "Let's get out of here."

There was the sound of a helicopter approaching and they could see lights flashing through treetops. It would be landing shortly with their reinforcements.

McGaven looked at his watch. "Right on time."

Katie felt so many emotions hijacking her body she wasn't quite sure what was real and what wasn't. But that exact moment, she knew she would remember forever. She didn't care; her family was still here and they would be okay. That's what mattered.

McGaven leaned down and took off Katie's cuffs. "Let's get this killer in handcuffs instead."

Katie managed to get to her feet and helped John up. They leaned on each other as they watched McGaven jump down into what was once a family burial plot and arrest Clark.

FIFTY-FIVE

Monday o145 hours

The group headed to Devin's property—Katie and John, with Cisco and McGaven escorting Clark—looking like they all had been in a war, battered, beaten, and bloodied. But they had overcome the killers together.

Devin's driveway was filled with emergency vehicles: two ambulances, two state vehicles, FBI, and more were coming. The helicopter from the Pine Valley Sheriff's Department landed in the middle of the field.

Sheriff Scott was the first to meet up with group. Without a word, he ran to Katie and hugged her tight.

"I'm so glad that you're okay," he said in her ear. "I'm sorry we're late, but the storm posed a problem."

Katie fought back the tears. She'd missed her uncle so much. "I'm fine," she managed to say.

"Are you all okay?" the sheriff said.

"Been better," said McGaven.

"I'm fine," said John.

"Cisco's doing great though," said McGaven in good humor.

Two FBI officers took Clark. He would go to the hospital under arrest and when he was better they were going to interrogate him before keeping him in federal prison.

"Let's get you all checked out," said the sheriff. "After that, there will be a debriefing on everything that has happened."

"There's a body about a quarter mile back of Dr. Jack Thomas—he was shot by FBI Agent Clark. And Police Chief Cooper was taken to the local county hospital by the owner of the property, Devin Bradley, after we found him locked in a shed where he'd been for a number of days," said Katie. "He doesn't look good."

"Got it," said one of the agents before he moved on to the cabin.

"C'mon," said the sheriff.

Katie thought once more about how TJ and Theresa didn't get to enjoy their reunion as sisters and that deeply saddened her.

Katie, Sheriff Scott, McGaven, John, and Cisco walked to the ambulances. More FBI agents descended upon the property and began to work the area.

FIFTY-SIX

Two weeks later…

The blue sky and the emerald water was an incredible backdrop. Katie finally was able to get some serious rest with no crime scenes or killers to catch—at least for now. She did opt to go somewhere warmer and calmer this time.

Wearing a sundress and beginning an island tan, Katie walked the beach with her bare feet in the water, feeling the warm ocean lapping over her ankles. The warmth on her skin felt more wonderful than she had imagined and was definitely what the doctor ordered. Her physical wounds were healing nicely and she was working on her hidden emotional ones.

Everything felt different, but yet, some things were still the same. One thing was for sure, she was going to live her life and take things slowly, enjoying every moment.

"Hey," said John as he jogged up to her. "Want some company?"

"Sure," she said. Katie admired John's tanned body, his tattoos showing in his T-shirt and shorts. His strength physically and mentally was so evident to her. He was more than a friend, but they weren't going to jump into an exclusive relationship—at least not yet. The dust had to settle and she still had some raw wounds from being left by her fiancé Chad. She didn't want her relationship with John to be a rebound.

"Don't you love it here?" he said, admiring the view.

"It feels like a dream." She smiled.

"It really does."

"At least now that I'm officially taking my two weeks, I can enjoy it to the fullest." She chuckled.

"I imagine you miss Cisco."

"Of course, but my uncle and Gav are taking turns spoiling him rotten."

"I've seen the photos."

Katie stopped. "Thank you for saving my life and watching after Cisco."

John became serious, staring at Katie and brushing her hair from her face. "I will always have your back."

"And you know I've got yours." Katie leaned in and they shared a long passionate kiss.

A LETTER FROM JENNIFER CHASE

I want to say a huge thank you for choosing to read *The Whispering Girls.* If you did enjoy it, and want to keep up to date with all my latest releases, please feel free to sign up at the following link. Your email address will never be shared and you can unsubscribe at any time.

www.bookouture.com/jennifer-chase

This has continued to be a special project and series for me. Forensics, K9 training, and criminal profiling has been something that I've studied considerably and to be able to incorporate them into a crime fiction novel has been a thrilling experience for me.

One of my favorite activities, outside of writing, has been dog training. I'm a dog lover, if you couldn't tell by reading this book, and I loved creating a supporting canine character, Cisco, to partner with my cold-case police detective. I hope you enjoyed it as well.

I hope you loved *The Whispering Girls*, and if you did, I would be very grateful if you could write a review. I'd love to hear what you think, and it makes such a difference helping new readers to discover one of my books for the first time.

I love hearing from my readers—you can get in touch through my Facebook page, X, Goodreads, Instagram, or my website.

Thank you,

Jennifer Chase

www.authorjenniferchase.com

 facebook.com/AuthorJenniferChase

 x.com/JChaseNovelist

instagram.com/jenchaseauthor

ACKNOWLEDGMENTS

I'm grateful to all my law enforcement, police detectives, deputies, police K9 teams, forensic units, forensic anthropologists, and first-responder friends—there's too many to list. Your friendships have meant so much to me over the years. They have opened a whole new writing world filled with inspiration for future stories for Detective Katie Scott and K9 Cisco. I wouldn't be able to bring my crime fiction stories to life if it weren't for all of you. Thank you for your service and dedication to keep the rest of us safe.

Writing this series continues to be a truly amazing experience for me. I would like to thank my publisher Bookouture for the incredible opportunity, and the fantastic staff for continuing to help me to bring this book and the entire Detective Katie Scott series to life.

Thank you, Kim, Sarah, and Noelle for your relentless promotion for us authors. A thank you to my absolutely fantastic editor Harriet and my amazing editorial team—your unwavering support has helped me to worker harder to write more endless adventures for Detective Katie Scott and K9 Cisco.

PUBLISHING TEAM

Turning a manuscript into a book requires the efforts of many people. The publishing team at Bookouture would like to acknowledge everyone who contributed to this publication.

Audio
Alba Proko
Sinead O'Connor
Melissa Tran

Commercial
Lauren Morrissette
Hannah Richmond
Imogen Allport

Cover design
Head Design Ltd

Data and analysis
Mark Alder
Mohamed Bussuri

Editorial
Harriet Wade
Sinead O'Connor

RAISING READERS
Books Build Bright Futures

Dear Reader,

We'd love your attention for one more page to tell you about the crisis in children's reading, and what we can all do.

Studies have shown that reading for fun is the **single biggest predictor of a child's future life chances** – more than family circumstance, parents' educational background or income. It improves academic results, mental health, wealth, communication skills, ambition and happiness.

The number of children reading for fun is in rapid decline. Young people have a lot of competition for their time, and a worryingly high number do not have a single book at home.

Hachette works extensively with schools, libraries and literacy charities, but here are some ways we can all raise more readers:

- Reading to children for just 10 minutes a day makes a difference
- Don't give up if children aren't regular readers – there will be books for them!

- Visit bookshops and libraries to get recommendations
- Encourage them to listen to audiobooks
- Support school libraries
- Give books as gifts

There's a lot more information about how to encourage children to read on our websites: **www.RaisingReaders.co.uk** and **www.JoinRaisingReaders.com**.

Thank you for reading.